The House on the Cliff

The House on the Cliff

by D. E. Stevenson

Holt, Rinehart and Winston

New York / Chicago / San Francisco.

Library of Congress Catalog Card Number: 66-23225

Published, September, 1966
Second Printing, January, 1967
Third Printing, April, 1967

Designer: Ernst Reichl
88142-1216
Printed in the United States of America

Part One

1

Messrs. Riggs, Sandford and Wilkins is an old-established firm of lawyers whose offices are to be found in a quiet street not far from the Palace of Westminster. The firm has moved with the times and inside the old-fashioned buildings there is modern comfort. This modernisation of the premises has been carefully done, so that it does not offend old clients who like old ways, and yet attracts new clients who appreciate the genial warmth of central-heating, the convenience of a lift and the cleanliness of the rooms.

The original partners have been dead for years, but their descendants sit in their seats and carry on the tradition. Mr. Sandford, who was once "young Sandford," is now the senior partner; his nephew, Ronald Leighton, is the junior partner. Between these two extremes there is Arnold Riggs, his son Peter, and two Blaygrove cousins—grandsons of the first Mr. Wilkins. There is also a young Wilkins, but as he is reading law at Cambridge, it will be some time before he is qualified to take his rightful place in the family firm.

One aftenoon in March, Mr. Sandford decided to go home early and play golf. The day was mild and spring-like, there was nothing of importance in the office and Mr. Sandford had not played golf for weeks. Mr. Sandford was a bachelor; he lived at Uxbridge in a pleasant house with a delightful garden; his youngest sister kept house for him and made him very comfortable indeed. In fact Millie Sandford was so devoted to her brother that she was apt to spoil him . . . but that was their own affair.

Mr. Sandford put away his papers, locked his safe and looked in to see his partner, Arnold Riggs, and explain his plan. Then he made his escape.

There was nobody in the entrance hall, but as he went out through the revolving door he saw a girl standing at the bottom of the steps gazing at the brass plate which was fixed to the railings. The plate was old and the legend, MESSRS. RIGGS, SANDFORD AND WILKINS, was partially obliterated by years of hearty polishing. . . .

When the girl saw Mr. Sandford coming down the steps, she turned and walked away.

Mr. Sandford hesitated, wondering whether to speak to her; he was still hesitating when she turned and came back. She was thin and pale, not pretty, but graceful and well dressed.

Mr. Sandford had a vague sort of feeling that he had seen her before. "Can I help you?" he asked.

"Well . . . I don't know. I really came . . . but I don't think I'll bother today." She blushed as she spoke and he realised that she was younger than he had thought.

"Are you looking for someone?"

She nodded. "I really came to see Mr. Robert Sandford, but—but I don't think I'll bother."

"You see him," said Mr. Sandford.

"Do you mean you're Mr. Sandford? I thought . . ."

"What do you think?"

"I thought he would be old," she replied frankly.

Mr. Sandford was old enough to feel pleased. He smiled very kindly and said, "What can I do for you?"

She held out a copy of *The Daily Telegraph*. "It was that," she explained. "Did you put in the advertisement? I suppose you must have put it in if you're Mr. Robert Sandford. It says you want news of Marjory Thistlewood and—and I thought it must mean my mother."

"Your mother?"

"Yes, it isn't a common name, so I thought . . ."

Mr. Sandford hesitated, but only for a moment. "You had better come in," he said.

She followed him into the hall and they went up in the lift together without speaking. Although he had been looking forward to his golf, Mr. Sandford was too much interested in his visitor to mind the delay. If she were really Marjory Thistlewood's daughter, it would be very interesting indeed . . . but he must make sure of course.

He waited until they were seated in his comfortable room and then said, "Yes, it was I who put in the advertisement; I have been advertising for months in all the daily papers. Where have you been?"

"Where have I been?" asked the girl with a surprised look. "I've been here, in London."

"Why didn't you see my advertisement before?"

"Oh, I see what you mean! As a matter of fact I wouldn't have seen it today if it hadn't been for a friend who drew my attention to it. She always takes *The Daily Telegraph* and reads it carefully. I didn't want to come and see you—there didn't seem any object in my coming—but Miss Martineau insisted on it. In fact she wanted to come with me but—but I thought that would be a mistake."

"Better to come by yourself."

"That's what I thought. I brought my birth-certificate and some other papers in case you wanted proof of my identity . . . but first I should like to know why you put in the advertisement."

"Mine is a long story," said Mr. Sandford cautiously. "Before I embark upon it I should like to make sure I'm telling it to the right person."

She nodded and, opening her hand-bag, produced a large Manila envelope. "I don't know if these papers are what you want," she said doubtfully.

He took the papers and examined them: the marriage certificate of Frederick Thistlewood and Marjory Mountjoy Ware;

the birth certificate of Elfrida Jane Thistlewood. In addition there were half-a-dozen snap-shots and a cabinet-size photograph of a woman and a child of about ten-years-old.

Mr. Sandford smiled. He was convinced that his visitor was Elfrida Jane, not so much on account of the certificates (which might have been obtained from someone else), but because the face on the other side of the table, which was looking at him anxiously, bore an unmistakable resemblance to the face of the little girl in the photograph . . . and because, long ago, he had known Marjory Ware and this girl was like her. Very like her, thought Mr. Sandford with a sigh . . . the same blue eyes, the same wide forehead and generous mouth, the same shade of light-brown hair. There was a difference, of course, for Marjory had been a beautiful creature with a clear healthy skin and pink cheeks; her hair had been curly and full of golden lights; her eyes had been gay and sparkly, whereas this girl . . .

He said suddenly, "You're much too thin."

"Too thin?" she asked in surprise.

"Too thin and pale and—and tired. Have you been ill?"

"Oh no, not ill," replied the girl. "Things have been difficult lately and I've been working terribly hard. It doesn't matter. If you're satisfied that I'm the right person, please tell me why you advertised for information about Mother."

"It's a long story," said Mr. Sandford. "It really begins when your mother was a girl. I knew your grandparents and used to go and stay with them in Devonshire. Perhaps you are aware that your grandparents didn't want your mother to marry Frederick Thistlewood?"

"They were in love with each other so she ran away and married him. Why shouldn't they?"

"Go on," he said. "What happened to them?"

"Father was an actor—you knew that, I expect. He wanted Mother to go on the stage and for a time she studied at a Dramatic School but—but it was no good. She looked lovely of course, but acting wasn't her line. She used to get little jobs behind the scenes. I remember touring about the country when

I was a child, living in lodgings. I got small parts off and on."

"A hard life," said Mr. Sandford compassionately.

"Hard and—and anxious," she agreed. "You never know what's going to happen. I'm in a play now, *The Motor Car.* I was terribly pleased when I got the part because it was the first big part I had managed to get, but it's a silly play and badly produced, so it isn't going to last long. The critics tore it to pieces."

Mr. Sandford knew very little about the theatre, but he remembered that his sister had mentioned *The Motor Car.* He said vaguely, "There's a very good man in it, isn't there?"

"Glen Siddons? Yes, he's very good indeed, but one man can't carry everything on his shoulders, besides . . . well, it isn't the right sort of play for him; it doesn't give him enough scope. He was splendid in *The Beggar King.*"

For a few moments the girl was animated—she had come alive—and her resemblance to her mother was intensified. That's why I had a feeling I had seen her before, thought Mr. Sandford.

He said, "Where are you living?"

"In a boardinghouse. It's run by Miss Martineau; she's interested in the theatre—all her boarders are on the stage."

"You mentioned Miss Martineau before."

"Yes, she's the friend who saw your advertisement and advised me to come and see you. She's very kind and—and interested in people."

"Does she make you comfortable?"

"Oh, yes."

There was a short silence. Mr. Sandford took off his spectacles and polished them with a silk handkerchief. "Well, now," he said. "You want to know about your grandparents. They were friends of my parents so the connection goes back a long way and we have always done all their business. Your grandfather died last August; he had been seriously ill for some time so his death was not unexpected. In October I received word that your grandmother would like to see me; needless to say I went at once."

"You went to Mountain Cross?"

"Yes, I got my nephew to drive me down. It's a long way. I suppose your mother has told you about the old house."

"She talked about it a lot, especially when she was ill. She told me stories about her childhood. There's a little photograph of Mountain Cross in that envelope."

Mr. Sandford picked it up and looked at it. "Yes, it's quite a good photograph. I know the house well, of course. It's a solid, well-built house, comfortable but rather old-fashioned. Mr. Ware was one of the old school, he hated anything to be changed. It isn't a house I should care to have," added Mr. Sandford, thinking of his own modern, labour-saving little house at Uxbridge.

"Mother loved it."

"Yes, it was her home," agreed Mr. Sandford. "She was happy there when she was a child. Well, as I told you, I went to Mountain Cross and saw your grandmother; she was ill in bed, so I saw the doctor and made sure she was being properly looked after. I had several long talks with her. She asked me to find her daughter."

"She wanted to see Mother?"

"She told me that she had wanted Marjory for years; she had tried to persuade Mr. Ware to forgive Marjory and make up the quarrel, but Mr. Ware was obdurate; he refused to speak of her, he had removed her portrait from the drawing-room wall. Your grandfather was a very determined man, Miss Thistlewood."

"Hard and unforgiving," said Elfrida bitterly.

Mr. Sandford hesitated and then said, "It's difficult for you to understand because you didn't know them. The Wares were not young when Marjory was born, she was their one ewe lamb. Mr. Ware adored Marjory; he was immensely proud of her, nothing was too good for her. In his eyes she was perfect . . . so you can imagine what a terrible blow it was when she ran away with Frederick Thistlewood. However, it's no use talking about that. When I saw your grandmother, she was ill and lonely and wanted her daughter. She thought about Marjory constantly; she had had Marjory's portrait hung over the chimney-piece in her bedroom, so that she could see it from her bed. She besought me with tears to find Marjory. I said I would find her—as a matter of fact I didn't think there would be much difficulty in finding her. That was in October and I've been searching for her ever since, advertising in the papers in London and in the Provinces, in America, Australia, Canada and New Zealand. I engaged a private enquiry agent to search for Marjory Thistlewood . . . what else could I do?"

"Mother died on Christmas Day."

"Oh!" exclaimed Mr. Sandford in dismay. "Oh dear, I was hoping . . ."

"I'll tell you about it—if you want to know."

"Yes, of course I want to know. Oh dear, this is very sad news. I had hoped so much . . ."

"We had a flat," said Elfrida in level tones. "We lived there together. The flat was at the top of an old house; it was little more than an attic, too hot in summer and very cold in winter, but Mother made it a home. I was able to get small parts and Mother did sewing for one of the big shops. Then Mother got a cold which developed into bronchitis and the coughing affected her heart. She was ill for weeks; she couldn't sleep and became weaker every day. At last she was so ill that the doctor said she must go into a hospital. Mother didn't want to leave me, but there was nothing else for it—I was too busy rehearsing for *The Motor Car* to look after her properly—so they brought a stretcher and took her away. She was in hospital for a fortnight . . . and then died. After that I gave up the flat and went into lodgings. I couldn't bear to be alone in the little flat . . . we had been so happy together . . . it wasn't a home . . . any more."

"I'm sorry," said Mr. Sandford sadly. "It must have been dreadful for you. Believe me, Miss Thistlewood, I sympathise with you most sincerely." He hesitated and then added, "What

I can't understand is why we didn't manage to find your mother. The private enquiry agent tried all the hospitals over and over again; it was one of the first things we thought of."

"You were looking for Mrs. Thistlewood, I suppose?"

"Of course!"

"We called ourselves Ware."

Mr. Sandford gazed at her in surprise.

"I used it as my stage name," she explained. "I've used it as my stage name ever since I was a child. You see Elfrida Thistlewood is a frightful mouthful. Mother said Jane Thistlewood sounded quite well, but Elfrida Ware was better. Then, when Father died, Mother decided that it would be a good plan for us to be called the same; it was such a bother explaining to people that she was my mother."

"Your mother called herself Mrs. Ware?"

"Yes, it saved trouble. I can see it seems funny to you, but it's quite usual for stage people, you know."

It seemed very funny to him. "What about your father?" he asked. "You said he died. How long ago was that?"

"He died years ago in Australia. He went to Sidney with a touring company and for a time he wrote to Mother . . . then we didn't hear any more and Mother's letters were returned."

"Didn't you make any attempt to find out what had happened to him?"

She shook her head. "We couldn't spare the money and Mother was sure he was dead. Mother said he would have written to us if he could, so what was the use of making any enquiries?"

Mr. Sandford was often surprised at the extraordinary things people did—or left undone—but this was almost incredible. He said, "You should have taken steps to trace your father; you could have done it through the police."

"Mother was sure he was dead."

"How long ago did this happen?"

"I don't know," she began. "I can't remember much about it; I was just a child . . . Oh, wait a minute! I must have been ten-years-old because Mother had that photograph taken to send to him. That makes it eleven years ago," she added.

Mr. Sandford was surprised; he had thought her younger. He said, "I can't think why you didn't see any of my advertisements, Miss Thistlewood. Don't you ever read the papers?"

"Not your sort of papers," replied Elfrida, with a sad little smile.

"Oh, well, it can't be helped. I've found you now."

"It's too late. Mother died at Christmas." She rose and added, "You can write and tell Mrs. Ware the whole story. Tell her that Mother often thought of Mountain Cross, especially during her last illness. She used to say, 'The air is so lovely at Mountain Cross; I would get well quickly if I could breathe that lovely fresh air.' We were very poor, you see. I couldn't give her nourishing food or—or proper attention. Tell Mrs. Ware all that . . . and tell her that in spite of everything we were happy together because we loved each other so dearly."

"Your grandmother died two days ago."

"Oh!" exclaimed Elfrida with a little gasp.

There was a short silence.

"Please sit down, Miss Thistlewood," said Mr. Sandford at last.

"What's the good?" she asked bitterly. "It's over and done with. They're all dead—all except me—and sometimes I wish I were dead too."

"Please sit down," he repeated. "I know you've had a bad time, but perhaps we can make things more comfortable for you. Before Mrs. Ware died she made a testamentary disposition in favour of her daughter. Let me explain the matter simply. I told you that I went to see Mrs. Ware when she was ill. She was very frail, but her mind was perfectly clear; she told me that she wanted to make a new will, so I drafted it according to her instructions: there were some small legacies to friends and charities and a pension for the couple who were looking after her—they had been with the Wares for many years so it was right that they should be pensioned. Mountain

Cross and the residue of Mrs. Ware's estate she bequeathed to her daughter, Marjory . . . or to Marjory's children. As I told you, I felt certain I would be able to trace the family."

For a few moments Elfrida gazed at him in silence. Then she said in a whisper, "You mean . . . you mean it belongs to me?"

"Yes."

"Mountain Cross and—and——"

"Yes. I can't remember the actual wording—and I don't suppose you would be much the wiser if I sent for the document and read it to you—but the estate includes a farm, fields and woods, a large walled-garden containing fruit-trees and a greenhouse et cetera and the mansion-house of Mountain Cross and its contents."

"All mine?" asked Elfrida incredulously.

"All yours," nodded Mr. Sandford. "There's very little money, I'm sorry to say. At one time the Wares were very well off, but Mr. Ware was not a good business man so his income had dwindled considerably in recent years and, in addition to that, he seemed to be spending a good deal of money. I tried to find out what he was doing with it, but he was very secretive. In fact he told me, quite kindly, to mind my own business." Mr. Sandford sighed and added, "Latterly the Wares were spending capital."

Elfrida was silent. She was so stunned by the news that she had become the owner of her mother's beloved home that she scarcely took in what Mr. Sandford was saying.

"Well, that's the position," continued Mr. Sandford. "It's unfortunate, but it can't be helped. Mountain Cross isn't the sort of place that will sell very easily, but we'll do our best to find a buyer. I shall put it into the hands of a house-property agent and——"

"You can't sell Mountain Cross!"

"It will be difficult, I admit, but we must do our best."

"I mean—I mean, if it's really mine I don't want to sell it."

"You don't want to sell it?"

She shook her head and said, "No."

"What do you propose to do with it?"

"I don't know," she said breathlessly. "I haven't thought . . . but if it belongs to me I want to keep it."

Mr. Sandford looked at her and his eyebrows rose. They were very dark eyebrows and they could show quite a number of different emotions. At the moment they showed disapproval.

"But my dear Miss Thistlewood," he said. "You are an actress, so I imagine that most of your time will be spent in London—or on tour. Mountain Cross would be a white elephant to you."

"I could go there when I was resting."

"You would be very ill-advised to let the house stand empty. An old house deteriorates very quickly if it isn't lived in and taken care of."

"We could get a caretaker, couldn't we?"

"I doubt if there will be sufficient money to pay a caretaker. There will be a little, of course; I can't tell you how much until Mrs. Ware's estate has been settled."

"Couldn't we wait and see?"

"At the moment the place is in reasonably good order, so it would be wiser to sell it as soon as possible."

"But I don't want to sell it!" cried Elfrida.

Mr. Sandford sighed. She really was very obstinate. "You had better consult your friends," he said patiently. "I'm sure your friends will advise you——"

"But I haven't any friends—at least I haven't anyone I could consult about that sort of thing."

"Nobody at all?"

She shook her head.

"Well, you had better think it over," said Mr. Sandford. "Let's see now: this is Friday. My junior partner has gone to Mrs. Ware's funeral; he'll be back on Monday, so I suggest you should come in on Tuesday and have a chat with him. He will be able to tell you all about Mountain Cross."

"I'll come on Tuesday afternoon," she agreed.

2

When Elfrida returned to Miss Martineau's boardinghouse, she was very tired, so she went upstairs to her bedroom. It was an attic-room, but it had a good window and was bright and comfortable. Elfrida took off her coat and hat and lay down on the bed. She was often tired nowadays—in fact she was tired all the time. Presently she heard the attic stairs creaking, as they always did beneath their owner's weight.

Miss May Martineau had been on the stage when young. In real life she was Mrs. Norman Potts and was now a widow, nearing fifty; she was still keenly interested in the theatre and ran her boardinghouse for members of "the profession," which kept her in touch with theatrical affairs. She was short and fat with improbably golden hair, tightly permed, and her pink-and-white complexion came out of jars and boxes . . . but in spite of her flamboyant appearance she had an extremely tender heart.

She knocked gently upon Elfrida's door and, on being invited to enter, came in and sat on the end of the bed.

"I just—wondered," she said breathlessly (the stairs made her puff like an old-fashioned steam-engine) "I just—wondered if you saw—that lawyer."

"Yes, I did. He was very kind."

"Is there money in it, dulling?"

"He said there would be a little and——"

"Oh, good!" cried Miss Martineau. "I was right to make you go and see him, wasn't I? Has somebody died, or what?"

"Yes, my grandmother died. She left some money and there's a house. It's Mother's old home in Devonshire."

"You could sell it, couldn't you?"

"That's what Mr. Sandford said . . . but I don't want to sell it."

"You don't want to sell it? What else could you do with it?"

Elfrida was silent. She did not see what else she could do with it and she knew she was being unreasonable, but all the same she was quite determined not to sell Mountain Cross.

"Why don't you want to sell it?" Miss Martineau enquired.

"I don't know—really," replied Elfrida thoughtfully. "It's just—well, it's just a sort of feeling I have. Mother loved her home; she used to tell me what a lovely place it was; she talked about it so much that I can almost see it. I'd like to tell you all about it if you aren't too busy."

This was what Miss Martineau had hoped for, so she settled herself more comfortably on the end of the bed and listened. She was not disappointed; Elfrida's recital of all that had happened from the moment when she had met Mr. Sandford at the bottom of the steps until the moment when she had shaken hands and said goodbye was quite enthralling. Even more enthralling was Elfrida's description of Mountain Cross, and the little photographs of the house on the cliff which were produced for her inspection.

"Yes, I see," said Miss Martineau, nodding her golden head. "It's a great big beautiful place, but what would you do with it, dulling? Mountain Cross is a dream—that's why you don't want to sell it—but this is real life, you know. I should wait a bit if I were you. I mean you don't have to make up your mind all of a sudden. I always say it's a good thing to sleep on a problem . . . though, as a matter of fact, I've found that if it's a very complicated problem, you're more likely to lie awake on it."

"Yes," agreed Elfrida, smiling in spite of herself.

"You're to go back on Tuesday," Miss Martineau pointed out. "Well, something may happen before Tuesday."

"Something may happen?"

"Something to help you to make up your mind. And anyhow," added Miss Martineau, "anyhow you'll have to discuss it with *him*, won't you?"

"Him!" exclaimed Elfrida in alarm. "Whom do you mean?"

"I don't know, dulling. All I know is there's a man somewhere about. I've seen a good deal in my time, so I know the symptoms. You're as thin as a lath; you don't eat your food; you don't listen when people talk to you. They say it's love that makes the world go round, but I've always found it stops the world going round . . . for most girls."

Elfrida hesitated. Then she said, "Yes, I suppose it's true . . . in a way."

"Are you engaged?"

"Oh, no!"

"Does he love you?"

"No, I don't think so. At least . . ."

"But you must know," said Miss Martineau sensibly. "Any girl can tell by the way a man looks at her."

"He smiles at me as if there were nobody else in the world."

"Well, then, what more do you want?"

"He smiles at other people too."

"That's not so good."

Elfrida sat up and pushed back her hair. She said, "It's no use talking about it because it's quite hopeless . . . it's Glen Siddons."

"Goodness, that's a bit of a facer!" exclaimed Miss Martineau. "I don't know him, of course, but I've seen him on the stage and he's certainly a charmer. Well, I never thought it could be him! He's everybody's idol."

"I know," said Elfrida nodding. "I know quite well that I'm a perfect fool, but I can't help it. You see it happened quite suddenly the first time I saw him. I wasn't expecting it . . . but it just . . . happened."

It had happened like a flash of lightning at the first rehearsal of *The Motor Car*. Elfrida had been feeling cold and miserable and frightened . . . then Glen Siddons arrived. He was tall and slender with brown eyes and dark hair brushed back from his forehead in a shallow wave. The others knew him—they had been with him in *The Beggar King*—so they gathered round, talking and laughing delightedly. Elfrida did not know him; she stood apart waiting for the rehearsal to begin. Suddenly Glen Siddons turned his head and saw her . . . and smiled to her. He had smiled to her as if they two were alone in the world and she had fallen in love with him then and there.

Afterwards, when the rehearsal was over, he had spoken to her and asked why she looked unhappy. He had asked so kindly—as if he really wanted to know—that she told him her mother was seriously ill and getting weaker every day. It was easy for Glen to be kind; he had listened sympathetically and had given Elfrida a bouquet of pink carnations (which had been sent to him by one of his many admirers) and had asked her to give it to her mother with his love.

Perhaps if Elfrida had not been in such an emotional condition, she would not have been bowled over so completely.

"He's certainly a charmer," repeated Miss Martineau in thoughtful tones. "I saw him in *The Beggar King* and he was marvellous. I don't wonder at any girl falling for him, but—well—to tell you the truth I'd rather have someone a bit less glamorous, someone who kept his smiles for *me*. Norman wasn't glamorous by any means, but he never looked at another girl—it was me he wanted—so I married him and I never regretted it for a minute. We were happy together, we were all in all to each other. Yes," said Miss Martineau, nodding wisely. "Yes, that's what you want in marriage, to be all in all to each other."

Elfrida was silent; she had never envisaged marriage with her idol. All she wanted was to be near him, to hear his voice and to see him smile at her.

"Glen Siddons is a widower," said Miss Martineau; there was nothing much she did not know about theatrical personalities.

"I never knew that!" Elfrida exclaimed.

"It was a boy-and-girl affair, long before your time. He met her in Ireland and they were married there. I never saw her, but someone told me she was beautiful and they were very much in love. His name isn't Siddons, of course."

"I thought he was related to Mrs. Siddons."

"That's what you're meant to think," replied Miss Martineau quite seriously. "Of course he may be related to her for all I know. I mean people are often related to people with different names. I knew a chap who said he was related to—to Risotto—or something."

"Rossetti?"

"Yes, that was it. You know a lot, don't you?" said Miss Martineau admiringly.

"Mother was very fond of the poems of Christina Rossetti," explained Elfrida. "She had a little book of them and read it so often that it has almost fallen to pieces. I could lend it to you if you like."

"Well, I'm not really very keen on poems, dulling, but thank you all the same. I was just telling you about Rossetti because of this chap I used to know. His name was Charlie Stubbs but he really *was* related to Rossetti through his grandmother or somebody—I can't remember exactly—so you see Glen Siddons *may* be related to Mrs. Siddons." She hesitated and then added, "Or may not."

Elfrida could not help smiling.

"But all that has nothing to do with it," declared Miss Martineau. "The important thing is do you think he's seriously fond of you?"

"Sometimes I've thought he was."

"Sometimes isn't much use."

"Oh, I know!" cried Elfrida. "I know I'm a fool—but what am I to do?"

"Get over it."

"Get over it? But I couldn't——"

"There's no future in it," Miss Martineau pointed out. "If there's no future in what you're doing, it's better to cut your losses and try a new line. That's what Norman and I did when we left the stage and bought this house . . . it was a plunge, but we took it together. Now listen, dulling: you aren't doing yourself any good dreaming about Glen Siddons; you're getting thinner and paler and more woe-begone every day. You'll get ill if you don't take care—and then what? You'd much better make up your mind to get over it. Oh, it won't be easy, but you'll be able to do it if you try hard enough. You'll feel pretty miserable for a bit, but it's better to be miserable now than miserable all your life . . . and miserable all your life is what you'd be with Glen Siddons."

"But Miss Martineau, I never thought——"

"No, listen, dulling! I've talked to you like this because you're different from the other girls."

"Different?"

"Yes, you're made of different stuff."

"You mean I shall never be an actress?"

"No, that isn't what I mean," said Miss Martineau, frowning in perplexity. "It's true that you'll never be a star with your name in electric lights over the entrance to the theatre—you haven't got it in you—but there's lots of girls who'll never be stars and they're quite happy playing small parts and having a good time, flirting a bit with Tom, Dick and Harry, going to parties every night."

"I don't enjoy parties."

Miss Martineau smiled. "I know that. I've watched you wriggling out of invitations more than once. Dolly was fed up when you refused to go to her Twenty-First Celebration."

"I just couldn't," declared Elfrida. "I've been to that kind of party before, so I knew what it would be like . . . hot and smoky and terribly noisy. They play pop music on the gramophone and everyone talks louder and louder . . . and nobody listens; people drink too much and get silly. I can't understand how anyone can enjoy it."

"Because you're made of different stuff, that's why."

"I suppose I must be," said Elfrida wearily.

"What you need is a nice kind husband," declared Miss Martineau. "Someone who'll look after you; someone who likes the same sort of things that you like."

"Where am I to find him?" asked Elfrida, with an involuntary giggle.

"Oh, don't you worry, there's plenty of time; Mr. Right will come along one of these days. Meanwhile you'll have to work Glen Siddons out of your system . . . and you'll never do that as long as you go on seeing him every night in *The Motor Car*."

"But I can't help——"

"I know!" cried Miss Martineau, with sudden inspiration. "I know what you'd better do. You'd better go to Devonshire and live in that old house."

"Live there!"

"Well, why not? It belongs to you, doesn't it? I don't suppose it would be very comfortable—you said it was old-fashioned, didn't you?—but you could go there and see what it's like. You could go and have a look at the place."

The idea was new to Elfrida, but now that Miss Martineau had put it into her head she realized that she was very anxious "to have a look at the place." In fact she was longing to see Mountain Cross (perhaps that was the reason why she had refused to let it be sold!).

"A change of air would do you all the good in the world," added Miss Martineau persuasively.

"Yes," said Elfrida—but she said it doubtfully. The mere thought of going away was almost unbearable. If she gave up her part in *The Motor Car* and went away, she would lose him completely . . . she might never see him again. "He would forget me in a week," she murmured unhappily.

"Forget you in a week!" cried Miss Martineau. "If that's the way of it, you'd better get over it as quickly as you can."

"I didn't mean it literally."

"Oh, I know that, but all the same . . ." She hesitated and then added, "We're told in the Bible that we ought to be meek, but that doesn't seem very sensible to me. A little pride never did anyone any harm."

"Pride?" asked Elfrida. "Do you mean——"

"I mean you shouldn't hang about and wait for a smile—that isn't the way to treat a man like him—there are too many girls hanging about and waiting for his smile. Well, goodbye for now," added Miss Martineau, rising and toddling to the door. "I take a pride in making my boarders happy and if I don't get a move on, there'll be no supper."

Elfrida lay and stared at the ceiling; there were curiously shaped cracks in it and a stain where water had come through the roof. She had often stared at it and sometimes it seemed that the stain was the shape of an elephant. She stared at the elephant and thought of all that Miss Martineau had said; every word was true. Especially true were her parting words about pride. When Miss Martineau said "pride," she really meant self-respect, but she had got hold of the right idea. Elfrida remembered how often she had hung about in the draughty passage outside the door of Glen's dressing-room in the hope of seeing him for a few moments and hearing him say goodnight. After that she could go home with a warm feeling in her heart. There was not much "pride" about that.

3

Having decided that Miss Martineau's advice was sound, Elfrida proceeded to carry it out to the best of her ability and the following evening at the performance of *The Motor Car* she avoided Glen and chatted to other people. It was easily done; she was sure nobody had noticed, least of all Glen! However, when the play was over and she had changed, Glen was waiting for her in the passage.

"I want to speak to you," he said.

"I'm in a hurry, Glen."

"So am I," he replied. "But before I dash off to Tommy's party I want to know what I've done to upset you."

"Nothing, Glen! Don't be silly!"

She tried to evade him, but he took her by the arm. "Come into my room for a minute. There's always a howling draught in these passages . . . we can't talk here."

As she followed him into his dressing-room, it flashed across her mind that Miss Martineau had been right: to hang about and wait for a smile was not the way to treat Glen Siddons.

"There," he said, shutting the door. "That's better. I've been hanging about waiting for you—in a howling draught. Heaven knows why I ever decided to make a career on the stage; it's the draughtiest place in the world."

Elfrida smiled; she was aware of Glen's allergy to draughts. "This room is like an oven," she said.

"That's how I like it. Sit down, Elfie, and tell me what's the matter."

By this time Elfrida had recovered her wits. She said briskly, "Nothing is the matter. Perhaps I was a bit—a bit wandery tonight, but I'm rather excited. I've just heard that I've got a house."

"I didn't know you were looking for a house."

"Oh, I wasn't! It's—it's an old house on a cliff near the sea. My grandmother died and left it to me in her will."

Glen perched himself on the end of the sofa. "The ancestral home," he suggested.

"Yes, it is—really."

"Why do you get it?"

"Because there's nobody else," replied Elfrida. "At least there doesn't seem to be."

"I'm so glad Elfie," declared Glen, smiling at her very kindly. "You'll be able to sell it and get pots of money, won't you?"

It was funny how everyone had the same idea. "But I don't want to sell it," she told him.

"What are you going to do with it?"

"Live in it."

"That's a good joke!"

"It isn't a joke," said Elfrida. "I've decided to go and live there. I'm glad I saw you tonight because I wanted to tell you about it."

"You can't be serious! Darling Elfie, what do you think you would do with yourself sitting in a dilapidated old house on the top of a cliff—like Mariana at the moated grange or something?"

"I didn't say it was dilapidated."

"It's sure to be; moated granges are always dilapidated. I can imagine you sitting, gazing out of the window. 'There, at the moated grange, resides this dejected Mariana.' "

"Oh, I shan't have time to sit and look out of the window,"

replied Elfrida with spirit. "I shan't have time to be dejected. . . . I intend to keep ducks."

"Ducks?"

She nodded. It had only just occurred to her that she might keep ducks; they waddled and quacked and would be much more friendly and amusing than chickens.

"Good heavens, I believe the girl really means it!" exclaimed Glen.

"Of course I mean it. The house belongs to me; I'm longing to see it!"

Glen frowned. He said, "You aren't chucking *The Motor Car*, I hope."

"But, Glen!" she said hastily. "It's practically dead—you said so yourself! You told me you were on the look out for something else. It won't matter a bit if I give up my part—it won't upset anything—Dolly can step into my shoes tomorrow! She has been longing for me to be ill so that she can play Mrs. Carruthers. Oh, I want to get away *soon!* I want peace and quiet; I want a holiday near the sea——"

"My dear girl, you had better calm down and tell me about it properly."

"I told you," she said, trying to speak reasonably. "It's an old house and probably a bit old-fashioned, but it was Mother's home when she was a girl and she loved it, so I shall love it too. Mother used to talk about it to me, she longed for the lovely fresh air. There's a path down the cliff, leading to a sandy beach; there's a little wood and a farm and fields and a walled-garden with apple trees. It's called Mountain Cross."

"There's a village called Mountain Cross in Devonshire."

"Yes, that's it! Do you know it, Glen?"

"I've been there once or twice. Sometimes I have to go down to that part of the country on business and I remember passing the village and seeing the name on the post office. It's a very isolated place—dead as mutton. Have you got enough money to live on?"

"I don't know, exactly. The lawyer said there wouldn't be much."

"You can't live on fresh air—and apples."

"I can live on very little."

"Darling, listen to me," said Glen, smiling at her with his slow lazy smile. "It strikes me that you're looking at your ancestral mansion through rose-coloured spectacles. You see yourself sun-bathing in a bikini, picking apples attired in a sunbonnet, and scattering corn for the ducks . . . whereas in reality the house will be full of rats, the roof will leak, the chimneys will smoke and a howling draught will blow in under the badly-fitting doors."

She laughed.

"Oh, well, perhaps I'm exaggerating a bit," admitted Glen. "But, honestly, I'm sure the right thing to do is to sell the place. You think the simple life would be fun, but it would be lonely and dull—you would be sick and tired of it in a month."

"I'm lonely in London," she murmured.

"Of course you are! We're all lonely sometimes, but there's no need to sit down and mope. You can always get hold of someone to talk to . . . or you can throw a party and ask the gang and have a cheery time."

"I don't like parties."

"Well, you don't exactly shine at parties," he admitted, smiling at her. "You don't make any effort to be sociable. You could if you liked, you know."

Elfrida was silent.

"Listen, Elfie," said Glen earnestly. "You needn't decide at once, need you? Let's talk it over together—let's have a real good chat about your plans. This play is a mess, but I happen to know that something pretty good is coming along soon. I can't tell you about it because it's top secret, but——"

"Do you mean there might be something in it for me?"

He nodded mysteriously. "Promise not to fix anything until we've had a talk."

"I have to decide before Tuesday."

"Oh, well, that gives us lots of time. Let's see, now: tomorrow is hopeless, of course (how I hate Saturday matinées!); but we could go for a spin on Sunday afternoon and have tea somewhere. You'd like that, wouldn't you?"

She nodded. Of course she would like to go for a spin with Glen in his car.

"That's settled then," he said. "If by any chance I can't manage Sunday afternoon, we could meet and have lunch together on Monday. I had better ring you up and let you know definitely. What's your number?"

Elfrida gave him Miss Martineau's number and repeated that she must decide upon her plans before Tuesday.

"There, I shan't forget that," he said, as he wrote the number in his engagement book. "Yes, I know Tuesday is the day of decision; you told me that before. I'm going to think of all sorts of reasons why you shouldn't bury yourself in the moated grange, and I may be able to tell you a bit more about the good thing that's coming along. No time to argue with you now; I'm half-an-hour late for Tommy's party and it will take me at least twenty minutes to get there." He put his arm round her shoulders and added, "You mustn't go, Elfie. I should miss you dreadfully. You know that, don't you?" Then he kissed her lightly on the cheek and strode off down the passage.

It meant nothing, of course; she knew it meant nothing, but all the same she felt dizzy and her heart was beating against her ribs like an imprisoned bird. She had to lean against the wall for a minute or two until she recovered sufficiently to make her way home.

Elfrida slept very badly that night; her mind was in a turmoil. She had decided to take Miss Martineau's advice and "get over" Glen Siddons; she had decided to give up her part in *The Motor Car* and go to Mountain Cross. This was the right thing to do—Elfrida knew it—but her interview with Glen had upset these sensible plans. I'll wait and see, thought Elfrida. It will be lovely to go out with Glen on Sunday. I'll see what he says . . .

There were two performances of *The Motor Car* on Saturday, but Elfrida had no opportunity to speak to Glen. On Sunday morning she felt ill and wretched; she stayed in the house, hoping for a telephone message . . . but there was none. She thought of ringing him up, but pride came to her aid and she refrained. Glen knew her plans; he was aware that Tuesday was "the day of decision," so he was sure to ring up on Monday morning and arrange a time and place for lunch.

She hung about near the telephone all morning, but the only call was for Dolly Garden.

4

When Elfrida was shown into Mr. Sandford's room, he rose from his desk and came forward to shake hands with her.

"How cold you are!" he exclaimed. "Come and sit near the fire, Miss Thistlewood. My partners think I'm mad to have a coal fire, but in spite of their wonderful central-heating, my room is the most comfortable and best ventilated in the house. I want you to meet my partner, Mr. Leighton, who returned from Mountain Cross last night."

Mr. Sandford rang the bell and in a few minutes the door opened to admit a very large young man; his fair hair and blue eyes and ruddy complexion made him look very young indeed; Elfrida could scarcely believe he was the partner referred to by Mr. Sandford.

"Mr. Leighton will tell you all about it," said Mr. Sandford as he introduced them. "I have an appointment, so perhaps you'll excuse me if I leave you for twenty minutes or so. You aren't in a hurry to get away, I hope."

"Oh, no, I can stay as long as you want me," she replied.

When Mr. Sandford had gone, Mr. Leighton took up the poker and livened up the fire, then he sat down beside Elfrida on a stool and said, "I like coal fires, there's something very friendly about them."

There was something very friendly about Mr. Leighton, so

she smiled at him and agreed. "But people say they make a lot of dust," she added.

"That's what Mother says," declared Mr. Leighton. "I live with her; it's an all-electric house; labour-saving, but not very cosy. Sometimes I wish I had lived in the times when you had oil lamps and coal fires in every room."

"And lots of servants," suggested Elfrida.

"Of course," he agreed. "What fun it would be to pull a bell when you wanted something! . . . But we're wasting time, aren't we? You want me to tell you about your grandmother's funeral."

"I'd rather you told me about Mountain Cross."

"You've seen the place, haven't you?"

"No, but I heard a lot about it from Mother. I've decided to go and live there."

"Live there? Mr. Sandford said you were selling it!"

"It's mine," declared Elfrida.

"Oh, definitely yours, but——"

"Listen, Mr. Leighton, I don't want to be—to be stubborn and unreasonable, but you see I've never had a house of my own before—I've never owned a square yard of ground—so I feel rather excited about it."

"I should think so!" he exclaimed. "Of course it's exciting! I've never owned a square yard of ground and I'm not likely to—until I can afford to buy a miserable little villa in the suburbs. If Mountain Cross belonged to me, I'd be crazy with delight."

"You liked it?"

"Liked it isn't the word," declared Mr. Leighton enthusiastically. "It's a real house. It has been there, sitting on the top of the cliff for hundreds of years; it looks as if it had grown there, like a mushroom . . . no, not like a mushroom (they're impermanent); it's more like a fine old tree, deeply rooted in the soil. I suppose your ancestors have always lived at Mountain Cross?"

"I don't know."

"We must ask Uncle Bob; he'll be able to tell us."

"Uncle Bob?"

"Mr. Sandford," explained Mr. Leighton. "I call him Mr. Sandford in the office because he's the boss, but in private life he's Mother's brother—see?"

Elfrida nodded.

"But that reminds me," said Mr. Leighton, pulling himself together. "That reminds me that I'm supposed to be trying to persuade you that Mountain Cross ought to be put into the hands of a house-property agent and sold as soon as possible."

"You would be wasting your time."

"It's a biggish house, rather old-fashioned, and it's very isolated. You would find it lonely. I mean you're used to a gay life, lots of people and parties and things."

He looked so worried that Elfrida could not help smiling. She said, "Well you've done your duty—you've warned me—so now you can go on telling me about Mountain Cross."

"Uncle Bob will be annoyed with me."

"No, he won't," said Elfrida in comforting tones. "Tell me all about Mountain Cross. Did you have a look round the place when you were there?"

"I had a good look round. We wanted a report upon the condition of the roof, so I got the local builder and he found it in very good order. The farm buildings are all right . . . in fact the whole place is in good condition except the little wood on the hill where some of the trees have been blown down. I expect it would take time and money to clear it up properly. I went round the garden too; it's in a sheltered position behind the house and there's a high wall all round. There are fruit trees: peaches and plums and apples. They have been well cared for, but the rest of the garden is pretty wild, and the greenhouse has practically fallen to bits . . ."

He was still telling her about Mountain Cross when Mr. Sandford returned.

"Well now," said Mr. Sandford cheerfully. "You've fixed it all up, I expect?"

"Not really," replied Elfrida. "Mr. Leighton says it's a big house and rather isolated, standing on the cliff. He thinks it would be difficult for me to live there alone, but——"

"It would be impossible!" interrupted Mr. Sandford in horrified tones.

"Well, perhaps . . . but it was Mother's home and I can't decide anything until I've seen it."

"It would be better to sell it at once."

"That's what Mr. Leighton said, but I can't sell it without seeing it."

He saw by her attitude that it was useless to argue with her. "You're very determined," he said with a sigh.

"I don't want to be unreasonable," said Elfrida, smiling at him persuasively. "But, honestly, Mr. Sandford, is it unreasonable to want to see my mother's old home?"

"Well, perhaps not," he replied. "Would it be possible for you to get a few days' holiday? If so you could go and have a look at Mountain Cross. I'm sure you would realise that you couldn't possibly live there."

"I can have as long as I want."

"Do you mean you are free? Have you given up your part in that play?"

She nodded. "I just felt I couldn't . . . couldn't go on with it."

"Was that wise?" asked Mr. Sandford, frowning.

Mr. Leighton had been silent, but now he intervened, saying hastily, "I went and saw it last night; it's a silly play and it's going down the drain. Miss Thistlewood is well out of it."

"Oh, I see!" said Mr. Sandford. "I'm bound to admit that I know very little about theatrical matters. I suppose there will be no difficulty in Miss Thistlewood obtaining a part in some other production?"

Elfrida was silent. She was aware that it would be very difficult indeed. By walking out of *The Motor Car* she had burnt her boats.

The manager had been quite pleasant to her when she told

him that she wanted to break her contract (glad to get rid of me, Elfrida had thought!), but Glen would be very angry when he heard what she had done; Clarissa Downes would be angry. In fact the whole cast would be annoyed with her . . . all except Dolly Garden who was stepping into her shoes.

"I mustn't take up too much of your time, Mr. Sandford," said Elfrida. "There are just one or two things I want to know. Mother told me she had a cousin; she thought he would inherit Mountain Cross."

"Ah, yes, young Whitgreave!"

"Is he dead?"

"Dear me, no! He's very much alive." Mr. Sandford put his elbows on the table and fitted his fingers together. "It's like this," he said. "Your grandfather's sister, Doris Ware, married James Whitgreave and they went to Canada. They had one son, called Walter, who was about the same age as your mother—they were cousins, of course. For some reason Walter's parents sent him to an English Public School and he often spent his holidays at Mountain Cross."

"Did you know him?"

"Yes, I met him at Mountain Cross quite frequently. Your grandparents were very kind to me and I used to go and stay there whenever I could . . ." Mr. Sandford hesitated and then continued, "But we were talking about Walter Whitgreave. When he left school, he went to Canada to join his parents and your grandfather gave him sufficient capital to set him up in business. I can't remember the exact amount, but it was a substantial sum. In those days Mr. Ware was well off, so he could afford it and I remember his saying to me, 'It's better for the boy to be given money now, when he needs it, instead of having to wait until I'm dead.' "

"Will he be disappointed when he hears that he isn't going to get Mountain Cross?"

"I doubt it," replied Mr. Sandford. "His business is in Montreal, so Mountain Cross wouldn't be much use to him. At any rate he has no cause to complain. Mr. Ware gave him capital when he needed it to start him off in business; not many uncles would do that."

"Whitgreave isn't the only man to have a generous uncle," put in Mr. Leighton.

Mr. Sandford looked at him and frowned in a forbidding manner.

There was a short silence.

Elfrida was the first to speak. "Did Mr. Whitgreave succeed in business?"

"From what I hear he's very well off."

"Have you heard from him lately?"

Mr. Sandford nodded. "Yes, I wrote to him advising him of your grandfather's illness and mentioned that the Wares had lost money recently and had been obliged to use capital for the repair of the roof."

"Did he take the hint?" asked Mr. Leighton.

"It wasn't really a hint . . . or at least it was only a very gentle hint," replied Mr. Sandford. "I had no right to do as much as that (Mr. Ware wouldn't have liked it), but it seemed to me that Whitgreave should be informed of the state of affairs. His uncle had been extremely good to him, so I hoped he would feel it his duty to come over and put things right. People can get about the world so easily nowadays. He replied to my letter very unsympathetically, saying that it was impossible for him to come over at the moment as he was in the midst of a very delicate business transaction."

"That was all?" asked Mr. Leighton.

"That was all," agreed Mr. Sandford. "As a matter of fact I thought 'delicate' was a curious word to use in connection with a business transaction—but that's neither here nor there. I discovered afterwards that Mr. Ware had written, telling Whitgreave about his illness and asking him to come. He received the same reply."

"Ungrateful beast," murmured Mr. Leighton under his breath.

Mr. Sandford pretended not to have heard; he changed the

subject by asking Elfrida to let him know when she wanted to go to Mountain Cross, so that he could ring up the couple who were looking after the place and warn them of her arrival.

"Shall I find out about trains for Miss Thistlewood?" suggested Mr. Leighton. "She'll have to change at Exeter, I expect."

"That would be very kind of you," said Elfrida gratefully.

"No bother at all," declared Mr. Leighton. "I'll ring you up and let you know. What's your number?"

She gave him Miss Martineau's number and watched him write it upon the back of a used envelope. Three days ago she had given Glen the same information . . . Glen had written it in his engagement book and had said, "There, I shan't forget that."

Mr. Leighton made no such promise.

Having fixed up these matters, Elfrida said goodbye and hurried home. She had a feeling that Glen might have rung up in her absence, but Miss Martineau assured her that there was no message for her.

That settles the matter, thought Elfrida and she went to look out her clothes for packing. Her clothes were "town clothes," and she came to the conclusion that she had nothing suitable to wear in the country, so the following morning she went shopping and bought a pair of strong brown shoes, a tweed coat and a skirt to match. It was a light-brown tweed, flecked with white, and she was rather pleased with it. She also bought a couple of pullovers and some stockings.

Miss Martineau was interested and came upstairs to watch her try on her purchases.

"Yes," said Miss Martineau nodding in approval. "You look well in tweeds, which just shows I was right."

"What do you mean?" asked Elfrida, as she surveyed herself in the mirror.

"You're County, that's what you are. It's a bit difficult to explain," she continued, wrinkling her brows thoughtfully. "I haven't met many County people—they haven't come my way

—but you can recognise them a mile off. They've lived in the same place for hundreds of years and they sort of belong to their land. I expect your mother was County, wasn't she?"

"Well, her family has lived at Mountain Cross for hundreds of years," admitted Elfrida, smiling.

"I thought so. County people can dress up and look smart if they want, but they're better in tweeds and pullovers with a string of pearls round their necks. You'd better get a string of pearls, dulling," added Miss Martineau. "Ciro's if you can run to it, but if not, you'll get quite a nice one at Woolworth's."

This was the only piece of advice Elfrida did not take.

At lunch-time Mr. Leighton rang up; he sounded very business-like and Elfrida felt sure he was not alone.

"Miss Thistlewood?" asked Mr. Leighton. "Oh, good afternoon, Miss Thistlewood. I haven't looked up the trains for you because Mr. Sandford has suggested that I should take you down to Mountain Cross by road. He thinks it would be more pleasant for you."

"Oh, yes!" replied Elfrida. "It would be lovely."

"Mr. Sandford wishes me to say he would take you himself, but it's difficult for him to get away from the office at the moment."

"Oh, I know how busy he is!"

"Yes, he's very busy. As you know I've been to Mountain Cross quite recently, so I could give you any information you require."

"But wouldn't it be a bother for you?"

"Not at all. When would you like to go?"

"Could we go tomorrow, Mr. Leighton?"

Mr. Leighton replied that tomorrow would suit him admirably and added that he would call for Miss Thistlewood at six-thirty because the roads would be less crowded in the early morning.

5

The expedition to Mountain Cross had been settled so quickly that Elfrida felt quite breathless—she could not believe she was going to Mountain Cross tomorrow! And why had she said tomorrow? There were all sorts of things to be done. She could not possibly be ready at six-thirty tomorrow morning!

"Of course you can be ready," Miss Martineau declared. "You won't have to press your frocks or wash your nylons . . . I suppose there'll be water at that place and an iron of some sort. When you've made up your mind to take a plunge, it's better to go straight in—not stand and shiver on the brink."

Elfrida laughed.

Miss Martineau laughed too; she had a fat, jolly laugh. "Well, I've watched them at Margate," she said. "People standing in a bitter east wind with nothing on but a bathing-dress, trying to make up their minds. It's enough to make a cat laugh! You go and pack your things like a sensible girl."

The following morning Elfrida was up at five so she was all ready by six-thirty . . . and in spite of the early hour Miss Martineau came downstairs attired in a bright pink house-coat with blue flowers all over it, her hair firmly encased in a bright pink net.

"I wanted to give you a send-off," she explained. "I feel a bit guilty, because you wouldn't be going to that place if it hadn't been for me talking to you like an old granny. I just hope it's the right thing. If you can't stand it, you must come back here; I'll always find a bed for you . . . I mean that, dulling."

"Thank you," said Elfrida huskily. "You've been terribly kind to me, Miss Martineau."

"What am I to say to Glen Siddons if he rings up?"

" 'Annie doesn't live here any more,' " replied Elfrida. She was in a somewhat hysterical condition, hovering between laughter and tears.

"Very well," agreed Miss Martineau. "You're wise to make a clean break; that man is no good to you."

Elfrida had come to the same conclusion; she had decided to push Glen out of her mind . . . but she had a feeling that it was not going to be easy.

"Now, are you sure you've got everything?" Miss Martineau enquired. "You haven't forgotten your hot-water bottle, have you? It'll be cold in that big empty house."

By this time it was six-thirty. "Supposing he doesn't come?" said Elfrida. She was in such a state of apprehension that she hoped he had forgotten all about it.

"He'll come," declared Miss Martineau in soothing tones. "That clock is a bit fast . . . and anyhow you can't expect an elderly gentleman to get up at dawn, can you?"

Elfrida was about to explain that the junior partner of Riggs, Sandford and Wilkins was not "an elderly gentleman" when Miss Martineau, who had been peeping out of the dining room window, gave a loud squeak.

"Here's the car!" she cried. "Oh, what a lovely big black shiny car! Run, quick, and open the door! We don't want him ringing the bell and wakening everyone in the house!"

Elfrida opened the front door and exchanged greetings with Mr. Leighton.

"We're lucky," he said. "It's going to be a lovely day. Don't bother about your suitcases, I'll get them."

He looked a little startled when he was introduced to Miss Martineau . . . but Miss Martineau looked even more astonished. For a moment or two they gazed at each other speechlessly.

"We had better be going," said Elfrida. She kissed Miss Martineau fondly and ran down the steps to the car.

Mr. Leighton followed with the luggage, stowed it in the boot, got in beside his passenger and drove off.

For a time they were silent.

At last Elfrida said, "I know she looks funny, but really and truly she's a darling."

"Oh, of course," he agreed hastily. "I mean I'm sure she's a good sort; it was just seeing her suddenly . . . so early in the morning."

"She's the only friend I've got in the world."

"The *only* friend?"

"Yes."

"There's me," suggested Mr. Leighton diffidently. "I mean we aren't in the office now—and we're going to drive a long way together—so, if you're interested, my name is Ronald. Ronnie to my friends, of course."

Elfrida was feeling tearful again and was annoyed with herself. What on earth was the matter with her this morning? She swallowed a lump in her throat and said, "How nice of you, Ronnie. I'm Elfrida . . . but you know that, don't you?"

"Elfrida Jane," he replied, "Elfrida isn't quite right for you, somehow, but Elfrida Jane is perfect. When I saw your name in Uncle Bob's notes I was sure you would be you. Names are awfully important, aren't they?"

Elfrida thought of Glen Siddons and agreed. She could not imagine him with any other name.

"Elfrida is a very uncommon name," added Ronnie.

"Mother found it in an old book and she thought it was the feminine of Frederick."

"Oh, I see! And Jane was after your grandmother, of course."

Elfrida was silent. This was a new idea to her . . . and a very interesting idea. If her mother had given her the name of Jane *because it was her grandmother's name,* it meant that there was no feeling of resentment in her heart. It meant that Elfrida Jane's mother still loved old Mrs. Ware in spite of everything.

"This is a lovely car," said Elfrida after a short silence. "Does it belong to you, Ronnie?"

"Goodness, no! It belongs to Uncle Bob; that's why I'm being super-careful. I've got a Wisp—it's quite a good little bus, but it isn't comfortable for long trips. At least not for a girl. All the same I was a bit surprised when Uncle Bob said I was to take you in his Jag."

"It was awfully kind of him."

"He's fond of you; that's the reason."

"Fond of me!" exclaimed Elfrida. "He can't be fond of me; I saw him for the first time on Friday afternoon—and I refused to take his advice. He thinks I'm foolish and unreasonable."

"He's fond of you," repeated Ronnie with conviction. "I know him pretty well and I could see that he was very fond of you. I thought he had known you since you were a child—dandled you on his knee when you were an infant. Are you sure——"

"I'm perfectly certain."

They were out of the town by this time, so Ronnie was able to put on speed, but the big car ran so smoothly that the pace was not noticeable.

"Am I going too fast for you?" asked Ronnie.

"Not a bit. It's lovely."

"Good. This is such a marvellous machine that you don't notice the speed. I promised Uncle Bob that I wouldn't go too fast . . . but of course it depends upon what you call 'too fast,' doesn't it?"

She smiled and agreed, adding, "It's very kind of you to take me like this—ever so much nicer than the train."

"Kind of me! I was just thinking how lucky I am to be here instead of cooped up in the office."

"Don't you like being a lawyer?"

"Oh, it's quite interesting," replied Ronnie, without enthusiasm. "I'd have liked an out-door life. I'd have liked to have a farm—growing things and breeding animals—but you must have capital behind you if you're going to make anything out of farming."

"You said you lived with your mother."

"Yes, she has a little house at Uxbridge, quite near Uncle Bob. As a matter of fact Uncle Bob bought it for her. Father died when I was a small child."

"Oh, I'm sorry!" exclaimed Elfrida. "It must be especially sad for a boy not to have a father."

"Yes, I suppose so, but I was so young when he died that I never missed him . . . besides I had Uncle Bob. He was always there—if you know what I mean—so I could ask him things. When I was at school, he used to come and take me out to lunch. I've known lots of fellows whose fathers weren't nearly such good value. I could always depend on Uncle Bob. I can still depend upon him," added Ronnie.

"Have you got any other relations?" asked Elfrida.

"Too many."

"Too many?" she echoed incredulously. "But it must be lovely to have lots of relations!"

He remembered that this girl had no relations—none at all—and realized that she must be lonely. "Oh, well," he said. "You see Uncle Bob has four sisters. The two eldest are married and have families and live quite near us at Uxbridge. Then there's Mother and Aunt Millie—she's the youngest sister and lives with Uncle Bob and keeps house for him. It wouldn't be so bad if they weren't all very sociable and fond of parties."

"Don't you like parties?"

"I like a few—now and then—but not all the time."

They overtook and passed an enormous lorry, laden with iron bars. If "Uncle Bob" had been in the car, he would almost certainly have thought that Ronnie was going too fast . . . even Elfrida, who enjoyed speed, felt her toes curling up in her new brown shoes.

Nothing more was said for quite a long time. Elfrida was

enjoying the swift rush along the Great West Road and the fresh breeze from the open window. They sped along past woods and fields and villages, all bathed in the morning sunshine.

"Let's see, now," said Ronnie at last. "There are several things I've got to ask you. It was Mrs. Ware's wish that the owner of Mountain Cross should take the name of Ware."

"I took it years ago."

"I know you called yourself Ware, but it isn't really your name. It will have to be done by Deed Poll. People can't just change their names whenever they feel inclined."

"Stage people do."

"You aren't a stage person any more. If you intend to live at Mountain Cross you'll have to ——"

"I mean to live there if I possibly can," declared Elfrida. "And I'll be Elfrida Ware. I've been Elfrida Ware for years, so it sounds queer when people call me Thistlewood . . . as if it wasn't me."

"We'll have to wait until——"

"I'm Elfrida Ware from now on," said Elfrida firmly.

He glanced at her sideways and, seeing her determined expression, decided to change the subject. "There's another thing," he said. "Uncle Bob told me that I wasn't to stay at Mountain Cross, I was to put up at the Inn in the village, but it seems to me that you might like to have someone you know staying with you. I mean it's pretty dismal for you to arrive at a strange place amongst strange people. You don't know the Chownes, do you?"

"The Chownes?"

"That's the name of the couple who are looking after the place. They've been there for years."

"Oh, I see! It's a funny name, isn't it? Yes, of course you must stay at Mountain Cross. I suppose there will be a bed?"

"Half-a-dozen beds," replied Ronnie, smiling. He hesitated and then added, "I shall have to tell Uncle Bob that you wanted me to stay."

"Oh, I do," declared Elfrida. "Please stay, Ronnie. The

Chownes may be horrid for all I know. You could cope with them, couldn't you?"

"They aren't horrid, but if there's any coping to be done I'm quite willing to do it." He slowed down to a crawl, turned in at a wide gateway and added, "This is where we're having lunch."

It was a beautiful old country house which had been turned into a hotel. There was a park with fine trees, and a sweep of gravel in front of the pillared portico; half-a-dozen large, shiny cars were parked in an open space.

"It looks terribly expensive," murmured Elfrida apprehensively.

"It is," said Ronnie. "But not to worry; Uncle Bob said to lunch here and gave me lots of money. I'm ready for a good blow-out—so I hope you are, too. We had breakfast terribly early, didn't we?"

The hotel was luxuriously furnished with thick carpets, easy chairs and shining mirrors. Elfrida went to the Ladies' Room to tidy up and when she returned she found Ronnie waiting for her in the hall. He led the way to the dining-room where they were given a table in an alcove and presented with an extensive menu.

"Not many people here today," said Ronnie to the waiter.

"You're early, sir," explained the man. "The place will fill up later on. Would you like the luncheon or would you rather choose something *à la carte*."

"We'll have the luncheon," replied Ronnie. "We left London at dawn so we're hungry . . . at least I am."

"You've made good time," said the waiter, smiling.

When they had ordered their meal, Ronnie leant forward and said, "I rang up Mrs. Chowne. I told her I was bringing you in Mr. Sandford's car and would stay the night at Mountain Cross. She's going to make up a bed for me."

"Good," said Elfrida, nodding.

"She knows me, of course. I've been there before, several times."

"What is she like?"

"Oh, she's nice—I'm sure you'll like her—but she's an awful talker. She never stops talking for a moment; I expect she talks in her sleep. The only thing that annoys me is that she treats me as if I were ten-years-old. When I was looking through Mrs. Ware's papers—after the funeral—she came in and gazed at me in a funny sort of way."

"What did she want?"

"I asked her what she wanted and she replied, 'We thought Mr. Sandford would come—or else send a proper lawyer.' I ask you!" exclaimed Ronnie in disgust.

"It's just that you look young," said Elfrida in soothing tones.

"Don't I know it! Your friend, Miss Martineau, was staggered when she saw me."

"You were staggered when you saw her," Elfrida pointed out.

"That was different. I mean that was because she was such an astonishing sight . . . so early in the morning."

"I know."

Ronnie sighed. "People expect a partner in Riggs, Sandford and Wilkins to be a grizzled dotard or, at the very least, a middle-aged gentleman with stooping shoulders, a bald patch and a pot belly. I'm not really young, you know. I'm nearly twenty-seven and—and I took a First at Cambridge."

"How clever of you, Ronnie!"

"Not clever, just hard work. You see Uncle Bob was paying all my expenses so I felt I had to swot."

Elfrida nodded. "That's what you meant about generous uncles!"

"He was annoyed, wasn't he? I don't often mention it, but sometimes it comes over me and I feel I have to."

"He was only pretending to be annoyed."

"Oh, do you think so?" asked Ronnie, surprised. "That hadn't occurred to me. Perhaps you're right."

"I'm right," she said with conviction. "I haven't got your

kind of cleverness, but I've knocked about a good deal so I know human beings."

"Yes," agreed Ronnie thoughtfully. "You were clever with Uncle Bob; you managed him beautifully. You put things right, so that he wasn't angry with me and you've got your own way about Mountain Cross . . . but we've strayed from the point."

"What is the point?"

"The point is that if I'm going to stay at Mountain Cross you'll have to explain to Mrs. Chowne that I'm a lot older than I look—a very staid and respected member of the firm. You must call me Mr. Leighton and pretend to be a little bit frightened of me."

Elfrida thought this would be difficult—and said so.

"You're an actress," Ronnie pointed out. "So you ought to be able to do a little thing like that quite easily."

"But I'm not an actress any more; you said so yourself."

Ronnie was bending down to pick up his table-napkin which had fallen on the floor and when he straightened himself he had a flourishing brown moustache. He had put it on hastily and it was slightly crooked. "That makes me look older," he said.

"It makes you look like a little boy at a Christmas party."

"Oh, I say!"

She was laughing so much that she could scarcely speak, but she managed to gasp, "Take it off quickly—the waiter is looking."

Ronnie removed it and put it away in his pocket. He said, "Perhaps if I tried to grow one——"

"I don't think it would suit you," objected Elfrida. "Besides, lawyers don't go in for moustaches. Don't worry, you'll get old soon enough."

"Oh, I don't want to *be* old, I just want to *look* a bit older," Ronnie explained. "Peter Riggs is only a year older than I am, but he's dark, with a long, bony sort of face and receding hair."

"He doesn't sound attractive. Is he a friend of yours?"

"He's the son of Arnold Riggs and a partner in the firm," explained Ronnie. "I've known him for years and years, of course. They live quite near us at Uxbridge. . . . I say, don't you like that pudding?"

"It's very nice, but I can't eat any more."

"You ought to eat more," Ronnie declared, looking at her with a worried expression. "You haven't eaten enough to nourish a mouse . . . and you're much too thin."

After they had finished lunch, they had coffee in the lounge and then went out for a walk in the garden. It was pleasant to stretch their legs after sitting in the car all morning and the garden was well worth seeing. There were daffodils, standing up like regiments of soldiers, and there were buds on the trees; everything was much further advanced here than in London.

"I feel as if we were in a different country," said Elfrida. "Even the air seems different."

"It's 'the West Countree.' " Ronnie sighed and added, "I *do* envy you spending spring at Mountain Cross."

Thus reminded of their destination Elfrida suggested that they should continue their journey.

6

The car went like a bird. Ronnie adored driving the Jag (it was a very different machine from his own little second-hand Wisp) and if he had been by himself he would have sped on to Mountain Cross and would have arrived a great deal sooner, but he thought his companion was looking tired so he stopped at a small Inn for tea. It was after five when they turned off the main road, snaked their way through narrow lanes with high banks on each side and presently arrived in a small village nestling cosily in a dell. There was a triangular green surrounded by cottages with daffodils in their gardens. The old church and the vicarage stood back from the road, half hidden in a grove of beech-trees. On the right there was a post office and general store, on the left was an Inn with a signboard depicting Three Jolly Men.

"What a dear little village!" Elfrida exclaimed.

"Mountain Cross," said Ronnie. "And here is the entrance to your property, Elfrida Jane."

There were no gates, just a wide entrance with stone pillars on each side. Ronnie turned in and went slowly up the steep avenue which was more like a dry watercourse than a road.

"It's a bit rough," he commented. "But it would cost the earth to mend it properly and it would be as bad as ever after one or two winter storms."

Elfrida was too excited to speak.

The house was a long-shaped building of grey stone, with a

closely-fitting slate roof. There were only two storeys. It was not a pretty house, but it looked solid and permanent, as if it had been built to stand forever and a day.

Mrs. Chowne must have heard the car approaching for, as Ronnie drove up to the front-door, it opened and she stood there, smiling shyly.

"Here we are!" cried Ronnie. "This is Mrs. Chowne! I told you about her, didn't I? Mrs. Chowne . . . Miss Ware."

Elfrida got out of the car and shook hands with her.

"You must be tired," said Mrs. Chowne. "It's such a long way from London."

"Yes, but Mr. Leighton is a very good driver and the car went splendidly."

"Chowne had better come and help with the luggage," said Ronnie.

"He's coming," replied Mrs. Chowne. "I'll take Miss Ware straight upstairs to her room. You know your way about, don't you, Mr. Leighton?"

Elfrida followed Mrs. Chowne up the wide, shallow stairs. It was dark inside the house; the windows were small and the hall and staircase were panelled with oak, but when Mrs. Chowne opened the door of the bedroom, it was very bright. There were two windows, facing south and west, so the room was filled with the golden rays of the declining sun.

"Oh, what a lovely room!" Elfrida exclaimed.

"Yes, it's nice," agreed Mrs. Chowne. "It was Miss Marjory's room so I thought you'd like it. The furniture is nice and the bed is very comfortable and there's a bathroom next door. The view is nice, too."

The view was magnificent; the windows looked straight out onto calm blue sea which stretched to the far horizon where it merged almost imperceptibly with the cloudless blue sky.

"Lovely!" murmured Elfrida, standing entranced.

"It isn't always calm," said Mrs. Chowne. "Sometimes the waves are furious, dashing over the rocks, but the house is very solid. Mr. Leighton called you Miss Ware, but you're really Miss Thistlewood, aren't you?"

Elfrida nodded and explained the matter. "Perhaps you should use my christian name," she suggested.

"That will be nice, Miss Elfrida," said Mrs. Chowne, smiling happily. "You're Miss Marjory's daughter—and very like her —so I don't feel strange with you and I hope you don't feel strange with me. I was quite excited when Mr. Sandford telephoned and said you were coming . . . so was Ernie."

"Ernie?" asked Elfrida.

"Chowne," explained Mrs. Chowne. "Ernest Chowne his name is. We've been married for twenty-seven years . . ."

Mrs. Chowne certainly was a talker; she continued to chat while Elfrida washed her face and hands and unpacked some of her things. By this time Elfrida had had time to look at the housekeeper properly: she was of medium height, not exactly stout but shapeless, with sandy hair scraped back from her forehead into a large bun. Her eyes were blue and her cheeks hard and red like russet apples; she looked amazingly healthy and strong.

"You've been here for a long time, haven't you?" asked Elfrida.

"I came when I was fifteen—and that wasn't yesterday. Mrs. Ware took me as under-housemaid. I loved Mrs. Ware—she was very good to me—but Mr. Ware was different. He was proud and selfish and he got more selfish when he got older. Very difficult he was at times. For instance, when Mrs. Ware wanted a new rug for the hall he said he couldn't afford it, but he always had money to buy stamps."

"Did he write a lot of letters?" asked Elfrida in surprise.

"Oh, I don't mean stamps for letters; it was stamps for his book. He spent hours, pottering with his book; he used to show his book to Ernie and tell him about it. . . . You leave the rest of your things, Miss Elfrida. I'll unpack them for you later. I better run and see to the dinner now. I'm giving you soup and fried sole and chips and lemon sponge. It'll be ready at eight."

Elfrida was glad to be alone; she opened the window and lay down on the bed. She was very tired and her head was aching . . . but it was so quiet and peaceful, and the soft air drifting in through the window was so refreshing, that soon she began to feel better.

Mountain Cross, thought Elfrida. Mother's home . . . Mother's room . . . Mother's bed! If only Mother were here it would be perfect.

Ronnie and Elfrida were summoned to dinner at eight o'clock and sat down together in the large and somewhat gloomy dining-room. Mrs. Chowne had turned on the light which hung over the table but the rest of the room was in shadow, so it was not until they were half-way through their meal that Ronnie noticed the engravings hanging upon the pannelled walls and got up to examine them.

"They're pictures of the Spanish Armada," said Mrs. Chowne, who had come in with the lemon sponge. "Mr. Ware was very interested in history; there are lots of history books in the library. I'll put on the big light so that you can see the pictures better."

The engravings were in heavy oak frames: one depicted Drake playing bowls with his entourage; the others were scenes of battle, with huge ships firing guns or tossing about in stormy seas.

"It happened out there, of course," said Elfrida pointing to the window.

"It began out there," agreed Ronnie. "I've always been interested in the period; it must have been a terribly exciting time, especially for people living in this part of the world.

"Rather too exciting!"

"Yes. They knew the Spaniards were building an enormous fleet to attack England, but they didn't know when the attack would come. There were beacons on every headland all along this coast to give the alarm. Probably there was a beacon here at Mountain Cross."

Ronnie sat down and helped himself to lemon sponge.

"Tell me about it," said Elfrida. "I learnt about it at school, but I've forgotten most of it . . . and I'm going to live here, which makes it much more interesting."

"All right! You can go to sleep if you get bored. To begin with the Spaniards called the expedition, 'Enterprise England'; they looked upon it as a sort of crusade against the heretics. It took years to prepare but at last in 1588 it set sail—the biggest and most magnificent and best-equipped expedition the world had ever seen! The Spanish ships were enormous and carried thousands of troops; they sailed up the Channel in perfect order—a terrifying sight! The Spaniards had renamed their fleet 'The Invincible Armada' and they weren't far wrong for in a conventional sea-battle, which was what they expected, they could have smashed the English fleet and invaded England without much trouble . . . I don't suppose England has ever had such a narrow escape."

"Not even from Napoleon or Hitler?"

Ronnie shook his head and continued, "Fortunately Howard and Drake were fine sailors and their ships were smaller and easier to manage, so they were able to outsail the Spaniards and harry them with gun-fire, taking care not to come to close quarters. Their chief object was to prevent the Spanish Admiral, Medina Sidonia, from capturing one of the English ports. As a matter of fact he could have taken Plymouth quite easily and landed his troops—and the whole of the West Country would have fallen into his hands like a ripe plum—but his orders were to land at Margate and he dared not disobey them.

"After that everything began to go wrong for Medina Sidonia: the weather was against him; his stores of food and water were found to be badly packed and his ammunition was insufficient for this sort of battle. It was a new sort of battle; it continued off and on for days as the Armada sailed up the Channel. By the time the Spanish fleet reached Margate the ammunition was exhausted, so it was hopeless for Medina Sidonia to stage an attack and the only thing to do was to anchor his fleet in the roads off Calais where he hoped to get more powder and shot and provisions from the Duke of Parma.

"It was then that Drake got the idea of destroying the Spanish fleet with fire-ships—they were known as Hell Burners and were greatly dreaded by sailors—so he prepared seven, filling them with gun-powder and tar and other combustible material, and sent them down-wind into the middle of the Spanish fleet where they created havoc. It was supposed to be rather an 'ungentlemanly' expedient," said Ronnie smiling. "But the situation was pretty desperate."

Elfrida nodded, "It was lucky that the wind was in the right direction."

"Yes, the wind played a tremendous part in 'battles long ago.' The Hell Burners did a certain amount of damage to the Spanish fleet, but more to the morale of the men . . . and the fleet was driven out of the harbour before Medina Sidonia could lay in the necessary stores. It was driven northwards up the Flemish coast and into the North Sea with Drake hard on its heels, harrying it and 'plucking its feathers.' By this time Hope had given way to Despair so the great fleet disintegrated; it broke up into small groups which could easily be tackled by Drake. Many of the galleons were destroyed by storms as they struggled north round Cape Wrath, more were wrecked off the west coast of Ireland. Less than half the ships in 'The Invincible Armada' managed to limp home. It was a tremendous victory for England and a knock-out blow to the prestige of Spain."

"The weather helped us," said Elfrida thoughtfully.

"Of course it did! Nobody appreciated that more than Drake. The medals struck to commemorate the victory bore the inscription, 'God breathed and they were scattered.' "

"It was wonderful, wasn't it? After that people in England could go about their daily work without being frightened, and sleep peacefully in bed."

"Not for long," said Ronnie. "About seven years later Spain

launched another expedition against England and actually managed to land some troops in Cornwall, where they burnt houses and looted villages and behaved in their usual cruel and ferocious fashion. Drake was dead by that time and the English fleet was unprepared but fortunately there was no need for a sea battle . . . a frightful storm blew up suddenly and scattered the Spanish ships and finished them off. God isn't always on the side of 'the big battalions.' "

"I never knew about that!" exclaimed Elfrida.

" 'There are lots of history books in the library,' " quoted Ronnie laughing.

"I shall read about it," said Elfrida. "I shall have plenty of time to read. How lovely that will be!"

7

When they had finished their meal, Ronnie and Elfrida moved into the little sitting room next door where the curtains had been drawn and there was a cheerful fire.

Mrs. Chowne brought a tray of coffee and put it on the table, "This is a nice room," she said. "Mrs. Ware used it all the time after Mr. Ware died. She called it the parlour. It's cosy and you can heat it up quickly with a good fire. Mrs. Ware liked the view from the window and Ernie made a bird table so that she could sit and watch the birds coming for the crumbs and pieces of fat. Ernie is clever with his hands, but he can't talk. I thought I'd better tell you, Miss Elfrida, in case you thought he was surly."

Elfrida looked at her in surprise.

"It was the war," explained Mrs. Chowne. "He was in tanks and got blown up by a mine. He wasn't wounded except for cuts and bruises, but he was unconscious for days and days . . . and when he came round he couldn't talk—not properly, that is. I got to understand him all right and he's improved a lot, but he's shy about it. He talks a bit to people he knows, like Charlie Cobley and Alf Doubleday, but he won't talk to strangers in case they can't understand what he says. You'll thank Mrs. Perrimont for the daffies, won't you, Miss Elfrida? She's the vicar's wife. I thanked her this morning, but you'd better thank her yourself. Nice and fresh, aren't they?" added Mrs. Chowne, as she rearranged the bowl of flowers and put it on the table.

"Yes, of course I must thank her," said Elfrida. "It was awfully kind of her to think of me."

Mrs. Chowne finished arranging the daffodils and went away.

"Did you know he couldn't talk?" asked Elfrida in a low voice.

"Not really," Ronnie replied. "I just thought he was silent because she talked all the time. I mean it's difficult to get a word in edgeways, isn't it?"

"Yes, but I like her."

"Oh, so do I! Elfrida Jane, have you noticed that her legs go right down into her shoes. I mean she hasn't got ankles."

"No, I hadn't noticed."

"She's like Mrs. Noah. When I was a kid, Uncle Bob gave me a Noah's Ark; I loved it dearly and played with it for hours. All the animals and Mr. and Mrs. Noah and their family were carved in wood and painted. Mrs. Noah was just like Mrs. Chowne, sort of square with red cheeks and a white apron."

"And no ankles?"

"No ankles and no waist."

They had been perfectly serious but now, at the same moment, they broke down and laughed.

"All the same," said Elfrida. "All the same she's a pet—and I love her."

"Oh, she is! I adore her," declared Ronnie, chuckling. He added, "You do have funny friends, don't you?"

"Miss Martineau and Mrs. Chowne?"

Ronnie nodded.

"Mrs. Chowne is a very good cook, isn't she?" Elfrida continued, smiling happily. "It was a nice dinner—and everything was served attractively. The fish wasn't a bit greasy. I can't bear greasy fish."

"Horrible," agreed Ronnie. He hesitated and then said, "You had a chat with Mrs. Chowne before dinner. Did you arrange things with her?"

"Arrange things?"

"I was just wondering if you'd arranged how much you're going to pay them."

Elfrida gazed at him in silence.

"It's none of my business, of course," said Ronnie uncomfortably. "I just happen to know they were getting twelve pounds a week from Mrs. Ware. It's a good deal—but you've got money of your own, haven't you?"

"No."

"I thought you had!"

"I haven't a penny—except what I can earn."

It was Ronnie's turn to be silent; he did not know what to say. He had been quite sure, without really thinking about it, that Elfrida Jane was reasonably well off. She was well dressed and she behaved like a girl of independent means . . . she had thrown up quite a good part in that play! The play was rotten and wouldn't last long, but all the same it was rather mad to walk out like that when it was her bread and butter. Unlike his uncle, Ronnie knew a little about theatrical matters and was aware that good parts don't grow on every tree.

"Goodness, how silly of me!" Elfrida exclaimed. "I never thought about paying the Chownes. They seem part of Mountain Cross (as if they had always been here and always would be here); in fact when I was talking to Mrs. Chowne I felt as if Mountain Cross belonged to them and I was just a visitor. It sounds silly, but——"

"I feel exactly the same," Ronnie told her.

"Couldn't I manage somehow? Mr. Sandford said there would be some money."

"There will be a little, but it won't be enough for you to live on and pay the Chownes. I'm terribly sorry, Elfrida Jane. I shouldn't have encouraged you to come and live here. I thought you were fairly well off . . ."

"Why did you think so? I wonder."

"Various things . . . you chucked up your part in that play."

"I just couldn't go on with it. There was a reason."

Obviously she did not intend to disclose the reason so after a little pause Ronnie said, "You can't stay here without the Chownes."

"I might get a girl from the village."

"No, honestly, it wouldn't do. I'm afraid you'll have to reconsider the whole thing. There's no hurry about it, because it will take the Chownes some time to find another post and they can stay on at Mountain Cross in the meantime."

"Oh, Ronnie!" cried Elfrida in distress. "It will be dreadful telling them. They've been here for years and years; Mrs. Chowne remembers Mother when she was a girl. How can I possibly tell them they must go?"

"Did you say you would keep them on?"

"Well, not exactly, but it never occurred to me that they wouldn't be staying on, so I must have given her the impression that everything would be as before. Yes, I'm sure I did, because she said 'Ernie' was going to put up another shelf in the apple room before September and she told me how happy they were in their comfortable little flat. She asked me to go and see it and I promised to go in tomorrow morning. It will be frightful to tell them!"

"Would you like me to explain it to them?"

"Oh, Ronnie, that *would* be kind! You could explain much better than I could. Tell them I'm very stupid and unbusinesslike and I didn't understand. Would you mind doing it for me?"

He smiled ruefully. "That's what I'm here for, isn't it? You said I could cope with the Chownes."

"Yes, but I never thought it would be this kind of coping. It's really awful. They love Mountain Cross—it has been their home for years—and they aren't young. What will happen to them?"

"That's their problem."

"No, it's my problem!" she cried. "I've given them to understand that I'm keeping them here . . . and now I find I can't!"

"Don't worry too much; I'm sure Uncle Bob will be able to

get them another post. A caretaker's job would be best." Ronnie rose and added, "I'll go and speak to them about it."

"Now? But you said there was no hurry!"

"There isn't any hurry, but it's just as well for them to know that sooner or later they'll have to find themselves another post."

When Ronnie had gone Elfrida sat by the fire and considered the matter . . . how incredibly stupid she had been not to think of it before! What was she to do? If she agreed to sell Mountain Cross, the people who bought it might be able to keep the Chownes, but she did not want to sell it. She wanted to live here and make it her home—but could she live here by herself, alone in the house? She was not a nervous girl and would not have minded being alone at night in a cottage with other cottages round her . . . this house was too big, too isolated, too strange! It's because I don't know it, she thought. I shall get to know it quite soon . . . and I shall love it dearly . . . besides what else am I to do?

Yes, that was the trouble: what else was she to do? Go back to London, to Miss Martineau, and try to get some sort of work? She had no training for anything except acting and she was aware that she would never get very far on the stage. Miss Martineau had said, 'You haven't got it in you'—and Miss Martineau was right.

Elfrida was still thinking about it, worrying herself into a sort of frenzy, when Ronnie returned. He came in and shut the door.

"Were they terribly upset?" asked Elfrida in a low voice.

"They were prepared for it," replied Ronnie cheerfully. "They knew Mrs. Ware hadn't much money, so they've been thinking things out and making plans."

"Plans for moving?"

"No, plans for staying."

"But didn't you explain——"

"Of course I explained! They listened to all I had to say and then out came their plan, cut and dried. They don't want to leave Mountain Cross, so they're willing to stay on without any pay."

"What? But they can't!" cried Elfrida. "It wouldn't be fair! I couldn't let them——"

"Hold your horses, Elfrida Jane! It isn't as altruistic as it sounds; in fact it's an excellent plan from everyone's point of view. Your grandmother has left them a pension, and Chowne has a good war-pension on account of his disability, so they won't be badly off if you give them their rooms and fuel and milk and vegetables from the garden. In return he'll do light work on the farm and she'll do some cooking . . . but the main thing is they'll be here to look after you. I said I would tell you and see what you thought."

"I think it's marvellous!"

"I was sure you would agree."

"It's too good to be true!"

"It's true all right. The details will have to be worked out, but I don't think there will be much difficulty about it because they're very anxious indeed to stay on at Mountain Cross."

"Did they say why?"

"He never uttered, of course, just sat there and nodded occasionally, but she talked a lot and gave me all sorts of reasons. For one thing their daughter is married to the postmaster in the village; their name is Doubleday and they have a small boy called Henry James—isn't that nice? I was shown his photograph."

"I hope you admired it."

"Enthusiastically," declared Ronnie, smiling. "It wasn't difficult, really; he looks a nice kid. He's one of the reasons why they want to stay here; another is that Chowne's mother—or father—lives at Cherleigh and likes to be visited occasionally . . . but the most important reason is Chowne, himself. You see his disability makes him nervous of strangers and it would be difficult for them to find a place where he wouldn't have to speak. Mrs. Chowne didn't mention this until Chowne had gone out, but after that she opened up and told me a lot about him.

She has had very anxious times with him off and on. He has settled down now and is much better, but he still suffers from 'black-outs' if he's worried or upset . . . it would upset him to leave Mountain Cross."

Elfrida nodded. Her eyes were full of tears.

"She talked on and on," continued Ronnie. "She told me that last year they went to Bournemouth for a holiday; she thought it would be 'a nice change,' but it didn't suit Chowne because there were too many people about. He became 'so queer and nervous' that they had to come back after three days. Mrs. Chowne was annoyed with the landlady; they had taken the room for a week and the woman wouldn't refund the money. I gather there was a row. Well, that's about all," said Ronnie, frowning thoughtfully. "And I'm sure the Chownes will do all they can to look after you—she promised me they would—so if you want to stay here, you'll be able to manage. You can try it and see how you get on."

"I shall manage." She wanted to say more and to thank him for what he had done, but she could not trust her voice.

"Goodness knows what Uncle Bob will say!" added Ronnie apprehensively.

8

Elfrida had promised to go and see the premises in the east wing of the house which Mrs. Chowne referred to as "our flat," so the following morning after breakfast she opened the baize door and went down the stone-paved passage to the kitchen. Mrs. Chowne was not there, so it was a good opportunity to look about.

Everything was spotlessly clean. There was a kitchen range, so highly polished that it looked like a museum piece; obviously it was not used but was merely an ornament. The gas-cooker was in an alcove; upon it stood a kettle and a pan, simmering gently. The old-fashioned dresser took up the whole of the end wall; its shelves were filled with blue-and-white china. On the top shelf, high out of reach, there were half-a-dozen silver-plated dish-covers of different sizes, ranging from an enormous one, which would have covered a baron of beef, to a small one which might have been used for a plate. Elfrida stood with her head tilted back and looked at them. Long ago they had been used for big dinner-parties! This quiet kitchen had been a hive of activity, with cooks and kitchen-maids bustling about and scullery-maids to wash up the piles of dishes and prepare the vegetables!

Above the gleaming dish-covers hung a row of bells.

The door to an inner room was half open and led to the Chowne's sitting-room, which was furnished with a bright carpet, pictures on the walls, and easy chairs. The widow had a wide sill upon which stood a flourishing geranium in a fancy pot; there was a round table covered with a blue-and-brown patterned cloth. Above the chimney-piece was a shelf with a row of framed photographs standing on it. These included a cricket-team, a group of elderly people, a very good-looking young woman in a pretty hat and a couple who obviously had just been married for they were "all dressed up" and were clinging together desperately and wearing the somewhat dazed expression usual on these occasions. This photograph had faded with age, but it was easy to see that it depicted Mr. and Mrs. Chowne on their wedding day. In the middle of the shelf, and well in the forefront, was a large studio portrait of a small boy . . . Henry James Doubleday, of course!

Having seen all these furnishings and treasures, everything carefully chosen and beautifully kept, Elfrida felt that she understood the Chownes a great deal better. This was a home, dear to its occupants; they had made it and had lived in it for so long that it had become part of themselves.

She was still standing there, looking about her, when Mrs. Chowne came in from the garden.

"Oh, Miss Elfrida!" exclaimed Mrs. Chowne. "I didn't think you would be coming so early, with young Mr. Leighton here and everything! I was in the garden planting some seeds—it's a good day for planting. Did young Mr. Leighton tell you about Our Plan?"

"Yes, he told me last night. It's a very good plan—for *me*. I couldn't stay here alone, and I want to stay here."

"That's what we thought," said Mrs. Chowne nodding. "It's a good plan for us, too. I've been worried to death about what was going to happen to Mountain Cross. If it had been left to Mr. Whitgreave—which was what we were afraid of—we couldn't have stayed. I never liked Mr. Whitgreave. We'd have had to move and goodness knows what would have happened. Did young Mr. Leighton tell you about last year when we went to Bournemouth?"

"He said it didn't suit Chowne."

"Suit him! I thought he was going off his nut! I was scared to death, Miss Elfrida, really I was. He's all right here amongst people he knows, but strangers upset him terribly . . . besides this is our home and we couldn't bear to leave it and go away. This is a nice sitting-room, isn't it?"

"It's delightful."

"I was worrying and worrying about what was going to happen to us . . . and then we heard you were coming and I said to Ernie, 'Well, if she's anything like Miss Marjory she'll be all right.' So then we thought of THE PLAN. It was Ernie's idea, really; he can't talk very well, but he isn't silly—not by a long chalk! You'll have a cup of tea with me now you're here, won't you, Miss Elfrida?"

It was not long since Elfrida had finished breakfast but, as Mrs. Chowne had already begun to make preparations to entertain her, it would have been churlish to refuse.

"We'll fix up everything," said Mrs. Chowne, as she trotted to and fro with an activity surprising in a woman of her build. "You must tell me what you would like me to do, of course. I thought if you could manage your mid-day meal I'd do breakfast and supper for you . . . unless you have visitors, in which case I'll do lunch as well. We'll shut up the dining-room; it takes a lot of cleaning and you'd be more comfortable in a smaller room—Mr. Ware's library will make a nice little dining-room for you—and you'll use the parlour as your sitting-room. If you have a party we can take the drawing-room out of dust-sheets and get it aired quite quickly. We can share the kitchen . . . unless you'd rather do your little bit of cooking in the pantry. There's a small electric stove which would be handy for you. I'll show you where everything is kept; I'm all for keeping things in their proper places and I hope you're the same. Oh, what about your bedroom? Would you like to move into Mrs. Ware's room? It's bigger, of course. I put you in Miss Marjory's room, because she was your mother and I thought you'd feel more at home, but we can easily move your things."

Elfrida had become slightly muddled but the last question

was easily answered. "I like having Mother's room," she said.

"I thought you would," said Mrs. Chowne happily. "Besides it's nice for you having a bathroom next door. That bathroom was put in specially for Miss Marjory when she came home from school—it was a birthday surprise. Now I must tell you Ernie's plans and then we'll all know exactly where we are. 'Light work on the farm' is his intention—as I told young Mr. Leighton—but if I know anything about Ernie—and I've been married to him for twenty-seven years—he'll go on as usual. It isn't Ernie's nature to take things easy; he'd be better if he could—that's what the doctors said. They may have been right or they may have been wrong, but I could have told them they were wasting their breath." With that she gave a hoot of laughter and vanished through the door which led into the kitchen.

The hoot was so loud and sudden and so unexpected that Elfrida was quite startled. Later she got used to Mrs. Chowne's hoots, but it took some time.

While her hostess was absent Elfrida looked out of the window and saw a little garden fenced in with wire-netting; it was divided into halves by a gravel path. The beds were smoothly raked.

"It's mine," said Mrs. Chowne, returning tea-pot in hand. "I've always wanted a little bit of garden of my own to grow snapdragons and sweet peas and canterbury bells and hollyhocks and love-in-the-mist, so I asked Mrs. Ware and she said I could and Ernie put up the netting. It's for flowers, mostly, but I've got a corner for herbs. The big garden isn't very tidy; Ernie grows potatoes and vegetables and looks after the fruit-trees. What with that and Pansy, he hasn't time to do much weeding. You'll find this chair comfortable, Miss Elfrida; I'll put it near the table. Just help yourself to milk and sugar."

"What lovely creamy milk!"

"Pansy."

"Pansy?" asked Elfrida in a bewildered voice.

"Yes. Mrs. Ware bought her about two months ago. You'll be keeping her, won't you? Young Mr. Leighton said you'd let us have milk."

Until this moment Elfrida had had no idea that she was the owner of a cow; she was delighted at the news but hid her surprise and said, "Yes, of course, Mrs. Chowne."

"You must drink lots of milk," said Mrs. Chowne. "You're thin and peaky."

"I've had a very worrying time; Mother was ill for weeks and I couldn't look after her properly—I had to work, you see. I had managed to get a part in a play. It was a poor play and the producer kept changing it, which meant a lot of rehearsals. Then, when at last it was ready, it wasn't a success."

"*The Motor Car,*" said Mrs. Chowne.

Elfrida was surprised. She said, "Are you interested in the theatre?"

"I never get the chance of going to the theatre, but I take a weekly paper that tells you about theatrical productions and films—I wouldn't miss it! Ernie can't be bothered to read about film stars and their divorces and how many times they've been married, but Judy likes it so she gets the paper when I've done with it."

"Is Judy your daughter?"

Mrs. Chowne nodded. "Judith is her proper name; she's forever telling us to call her Judith, but it's difficult to remember. I'd like to come and go with you, Miss Elfrida. That's to say supposing you've got visitors I'll do more and when you're alone I'll do less. I like to take a run down to the village now and then to see Judy and the boy . . . and you won't mind us going to the pictures once a week, will you?"

"Of course not!"

"And another thing: Ernie said to tell you about the parent. It's a nuisance having to go over to Cherleigh—specially in bad weather—but the parent takes the huff very easily."

"Chowne's mother?" asked Elfrida.

"His father," replied Mrs. Chowne. "Between you and me,

Miss Elfrida, he's got a nice bit of money saved. He's ninety-one and Ernie is his only child, so it would be a pity if it went to a home for stray cats. That's what he says when he takes the huff."

"I don't suppose he really means it."

"Well, I don't know," said Mrs. Chowne thoughtfully, "He takes the huff very easily if he thinks we're neglecting him."

"You must go over and see him whenever you like."

Mrs. Chowne smiled happily. "You and me are going to get on like a house on fire. I'll make you cakes for tea and nice little suppers and I'll give you breakfast in bed. You'll soon fill out and put on weight."

"I see you're going to spoil me frightfully," declared Elfrida, laughing.

They had finished their elevenses by this time, so Mrs. Chowne showed Elfrida the other rooms in the flat: one good-sized double bedroom and two single bedrooms, all comfortably furnished. She explained that one of the smaller rooms was Judy's before she was married and the other was "for a visitor." There was also a good bathroom and a wash-house. As they returned through the kitchen Elfrida admired the row of gleaming dish-covers and asked if they were ever used nowadays.

"Oh, they're just for ornament; Ernie likes them," replied Mrs. Chowne. "They remind him of when he was boot-boy in a big house near Bath. The butler was nasty and Ernie was very unhappy; that's why he likes being reminded."

This was a new point of view to Elfrida and she said so.

"Because he's happy now," explained Mrs. Chowne.

"Oh, I see! But it must be a big job cleaning them."

"He does it. He fetches in the ladder and goes up and cleans them himself . . . I'm not allowed to lay a finger on them." She gave one of her wild hoots and trotted across the kitchen to answer the back-door bell.

Elfrida had been on the point of asking whether the bells were in working order or were "just for ornament" like the dish-covers and the old range, but now there was no need to ask; the bell was wagging violently and making a terrific din.

The rest of the morning was spent going round the house with Ronnie, opening drawers and turning out cupboards. During the search she happened to mention that she had not much money.

"Oh, that's all right," replied Ronnie. "Uncle Bob can easily send you a couple of hundred to tide you over until Mrs. Ware's estate has been settled up. Will that be enough?"

To Elfrida it sounded like riches.

9

Ronnie went off directly after lunch . . . Elfrida stood at the door and waved until the car vanished round a bend in the avenue with a spurt of loose gravel from beneath its wheels. She had told him not to drive too fast, whereupon he had grinned mischievously and replied, "It depends what you call 'too fast,' doesn't it?"

She sighed—she was sure he would drive too fast—and turned back into the house. For some reason she felt a little depressed.

"Why don't you go up to the farm and see Pansy?" asked Mrs. Chowne, appearing suddenly from the back premises.

The idea pleased Elfrida, so she put on her brown shoes and a chunky cardigan and, taking a blackthorn stick from the stand in the hall, set forth to view her property. The path led downhill at first; she came to a high wall with a green door in it. This was the garden, of course; she opened the door and went in. There were fruit trees here, and bushes and a tangle of vegetation; on the left, there was an unsightly looking pool of water covered with green slime. At the far end of the garden was an open space where a man was digging industriously.

Elfrida hesitated, wondering whether to go and speak to him. So far she had not spoken to him at all and she was a little nervous about it—how awful it would be if he said something and she could not understand!

Elfrida shut the door quietly and went on up the hill to the farm. A five-barred gate led into the yard, she opened it and went in and looked about. There was no sign of Pansy; in fact the whole place was empty. Elfrida found stables and a coach-house and two large barns . . . all these buildings were in good repair, but obviously had not been used for years. In the bigger barn there was a pile of straw and a rope dangling from a cross-beam in the roof. The afternoon sun streamed in through the sky-lights.

She was standing there, gazing round, when a husky voice behind her said, "Pigs."

"Oh!" she exclaimed, turning quickly.

It was Chowne. He must have followed her up the hill. For a moment or two she hesitated; she was almost sure he had said "Pigs." Perhaps he meant that in days gone by the barn had been used for pigs—but it was so clean and fresh that this seemed unlikely. Unfortunately she could not ask him what he meant; Mrs. Chowne had told her to talk to him, but not to ask him anything. The silence seemed to have lasted too long, so she pulled herself together and said, "It's a lovely afternoon for a walk. Mrs. Chowne told me about Pansy and I thought I'd like to see her."

Chowne nodded understandingly; he led her across the yard to another gate and opened it for her. She found herself in a paddock, enclosed by high banks with hedges on the top of them . . . a brown cow with white patches was lying down in the far corner; she rose slowly and came towards them across the grass.

"Oh, what a darling!" exclaimed Elfrida.

Pansy was a friendly cow; she allowed her new owner to admire her and to stroke her soft brown nose and then followed Chowne across the yard. It was milking time.

The process interested Elfrida—she had never before seen a cow being milked—and she decided to learn how to do it herself. Also, she was interested in Chowne. He was intent upon his task, so she was able to look at him properly. He was tall and thin with large hands and feet; his hair was plentiful, almost white, and had been cut by an unskilled hand. His eyes were dark brown, deeply sunk beneath jutting brows; his face was sad—it was easy to see he had suffered. His wife had said he was happy now, she wondered if it were true.

Elfrida walked on up the hill; she went through a field and found herself in a narrow lane with high banks on each side; on the top of the banks were bushes of blackthorn, their spiky black twigs covered with delicate blossoms. The banks were so high that there was no view of the country. In one place, however, where the bank was lower and blackthorn bushes had given way to hazel trees with little necklaces of yellow catkins hanging upon them, Elfrida scrambled up and had a good look round. There was a field with cows in it; beyond was a rough hill with big rocks and tufty grass and sheep. It would have been fun to go up there, but the cows in the field had horns and had raised their heads from the monotonous business of eating grass and were looking at her with interest—rather too much interest, thought Elfrida—so she jumped down into the lane and went on her way. The lane wandered this way and that in what seemed an aimless manner; then suddenly took a sharp turn downhill and became even deeper than before. On one side ran a little stream, fringed with tiny ferns; on the other side there were big flat stones which overlapped to make a causeway. It was very quiet here and so sheltered that the banks were full of primroses—great cushions of little yellow flowers—and there were bushes of pink blossoms which were sticky to the touch. In one place there was a large clump of violets with a delicious scent.

Elfrida was tired by this time, she was unused to walking, so she sat down upon the bank near the violets. How amazing it was to think that two days ago she had been in London! Even more amazing to think that only a week ago Mountain Cross had been a sort of fairy tale! She had never expected to see it, far less come here to live. She wished that all this had happened six months ago, before her mother was ill, so that they could have come to Mountain Cross together. How happy we would have been! thought Elfrida. How she would have loved showing me her home! Oh dear, if only we had known that the door was open . . .

The bond between mother and daughter had been unusually strong. Marjory was mother, father, sister and dear companion to her child; they had shared joys and sorrows and difficulties. They had always loved each other dearly, but it was only afterwards, when Elfrida was alone, that she realised the fullness of her loss; realised, too, that she was a part of her mother and owed all she possessed to her mother's care and companionship.

In spite of their anxieties and lack of money, they had managed to enjoy life in a quiet way. One of their chief pleasures was to take a bus to the country and to spend a long day walking together through fields and woods, talking to country-people, who were friendly and kind, and admiring the flowers in cottage gardens. Marjory loved flowers, but she never picked wild-flowers . . . she said they should be left to grow in wild places; they faded so soon if you picked them. If there happened to be a little money to spare, she liked to buy a few flowers from a boy who came to the door once a week.

Marjory's illness ended these pleasures; there could be no more expeditions; there was no money for flowers. At first it was "just a cold," nothing to worry about, but as the days passed, her strength failed. Gradually she became too weak to sew or knit—or even to read—and she would lie for hours in the dull little room with nothing but her thoughts to keep her happy. The strange thing was that she had been happy. Elfrida could not understand it—how was it possible to be happy, lying there alone all day doing nothing and seeing nobody?

"But I'm not alone," Marjory had said, taking Elfrida's hand and holding it against her thin white cheek. "God is everywhere —even in this dull little room—so you needn't worry about me."

One day on her way home from a rehearsal Elfrida had bought a bunch of violets from an old flower-woman in Piccadilly Circus and had run upstairs and burst into her mother's room in breathless haste.

"Darling, is something the matter?" asked Marjory in alarm.

"Nothing wrong—just a surprise—shut your eyes, Mother."

So Marjory had shut her eyes and, when told to sniff, had sniffed. "Violets!" she had said . . . and suddenly tears of weakness ran down her cheeks.

Elfrida could never forget that moment, for it was then she realised that her mother was hopelessly ill . . . and it was that night when supper was over and Elfrida had cleared it away that Marjory had begun to talk about Mountain Cross. She talked about the old house which had stood upon the cliff for hundreds of years; about the garden and the orchard and the farm and the dapple-grey pony, which she had driven in a little cart through high-banked lanes; about the woods carpeted with bluebells—so blue that it looked as if bits of the summer sky had fallen—but most of all about the sea and the waves breaking on the shore and the fresh breezes. It was then that she had said in her husky whisper, "If I could see it just once—and breathe that lovely air—I'd get well quite quickly."

"You'll soon be well," Elfrida told her. "I shall make a lot of money and we'll go to the sea-side for a long holiday. There are other places besides Mountain Cross."

"Yes, of course," agreed Marjory, smiling. "Let's decide where to go."

"We'll go to the Western Isles," Elfrida told her. "There's a railway poster of the Western Isles in the Underground Station; I saw it this afternoon. There's green grass, blue sea and white sands and seagulls. You'll like that, won't you?"

"It sounds heavenly . . . and it's such a lovely name: the Western Isles."

"That's where we'll go when I'm a star and I've made lots of money."

Alas, they both knew they were building a castle in the air.

Elfrida was still sitting on the bank beside the clump of violets, but her thoughts had travelled a long, long way and her eyes were full of tears. The castle had not been "in the air"; it had been here all the time, waiting for them to come. If only they had known . . .

It was late when at last Elfrida found her way home—she had got thoroughly lost amongst the winding lanes.

Mrs. Chowne prepared her supper and brought it into the parlour on a tray. The meal consisted of bread-and-butter pudding and a baked apple. Bread-and-butter puddings are often soggy and tasteless, but Mrs. Chowne's version was delicious; crisp on the top and creamy underneath. The apple was large and stuffed with dates and was accompanied by a jug of cream.

After this delectable meal, Elfrida sat by the fire and tried to read a book about Sir Francis Drake, which she had found in her grandfather's library; it was an interesting book, but her day had been tiring and she was so full of fresh air and bread-and-butter pudding that she could not keep her eyes open.

She was awakened by Mrs. Chowne who came in to tell her that Mr. Cobley had called about the copse.

"What did you say?" asked Elfrida, struggling out of a dream.

"Mr. Cobley . . . about the copse. Shall I let him in?"

"Oh, yes, of course!" Elfrida exclaimed. She was still half asleep and was under the impression that her unexpected visitor must be connected with Scotland Yard, but this somewhat alarming idea vanished when she saw him.

Mr. Cobley was a chubby man—a true countryman—with a round pink face, cleanly shaved, and pale blue eyes. His hair was brown and very thick except for a round bald patch on his crown . . . Elfrida would have cast him as Friar Tuck without the slightest hesitation.

"It's about the copse," said Mr. Cobley. "It's an eyesore—that's what it is. I walked up there on Sunday and took a look round. It used to be a nice little wood, but it's been neglected—

wants tidying up. I thought I'd just call in and mention the subject."

"Oh, I see!" Elfrida was sitting upright in her chair and trying to look intelligent. "Yes, Mr. Leighton said something about it. I haven't seen it yet."

"It wants tidying up."

"I know, but I'm afraid it's out of the question. It would cost a lot of money."

"Now, that's where you're wrong, Miss Ware. Of course it's natural that a lady like you don't understand copses. It takes a man that knows about wood. I've been in wood since I was a kid. What with Father being a carpenter and me being in forestry for a bit, you might say I know about wood from A to Z." He gave her a beaming smile and added, "I daresay you could act Romeo and Juliet to the life, but copses is a different matter."

"Quite different," agreed Elfrida, stifling an involuntary giggle.

"It isn't much good explaining," he continued. "The best thing would be for you to walk up the 'ill some morning—say Saturday, I'm not so busy on a Saturday—and I'd meet you there and take you round. In 'alf-an-hour you'd see for yourself. You'd see that some of the trees 'ave been blown down—it was that gale we 'ad last winter—and some of the trees 'ave been rooted up and blown against other trees. It's a mess."

"It sounds dreadful, but I couldn't afford——"

"But it wouldn't cost you nothing! Ernie Chowne and me and Tom Parkins—if we can get 'im—could do the job. It'll take some time, of course, but here isn't any 'urry."

"I don't understand, Mr. Cobley. You say it wouldn't cost me anything, but surely you'd want to be paid for your time and trouble?"

"There's good wood there and I'd give you a good price for it, see?"

Elfrida saw. She said, "I don't like the idea of cutting down trees."

"Nobody does," agreed Mr. Cobley. "Trees take a long time to grow and they're very pretty; I'm fond of trees. It's just because I'm fond of them that I don't like to see them in a mess. When they're getting past their prime and being torn up and blown down in every gale it's a mistake to let them lie and rot. You'd be better getting good money for them, wouldn't you?"

Mr. Cobley went on talking; he was very persuasive and Elfrida liked him, so she agreed to meet him in the copse on Saturday morning at ten o'clock.

10

Various arrangements had been made with Mrs. Chowne; it had been agreed that Elfrida should look after her own bedroom and bathroom so she set to work immediately after breakfast. She was astonished at the cleanliness—no smuts!—and the task did not take her long to complete. Yesterday she had gone inland and walked through the lanes; today she decided to walk by the sea, but first she went into the parlour where she found an old-fashioned and somewhat clumsy pair of field-glasses in a shabby black leather case and swung it over her shoulder.

There was a side-door at the end of the passage; Elfrida unlocked it and went out. The wind caught it from her hand and slammed it behind her . . . three steps led down to a stretch of bright green turf which sloped gently to the edge of the cliff. The wind was boisterous, it tore at her skirts and ruffled her hair, but Elfrida enjoyed the sensation; she stood there for several minutes breathing deeply. Then she went down the slope to the edge of the cliff and looked over. Below her was a little bay sheltered from the west by a promontory of rock which stretched out into the sea.

This was the bay of which her mother had spoken: "Such a lovely place to bathe . . . but you have to be careful, of course. The path down the cliff is rather steep . . . and the current is dangerous at ebb-tide."

Elfrida could hear her mother saying it, but being a town-dweller, she did not understand. She could see the remains of a path down the cliff; there were rough steps and a piece of wooden railing, hanging crookedly; in other places there seemed to be no path . . . but her mother had used this path so it must be all right, thought Elfrida.

At first it was fairly easy; the steps were rough but solid, the path wound between bushes. Then she came to a place where there had been a cliff-fall and the path had been swept away . . . but by grasping the roots of a stunted oak and letting herself down carefully she managed to pass. It was not until she was within about ten feet of the bottom that the path ended abruptly in a scree of gravel. Elfrida hesitated, clinging to a boulder which was imbedded in the cliff . . . it was maddening to have come so far and to be defeated! Then suddenly the ground beneath her feet gave way and the next moment she was lying on the beach amongst a small avalanche of loose stones

She lay there, laughing. It had been an undignified performance, but there was nobody to see . . . and she was not in the least hurt.

The little bay was sheltered from the wind; the sun was golden, the sea was deep blue. It was much too cold to bathe, but later, in May or June, it would be delightful.

There were several ships in view, but Elfrida was too ignorant of nautical matters to identify them. One, which was nearer, was small and shabby.

" 'Dirty British coaster with a salt-caked smoke-stack
" 'Butting through the Channel in the mad March days . . .' "

Elfrida said it to herself and smiled. How strange that you learned a poem, but never envisaged the image it was intended to create until you saw it with your eyes! She could hear a curious noise, thud-thud-thud, and realised that this was the sound of its engine.

There were two fishing-boats, lying off the point of the promontory, anchored and heaving to the swell of the waves, so she took out the field-glasses and tried to focus them on the boats . . . at first it was all a blur, then suddenly her fingers found the trick and a bright clear picture sprang into view: the black boats with white letters on their sides; the men in yellow oilskins. What were they doing? Elfrida's silent question was answered almost at once, for while she watched, one of the men began to haul in a line and there was a fish on the end of it . . . a wriggling fish, its scales glittering like silver in the bright sunshine!

I might have known! thought Elfrida.

How quiet and peaceful it was in the little bay! The dirty British coaster had passed and there was no sound except the swish of the waves as they broke on the beach and the rattle of pebbles as they retreated. Elfrida did not know whether the tide was coming in or going out; there was a great deal she did not know about the country and the sea . . . but she could learn, of course. She could use her eyes and ears, she could use her nose. The smell of seaweed drying in the sun was intriguing.

Glen had told her it would be dull—she would tire of it in a month—but how could you feel dull when there was so much to learn? Glen had said . . .

But it was a mistake to think of Glen; she had decided to take Miss Martineau's excellent advice and to banish him from her thoughts. It was not easy, of course; every now and then something would remind her and the longing to see him and to hear his voice rose like a flood and threatened to swamp her. The flood was rising now, but Elfrida refused to be swamped.

Although she looked younger than her age and had a gentle manner, there was an inner strength in Elfrida. She had been brought up to fend for herself in the world of the theatre—a world full of intrigue and undercurrents—she had known the pinch of poverty. During her mother's illness she had known agony of mind and had been obliged to hide her troubles—and appear gay—when her heart was breaking. She had learnt fortitude; she had learnt that sitting still and feeling sorry for yourself did you no good at all, it was better to pretend to be cheerful . . . so she jumped up and ran along the beach at the edge of the sea, dodging the waves, not always successfully, and poking about amongst the rocks and filling her pockets with little shells which she found in the gravel. Surprisingly soon the pretence of cheerfulness became reality.

Elfrida spent quite a long time playing about in this childish manner; she might have spent longer if she had not begun to feel rather queer. It was a slight faintness, accompanied by an emptiness in her inside. She had not experienced the pangs of hunger for so long that at first she did not recognise them . . . then she realised that she wanted her lunch! It had been arranged that she was to cook her own mid-day meal—there was a chop waiting for her in the larder.

Coming down the cliff had been difficult enough but going up was infinitely worse: first there was the scree of stones to negotiate; every yard she managed to climb she found herself slipping back with an avalanche of loose gravel. However, she was young and agile and full of determination, so she scrambled on and reached the boulder (from which she had fallen) with scratched hands and jagged rents in her stockings. She paused for a few moments to rest and then went on, climbing carefully—she had learnt to be careful—hauling herself up by the gnarled roots of the stunted oak, creeping past the dangerous places on her hands and knees, until at last she arrived at the top.

Mrs. Chowne was washing up dishes in the pantry when Elfrida went in.

"It's two o'clock and you haven't had your lunch——" began Mrs. Chowne reprovingly. Then she exclaimed, "Miss Elfrida, what on earth have you been doing! Look at your stockings!"

"I went down to the little bay."

"You went down to the bay? But the path has gone—there was a cliff-fall last winter. How did you get back?"

"Climbed," replied Elfrida, beginning to giggle hysterically. "It was more—difficult—than I expected. Don't worry, Mrs.

Chowne; I'm hungry, that's what's the—matter with me. I'll cook that chop and ——"

"Nothing of the kind!" cried Mrs. Chowne. "You'll sit down on that chair and I'll give you a nice slice of veal pie that's left over from our dinner . . . and don't you ever do such a silly thing again, it's dangerous! If you want to go down to the bay, Ernie will mend the path and make it safe. My goodness, you might have broken your leg!" declared Mrs. Chowne as she bustled round preparing the meal in her usual competent manner. "Ernie'll have fits when I tell him . . . promise me you won't do it again."

Elfrida promised. She realised that Mrs. Chowne was right—it had been silly.

When Elfrida had finished her belated meal Mrs. Chowne sent her off to bed—it was a new and extremely pleasant experience to be cared for in this way—she lay there, dozing off and on until tea-time and was just thinking of getting up when Mrs. Chowne walked in with the tea-tray.

"You shouldn't!" cried Elfrida. "You're making me lazy!"

"It's good for you to be lazy," declared Mrs. Chowne. "I want to fatten you up a bit. You've had a bad time—anyone can see that. A bit of cossetting is what you need."

Elfrida sat up and enjoyed her tea . . . and thought about Mrs. Chowne. At first she had thought Mrs. Chowne rather a foolish woman—one was apt to think that about a woman who talked so much—but Elfrida was beginning to see through the smoke-screen of chat and to discover the real Emma Chowne behind it. She was extremely intelligent. It seemed unfair that she had not received a satisfactory education. Nowadays the veriest chit, with no brain to speak of, was given the benefit of the best education the state could supply (free of charge with meals thrown in for good measure), but when Emma Chowne was a child things were different. She had told Elfrida that she was the eldest of a big family and her mother had often kept her at home to help. "They used to make a bit of a fuss," Mrs. Chowne had said. "The school officer used to come . . . but what could mother do? She needed me when the babies arrived; I was good with babies. It wasn't that I didn't like school, Miss Elfrida. If I could have been in two places at once, I wouldn't have missed a day. I'm not clever, you know, but I seem to be able to see as far through a brick wall as most people and I've learnt a lot on my own . . . a lot of useful things that you don't learn at school."

Elfrida had nodded. She too had learnt a lot on her own.

After tea Elfrida went out to do some more exploring. She let herself out of the side door and found a path which led along the top of the cliff to a clump of trees, stunted and deformed by age and weather. She passed through them, picking her way over the gnarled roots and came out on the other side . . . and there, before her eyes, was a small round hillock crowned by a large stone cross. The sun was declining amongst rosy clouds and the cross was outlined boldly against the sky.

Mountain Cross! thought Elfrida. That's the reason! Why did nobody tell me? It isn't a mountain, of course, it's a cliff . . . but Mountain Cross sounds better. Who put it here, and why?

When she had looked at it for a while, and had watched the rosy clouds fade and the sun disappear behind a thick bank of darker cloud, she went forward up the little rise until she was standing beside the cross. The base was built of stones, firmly held together; the cross towered high above her head. She saw then that the monument—if such it was—had been here for a very long time. On the landward side it was covered with lichen. The cross-piece stretched out, facing the sea and on one end of the cross-piece was the remains of an iron basket, rusty and broken. Why? What was its purpose? She must ask someone.

Turning seawards she found she had a vast view of undulating waves stretching to the far horizon.

11

The next day was stormy; the wind had risen to gale force, blowing from the south west and splashing rain against the windows as if it were being emptied out of buckets. Elfrida had always said that she "didn't mind weather," so she sallied forth in rubber boots, a waterproof and a polythene cap . . . but she had never experienced the full force of a sou'-wester and it was too much! The wind battered her and took her breath away, the sheer weight of water was quite alarming, so she struggled home and came in at the back-door which was comparatively sheltered. Fortunately Mrs. Chowne was in her own premises, giving her sitting-room a thorough turn out—and humming "The Voice That Breathed O'er Eden," slightly out of tune, which she always did when she was enjoying herself—so Elfrida was able to escape upstairs to the bathroom and divest herself of her soaking garments without being observed. She was aware that Mrs. Chowne would not approve of her expedition.

The wind and the rain continued all day without abatement; Elfrida went to bed with the roaring and the splashing in her ears and lay awake for some time, thinking about tomorrow morning . . . for tomorrow was Saturday and she was trysted to meet Mr. Cobley in the copse. If this went on it would be quite impossible, of course, and it seemed to have been going on for such a long time that she could not believe it would ever stop.

She awoke to see brilliant sunshine streaming in at the window and realised that the storm was over.

"What a blow!" said Mrs. Chowne as she brought in Elfrida's breakfast. "It's over now, but it has done a lot of damage the postman says. Trees down and slates flying about and old Mr. Copp's roof torn off—well, what did he expect? It's a thatch and he grudges the money for mending it properly. It would take more than a sou'-wester to tear the roof of Mountain Cross," declared Mrs. Chowne cheerfully. "And if you're going up to the copse to meet Charlie Cobley, you'll better put on your rubber boots. Everything will be as wet as water."

Elfrida was early for her appointment with Mr. Cobley; she had intended to have a look round before he appeared, but when she approached the little wood she heard the sound of voices and realised that already he was there—and not alone. There was no sign of him, but she found what had once been a path; it was almost hidden by a tangle of brambles and obviously had not been used for years, but she pressed on through the trees and came to a clearing where an oak had been torn up by the roots and was lying full length upon the ground. Here she found Chowne, Mr. Cobley and another man—a burly individual whom she had not seen before. A large two-handed saw, gleaming like silver in the sunshine, was leaning against the fallen tree.

It was Chowne who saw her first; he touched Mr. Cobley's arm and pointed.

"Oh, good-morning, Miss Ware!" said Mr. Cobley. "'Ere's another casualty—it's come down in the night and no wonder! That was the biggest blow we've 'ad this year. There'll be work for the slater, I shouldn't be surprised. I'm glad you've come this morning because we've got Tom Parkins and we're starting right away."

"But I didn't mean you to start!"

"Soonest begun, soonest done," said Mr. Cobley cheerfully.

"We've got Tom Parkins, which is lucky. We'll make a good job of it."

Elfrida hesitated, wondering what to say. Evidently Mr. Cobley was under the impression that she had given permission for the work to be carried out and had engaged the burly Tom Parkins to come and help—truth to tell she had been so sleepy that she could not remember what she had said! Mr. Cobley had told her that it would cost nothing to have the copse tidied up, but Elfrida was no fool and was aware that sometimes things turned out differently from what one was given to understand. At last she said tactfully, "Of course I should like the place tidied up—and I'm sure you would make a good job of it—but I must know exactly what it would cost."

"Well, it's difficult to say *exactly* in a job like this," replied Mr. Cobley. "Some of the wood is good and some of it is rotten . . . but I'll give you what's right. Ernie will see I don't cheat you, won't you, Ernie?" He slapped 'Ernie' on the back and laughed uproariously.

Apparently this was a joke—so Elfrida smiled.

"Look, Miss Ware," said Mr. Cobley, suddenly serious. "I'll make a bargain with you. I said it wouldn't cost you nothing and I'll stick to it. I might make a few pounds—over and above—or I might lose a few pounds. I'll take the risk. What about it?"

Elfrida agreed to the bargain. She had no idea whether or not it was fair, but she had become very anxious to have the little wood tidied up; it was a blot on the landscape of Mountain Cross.

"Right!" said Mr. Cobley. "Now we know where we are, so you two chaps can get on with it. I'll take Miss Ware round the copse and mark the trees."

He led the way and Elfrida followed as best she could; the undergrowth was thick and matted and soaking wet, so it was not easy and she was glad of her rubber boots. Mr. Cobley talked all the time: this tree was in good condition—he could give Miss Ware a fair price for it—that one was rotten at the core, but would make nice logs for the fire; yet another would have to be taken down because its roots had been loosened and the first winter gale would uproot it . . .

There was a little grove of beeches at the west end of the wood—and here they paused.

"You aren't going to cut down these trees, are you? They're lovely," said Elfrida.

"They're lovely, but they're cramped. A beech wants room to spread and grow into a 'andsome tree. See what I mean?"

"Yes, I see."

"It'll 'ave to be carefully done," said Mr. Cobley, looking round and frowning thoughtfully. "Would you be willing to leave it to me?"

"Yes," she replied. She had realised that Mr. Cobley knew his job. He knew his job inside out, so perhaps he knew other things as well. Perhaps he knew the history and the meaning of the cross on the hillock (she had asked Mrs. Chowne and Mrs. Chowne had said, "Oh, its just an old monument or something.")

"Mountain Cross," said Mr. Cobley nodding. "It's funny that you should ask me about that. I don't know who built that cross—it's been there 'undreds of years—and I doubt if anyone could tell you. No, it isn't a monument--not like a War Memorial—it's a landmark put there for sailors and fishermen and such-like. The iron basket is a cresset—at least it was in the old days. There was a chap lived in a little cottage near-by. You wouldn't notice it, for it's no more than a 'eap of stones covered over with nettles, but I dessay it was quite a nice little cottage at one time. The chap got the cottage free of rent, but one of 'is duties was to put a light in the cresset at night."

"An oil lamp?" asked Elfrida with interest.

"Well, I don't know," replied Mr. Cobley, scratching his ear. "An oil lamp wouldn't show up very well, would it? More likely to be a sort of torch—rags soaked in tar—but I wouldn't 'ave a bet on it. You ask me something about wood," suggested Mr. Cobley.

Thus reminded of the job in hand, they continued their tour of the copse and presently returned to the clearing, where they discovered that Chowne and Tom Parkins had stopped work and were having "a breather."

"It's a pity when woods is neglected," said Mr. Cobley in conversational tones. "They ought to be looked at regular."

"That's right," said Tom Parkins in a voice so deep that it seemed to come out of his boots.

"It's a funny thing," continued Mr. Cobley. "Everyone knows that trees grow—it's silly to say it, really—but in spite of that everyone plants them too close. Everyone forgets that when trees grow bigger, they'll need more space. This is a nice little copse and when we get it tidied up and the brambles cleared, it'll be a nice place to walk. You could 'ave a seat or two; you could bring your friends 'ere in the evening. That 'ud be nice, wouldn't it?" His round pink face smiled at Elfrida so engagingly that she was obliged to agree.

"Seats would be easy," he told her. " 'Ere's Ernie Chowne; 'e could knock up a few rustic seats as easy as pie. It wouldn't take 'im long once 'e's got the pens made. The pens is first, of course, we all know that."

"Pens?" asked Elfrida.

There was a moment's silence. Mr. Cobley looked at Chowne . . . and Chowne looked at Mr. Cobley.

"One of the barns wants some work done to it," Mr. Cobley said. "It's a nice barn; you want to keep it nice, don't you, Miss Ware?"

"Yes, of course."

"That's all," said Mr. Cobley.

It was not "all." Elfrida was sure there was a secret understanding between the two men . . . but Mr. Cobley and Tom Parkins had begun to saw with such tremendous vigour that she could not hear herself speak. She decided to leave it for the moment and ask Mrs. Chowne, who was sure to know what it was all about and was quite incapable of keeping a secret.

This plan, though excellent, was banished from Elfrida's mind when she returned to the house, for Mrs. Chowne was awaiting her with the news that Mr. Sandford was in Tavistock on business and had phoned to say they could expect him at tea-time and, if convenient, he would like to spend a couple of nights at Mountain Cross.

"Mr. Sandford?" asked Elfrida in surprise.

"Yes, Mr. Sandford himself," replied Mrs. Chowne portentously. "I thought we'd put him in the blue room; he had it when he came here before. There's a lot to be done, so we'd better get on."

There was a lot to be done: the bed to be made and aired with an electric blanket; "a nice little dinner" to be planned (Mr. Sandford could not be expected to eat bread-and-butter pudding, however delectable) and a bottle of Mr. Ware's claret to be fetched up from the cellar and put to warm gently by the fire.

"Oh, dear, I wonder what he's coming for," said Mrs. Chowne as she trotted about, upstairs and down, like a circus pony. "Oh, dear, I hope he's not going to say you can't live here by yourself, Miss Elfrida. We're getting along so nicely, aren't we?"

12

Mr. Sandford arrived in his large black Jaguar at four-thirty precisely. The car, which Elfrida knew so well, was driven by Mr. Sandford's man who carried in a suit-case and a brief-case and then went off to the village to put up at the Inn.

Tea was ready in the parlour, so Elfrida and her guest sat down by the fire and chatted comfortably together. Mr. Sandford seemed different today, less formal and more friendly; he asked permission to use Elfrida's Christian name, adding that he had known her mother.

"You're like her," he said.

"But Mother was beautiful when she was young," objected Elfrida. "Everyone says so—and there's that lovely portrait of her in Grandmother's bedroom."

Mr. Sandford smiled. "All the same you're very like her. It isn't so much the physical resemblance—although that is much stronger now that you aren't so tired and pale—it's more your voice and—and the way you think. I find it difficult to explain."

"I expect it's because we were so much together," Elfrida replied in a low tone. "Mother was a wonderful person and she was everything to me . . . I was like a lost spirit when she died. It's because of Mother that I want to live here; because this was her home and she loved it."

"I can see you're determined to live here. Well, there's no

harm in trying it. Ronnie told me about the arrangement with the Chownes . . . do you think it will work?"

"Oh, yes, it's working splendidly. They're very nice people."

"It's early days. You haven't been here long—but if you find it too lonely, we can make some other plan." He hesitated and then added, "It's such a very different life from your chosen career on the stage."

"I didn't choose the stage . . . I mean it just happened. Father was an actor, so he was able to get small parts for me and I had to go on with it because there was nothing else for me to do. I had to do something."

"Do you mean you don't like it?" asked Mr. Sandford in surprise.

"Not really . . . and I knew I should never be any good. There was no future in it for me." She thought of Miss Martineau as she spoke and added, "If there's no future in what you're doing, you should cut your losses and try another line."

Mr. Sandford nodded. "Well, you certainly don't lack courage, Elfrida. You must do as you feel inclined, but I hope you will look upon you as a friend and let me know if you aren't happy at Mountain Cross. I can see you don't want to go back to the stage, but I could help you to find some other employment if necessary."

"Oh, how kind of you, Mr. Sandford!"

"I daresay you were surprised to hear I was coming today, but the fact is I had to see a client in Tavistock, so I thought I would kill two birds with one stone. I've got some papers for you to sign, relating to your change of name, and I want to speak to the Chownes about their pension which, as you know, was bequeathed to them by your grandmother . . . but all that could have been done by letter."

Elfrida looked at him enquiringly.

"You remember you asked me about your mother's cousin, Walter Whitgreave?" continued Mr. Sandford. "He has come over from Canada for a short visit and he called at the office to see me. Unfortunately I happened to be out, so he saw young

Peter Riggs who hasn't much gumption. I wish I'd seen Whitgreave myself."

"Is he coming here?" ashed Elfrida apprehensively.

"Yes, he is visiting his friends, the Bannisters, who live in Plymouth and intends to come over to Mountain Cross. He used to spend his holidays here when he was a boy. I told you that, didn't I?"

Elfrida nodded.

"Now, it's quite unnecessary for you to worry," said Mr. Sandford soothingly. "I know you have an uncomfortable feeling that you've 'done him out of Mountain Cross,' but, as I explained to you before, he was generously treated when he was young and, what's more, if he had come over when his uncle was ill (as he should have done) the place would have been left to him."

This idea was alarming.

"Big issues hang on small pegs," added Mr. Sandford.

"Yes," agreed Elfrida. She added thoughtfully, "It's rather frightening when you think of what might have happened if you had done something different. For instance, if I hadn't come to see you—and I nearly didn't—I wouldn't be here now."

"Or if you had seen one of the advertisements which I put in the papers last October, you might have been here months ago."

"I thought of that, too," admitted Elfrida in a low voice. "We both might have been here . . . and perhaps Mother would have got better."

There was a short silence.

"Well, what about Walter Whitgreave?" asked Mr. Sandford.

"Yes," said Elfrida doubtfully. "Do you think I had better ask him——"

"I was about to suggest that you should ring him up and ask him to lunch tomorrow. With your permission I shall stay and see him."

"Oh, yes, please stay! It would be such a help if you were here when he comes."

"That will suit me very well. I want to see Walter—or Walt as he calls himself nowadays—and I missed him in London."

"Walt? Oh dear! And Walter is such a nice name."

Mr. Sandford nodded. If he had been of a younger generation, he probably would have said he couldn't agree more. He continued fretfully, "Peter Riggs omitted to make notes of his conversation with Whitgreave—which I consider very casual and unbusinesslike—and it wasn't until I had questioned Peter closely that I got any information out of him. Then, but not till then, I discovered that Whitgreave was coming to this part of the country to stay with the Bannisters and intends to pay you a surprise visit."

"Oh, how glad I am that you warned me!"

"Yes, it isn't pleasant to be taken by surprise."

"Why is he coming? I mean what does he want?"

"He told Peter Riggs that he was going to ask you for a small memento of his uncle."

"Oh, is that all!" exclaimed Elfrida in relief.

"Will you be able to find something suitable?"

Elfrida rose and, opening a drawer of the bureau which stood near the window, she produced a small leather box and handed it to Mr. Sandford. The box contained a gold watch and chain. "Ronnie and I found that when we were poking about," she explained. "It's a repeater—rather nice isn't it?—I expect it belonged to Grandfather."

"Yes, he always wore that watch; it's the very thing, couldn't be better!"

"Will you ring up Mr. Whitgreave?" asked Elfrida. "It will be easier for you because you know him."

Mr. Sandford agreed and went off to the library to ring up Walt Whitgreave and arrange for him to come over from Plymouth to lunch on the following day.

That night, when she had conducted Mr. Sandford to the blue room and made sure he had all he wanted, Elfrida set her alarm-clock to waken her at seven. She had decided to go to church at eight, not only because she enjoyed the peace and quiet of the Early Communion Service but also because she could go without any fuss and she would be back in time to breakfast with her guest.

This was in Elfrida's mind as she went downstairs so she was surprised to see her guest in the hall. He, also, was surprised and paused with his hand on the key of the front-door.

They greeted each other and walked down the avenue together.

"What a lovely morning!" said Mr. Sandford happily.

"Yes, lovely! And listen to the birds," returned Elfrida.

"We poor mortals who live in towns miss a great deal of pleasure."

"Would you like to live in the country, Mr. Sandford?"

"Not really," he replied thoughtfully. "I enjoy my work—it's interesting and rewarding—and I enjoy meeting my friends. I'm fond of golf and I like an occasional game of bridge . . . but I must say that a little more leisure would be pleasant. I should like to be able to get away for a holiday more often."

"You're terribly busy."

"Yes, I've more work than I can manage, but when Ronnie has acquired the necessary experience, he'll be able to take a great deal of it off my shoulders. He's a good boy."

"You have been very kind to Ronnie. He told me that he has never missed his father because he could always depend upon 'Uncle Bob.' " Elfrida said this hesitantly; she had wanted to say it but she was a little doubtful as to how "Uncle Bob" would take it.

"Did he say that?" asked Mr. Sandford. "I'm very glad to hear it . . . he feels he can depend upon me! Well, all I can say is I couldn't be fonder of Ronnie if he were my own son."

By this time they had arrived at the little church and as usual Elfrida became completely absorbed in the service. It was only afterwards—a long time afterwards—that she remembered this little talk with Mr. Sandford.

13

Walt Whitgreave arrived at Mountain Cross soon after twelve o'clock, driving himself in a hired car. Elfrida had been watching from an upstairs window; she had decided to let Mr. Sandford receive the unwelcome guest.

When he had parked the car in the drive, he got out and stood, looking at the house and smoking a cigarette. He was tall and thin with dark hair, turning grey, and a sallow complexion.

Elfrida wondered what he was thinking: was he angry with the Wares for changing the destiny of Mountain Cross? Was he angry with the girl who had appeared from nowhere and done him out of his inheritance?

Suddenly he turned and, instead of coming to the front-door, he walked round the east end of the house and disappeared from view. Her first reaction was surprise . . . but when she had reflected for a few moments, she realised that he had known and loved the place long ago, so it was natural that he should want to have a look round before meeting his unknown cousin.

Elfrida waited for some time, but at last she decided that she must get this meeting over, so she pulled herself together and went downstairs to the parlour where she found Mr. Sandford and Mr. Whitgreave drinking sherry and talking.

They broke off their conversation when she came in and Mr. Sandford made the introduction:

"Mr. Whitgreave . . . Miss Ware," he said formally.

"But we're cousins," objected Mr. Whitgreave, as he shook

hands with her. "There's no need to stand on ceremony. I shall call you Elfrida—it's a pretty name—and you must call me Walt, or Cousin Walt if you'd rather."

"Yes, of course," said Elfrida; what else could she say? She added, "I'm afraid I've interrupted your business talk."

"Not at all," replied Cousin Walt. "There isn't any secret about it. I was just going to show Mr. Sandford a letter." He took a letter out of his pocket and unfolded it.

"From Mr. Ware?" asked Mr. Sandford.

"Yes. I won't bother you to read the whole thing; it's a long screed. He begins by saying he's ill and wants to see me and goes on, 'As you know, I was devoted to your mother and have many happy memories of my boyhood days when my sister Doris and I used to play together at Mountain Cross. Then, later, you used to come and stay here for your holidays; it was a great pleasure to me to have you and to see you growing up to be a true Ware. Mountain Cross is very dear to me and, as I have no son of my own, I want you to have the place when I am gone. Your Aunt Jane and I have made wills leaving everything to each other, but we are getting old and it seems foolish to leave our affairs in this condition as it would entail double death-duties.' Then he goes on to bewail the high rate of taxation."

"I should like to see the letter," said Mr. Sandford, holding out his hand.

"I've read you the only important part," replied Cousin Walt, folding it up and putting it back into his pocket.

"Oh well, it doesn't matter. You didn't come and see your uncle when he was ill, so he changed his mind. He left everything to his wife and in my opinion he was perfectly justified in doing so. Mr. Ware had been exceedingly good to you and I think——"

"That's an old story!"

"Some people have short memories for benefits received."

"I couldn't come," declared Walt angrily. "You know that,

Mr. Sandford. You had written suggesting I should come and I told you I couldn't manage it. I told Uncle Roger the same."

"Business matters prevented you."

"Yes, at least . . . well, if you *must* know I was mixed up in a divorce case. I was co-respondent, so it was essential that I should be there."

"You didn't mention that to your uncle, I presume?"

"No, I didn't. It was my own affair—nobody else's."

"It was your own affair," agreed Mr. Sandford. He added, "Mr. Ware's will is perfectly clear, and a model of brevity. I shall be pleased to let you see it if you are in any doubt about his intentions."

"I've seen it at Somerset House," muttered Walt. He rose and added, "If you'll excuse me, I'll go and have a wash before lunch."

There was no need to show him where to go; he knew his way, of course.

"I can't stand the fellow—never could," declared Mr. Sandford.

"I know, but you're making him angry," Elfrida pointed out. "After all he has a right to be annoyed, so——"

"He has no right to be annoyed."

"Couldn't we just be polite and pleasant to him?"

"Polite and pleasant!" said Mr. Sandford with a short laugh.

"I'm sure it's the best way," she said earnestly.

Mr. Sandford walked over to the window and stood there, looking out. "I must say I should have liked to see that letter which he said was from Mr. Ware. It didn't sound like Mr. Ware—all that sentimental nonsense about the old days and his devotion to his sister Doris! Mr. Ware wasn't particularly fond of his sister as far as I can remember . . . and in any case," added Mr. Sandford, "the man had no right to read out a piece of the letter and then refuse to let me see it."

"You said it didn't matter," said Elfrida soothingly.

"It doesn't matter. We knew before that Mr. Ware had changed his mind about the disposal of his estate."

"In that case there doesn't seem to be any point in talking about it, does there?"

Mr. Sandford turned and smiled at her. He said, "We're to be 'polite and pleasant' are we?"

"Yes, please, Mr. Sandford. When he comes back, I'll give him the watch and—and we can talk about something else."

"Very well—if that's how you want it—but you'll have to do most of the talking, Elfrida; I find it extremely difficult to be 'polite and pleasant' to Walter Whitgreave."

When Walt returned, he seemed in a better humour; he sat down beside Elfrida and said, "I'm afraid you think I behaved rather badly, Elfrida, but I really couldn't come when Uncle Roger asked me. As a matter of fact I had no idea he was so seriously ill and I was very upset when I heard he had died. By that time the case was settled, so I wrote to Aunt Jane telling her how sorry I was and suggesting that I should pay her a visit; I felt sure she must be feeling lonely, and it would comfort her to see me and talk things over. She replied, thanking me for my letter, but said she wasn't very well and would rather I put off my visit until she was better. Well, that suited me all right because I was getting married and we were looking for a flat. It was quite a shock when I heard that Aunt Jane was dead. That's the story," added Walt. "So now you know all about it."

"You must be—disappointed," said Elfrida with a little gasp. "I mean—about Mountain Cross. I'm sorry, Cousin Walt." She had made up her mind to say this, and now it was said.

"I'm glad you mentioned it," he replied, smiling at her quite amiably. "I like straight talk—and it gives me an opportunity to explain my feelings. It's true that Uncle Roger promised to make me his heir and, at one time, I would have been very pleased to inherit Mountain Cross and live here, but in recent years circumstances have changed. All my interests are in Canada; my business is in Montreal and I'm married to a Canadian girl . . . so what on earth would I have done with Mountain

Cross? I suppose I could have sold it, but it wouldn't fetch much. Very few people want a big old-fashioned house on the top of a cliff."

"I told you he wouldn't want it," put in Mr. Sandford, who was still standing by the window.

"I know, but I was worrying——"

"Don't worry," said Walt. "I wouldn't live here if you paid me—and I can't see Marigold in this environment; she'd go crazy in a week."

"In that case may I ask what all the fuss was about?" enquired Mr. Sandford coldly.

"I don't know what you mean!" exclaimed Walt.

"It doesn't matter," said Elfrida hastily. She produced the small leather box and added, "Look, Cousin Walt! Mr. Sandford told me you wanted a memento of your uncle; I thought you might like this."

"Oh, his watch! That's very kind of you, Elfrida, but it's a valuable watch. I didn't mean you to give me anything valuable; I just wanted something to remind me of the old man . . . his stamp album, for instance. I used to see him sitting at his desk working with his stamps."

"Yes, of course you must have it, Cousin Walt. Do have the watch as well."

He took it and looked at it. "Yes, I remember this watch; Uncle Roger always wore it and it kept excellent time. Well, if you're sure you want to give it to me. . . ."

Elfrida was quite sure; she was so relieved to find he did not want Mountain Cross that she was willing to give him anything. She smiled and said, "I'm delighted that you should have it—and anything else you would like. I found rather a nice little seventeenth-century snuff-box when I was turning out a cupboard . . . or perhaps you would rather have some pieces of furniture for your new flat . . . or would you like a picture? There's a very good engraving of Drake playing bowls, I expect you remember it hanging on the wall in the dining-room."

"You don't know Marigold!" exclaimed Walt, laughing. "If I

were to go back home with a lot of old-fashioned junk Marigold would throw it out in the street."

"Oh, I see," said Elfrida faintly.

"It wouldn't fit in with Marigold's scheme; she's very up-to-date. She's done over the whole apartment and the result is fine. All our friends admire it."

"How nice!"

"I wish you could see it, Elfrida. You must fly over and visit us in the fall. You'd like Marigold."

Elfrida had a feeling that she would not like Marigold, but she murmured polite thanks for the invitation.

"We'll fix it up," said Walt. "I'll have to consult Marigold, of course; she has a great many friends and enjoys visiting but I'm sure we'd manage to fit you in." He put the little box into his pocket and added, "I appreciate your generosity in giving me the watch; you can't buy watches like this nowadays. The stamp album is of no intrinsic value, but I'd like to have it for sentimental reasons."

Elfrida nodded. "I expect it's in the library; Mrs. Chowne will know."

14

Already the big dining-room had been abandoned and all the furniture swathed in dust-sheets, so when the gong was sounded for lunch Elfrida led her guests into Mr. Ware's library which had been converted into a very pleasant little dining-room, brighter and warmer and amply large enough for a party of three to four. Mrs. Chowne had never liked Mr. Whitgreave (she had said so), but that had not prevented her from serving up an excellent meal.

Mr. Sandford had made it clear to Elfrida that he had no intention of being 'polite and pleasant' to the guest, but he enjoyed good food and soon began to feel more amiable.

"There has been a great deal in the papers lately about space-flights," said Mr. Sandford. "Are you interested in the subject, Walt?"

It appeared that Walt was extremely interested in the subject; he knew an American astronaut who had taken part in a space-flight and had told Walt about some of his experiences.

This was a safe topic of conversation, so Elfrida was able to sit back and eat her lunch in peace.

"You're very silent, Elfrida," said Walt. "It's a pity Marigold isn't here . . . you could talk about clothes. Women are much more interested in dress than in space-flights."

"Oh, I was very interested in what you were saying," she replied. "I didn't speak because I don't know anything about space-flights except what I've read in the papers." Then she turned to Mrs. Chowne, who had come in with the coffee, and asked where Mr. Ware had kept his stamps.

"Stamps, Miss Elfrida? I can give you some if you want them for your letters."

"Mr. Ware's album," said Walt loudly. "It's a big red book; he used to keep it in his desk."

"Oh, an album!" said Mrs. Chowne. "The albums are all in that cupboard under the big book-case." She went to the cupboard, took out the pile of albums and dumped them onto the table. Her face had become very red and she was breathing heavily.

"But these are photograph albums!" Walt exclaimed.

"Yes, they're full of photographs," agreed Mrs. Chowne. "Mr. Ware had a lovely Kodak, he was forever taking snaps. He took a lot of Miss Marjory; here's one of her when she was all ready to go to a wedding—she had such a pretty frock! Wait till I find one of you, Mr. Whitgreave; it's in this green album, I'm sure. Oh yes, here it is! Mr. Ware took it the day you and Miss Marjory quarrelled about a game of tennis. You didn't like her beating you. That's why you're looking so glum."

Elfrida said quickly, "Let's finish clearing the table, Mrs. Chowne. I'll come and help you to wash up."

"Don't bother. I'd rather do it myself," replied Mrs. Chowne. She piled the plates onto the trolley and wheeled it away.

"Stupid woman!" exclaimed Walt. "I don't know what she was talking about. She spoke as if she knew me, but I've never seen her before in my life."

"She's a bit fussed," said Elfrida apologetically. "If you'll excuse me, I'll go and help her . . . meanwhile you can have a look round and see if you can find the album."

"You don't mind my having asked for it?"

"No, of course not."

"The only reason I want it is because I used to see Uncle Roger working with it. He knew very little about stamps, it was just a hobby to pass the time."

"I should have thought it was a hobby to most people," put in Mr. Sandford.

Walt smiled in a pitying manner, "Obviously you aren't a philatelist, Mr. Sandford. You've got to study the subject seriously if you want to have a decent collection."

"I've never been interested, but my partner, Arnold Riggs, is a keen philatelist," said Mr. Sandford coldly.

Elfrida left them talking and pursued Mrs. Chowne into the pantry.

"I don't want any help, Miss Elfrida," declared Mrs. Chowne. "I told you I'd rather do the washing up myself."

Elfrida hid her annoyance and said tactfully, "I wish we could find that book; I should like Mr. Whitgreave to have it. You see Mr. Ware promised to leave him Mountain Cross and——"

"I'm very glad he changed his mind!"

"So am I," admitted Elfrida. "But it must be disappointing for Mr. Whitgreave and he has taken it very well. The book isn't valuable, but he wants it, and I should like to give to him before he goes home to Montreal."

"I don't know where it is, Miss Elfrida."

"But you remember it, don't you? You told me that Mr. Ware was interested in stamps."

"Yes, he used to potter about with that red book." She hesitated and then added. "I'm afraid I was a bit short with Mr. Whitgreave, but I never liked him—and I can't stand being shouted at—and this morning before lunch when he came round to the back-door he was horrid to Ernie."

"Horrid? What did he say?"

"I don't know what he said (I was busy in the kitchen) but Ernie was quite upset. . . and I'm not going to have people upsetting Ernie whether they live in Montreal or Timbuktu," declared Mrs. Chowne in belligerent tones.

"Of course not! No wonder you were angry!"

Mrs. Chowne was appeased. She handed Elfrida a plate to dry and said more quietly, "Yes, I lost my temper. I don't often lose my temper and I'm always sorry afterwards. Well it can't be helped (just leave the plates in a pile, Miss Elfrida; I'll put them away later). About that book: I haven't seen it for months, but it must be somewhere in the house. I'll get Ernie to help me and we'll have a thorough search."

It was not a peaceful afternoon. The Chownes began their search in the library which seemed the most likely place (Mrs. Chowne explained that "the red book" was always kept in the library and it might have slipped down behind the other books on the book-shelves). Chowne brought in the ladder and, starting at the top, proceeded to take out all the books and to hand them down to his wife who dusted them carefully and piled them in heaps on the floor. Cousin Walt stood and watched them in silence.

Mr. Sandford retired to the parlour and Elfrida followed him.

"That book might be here," she said, beginning to hunt round the room.

Together they emptied the drawers of the tall-boy but they found nothing of interest.

"I can't think of anything I dislike more than looking for things," said Mr. Sandford, sinking into a chair.

"Yes, it's an awful nuisance," agreed Elfrida. "I wouldn't bother if I didn't feel guilty about Mountain Cross."

"Will nothing convince you that you needn't feel guilty about Mountain Cross?" asked Mr. Sandford, with a heavy sigh.

"He has taken it very well, hasn't he?" said Elfrida, beginning to search in the drawers of the bureau. "I mean some men might have been horrid about it . . . and anyhow you seemed to be getting on better with him. I mean he was interesting about space-flights."

"Practically everything he said was untrue."

"Untrue?" asked Elfrida in astonishment.

"Oh, I don't know about the space-flights—all that may have been true—but many of his other statements were not. I should very much like to know why he made all that fuss at the beginning if he did not want Mountain Cross . . . but you prevented me from questioning him."

"It was because I hate rows; it frightens me when people are angry," explained Elfrida. She hesitated and then added, "Of course it wasn't true that he had never seen Mrs. Chowne before in his life . . . but he can't *do* anything, can he, Mr. Sandford? He can't turn me out of Mountain Cross."

"Your title to the place is absolutely secure," Mr. Sandford assured her.

She was standing still, gazing at him in alarm. "But Mr. Sandford, supposing Grandfather made another will, leaving Mountain Cross to Walt Whitgreave, and—and hid it somewhere? Perhaps that's what he's looking for!"

"You've been reading too many sensational novels, Elfrida," replied Mr. Sandford, smiling. "People don't make wills and then hide them—not in real life. What would be the sense of it?"

While they were talking Walt had become tired of watching the activities of the Chownes and had begun to rove round the house, searching in various rooms and poking into unused cupboards; he seemed very anxious indeed to find Mr. Ware's stamp album. Fortunately, however, he had an engagement in Plymouth that evening so he was obliged to abandon the search and drove away in his hired car soon after five o'clock.

Elfrida saw him off at the door and was so pleased to see him go that she promised to have another look for the album and to send it to him if it were found.

15

Mr. Sandford went back to London on Monday morning; his man brought the car to the door and carried down his suit-case.

"Don't worry about that wretched book," said Mr. Sandford as he took leave of his hostess.

"I wish we could find it."

"You've done all you could. You've given him the watch—it's a valuable watch. You've offered him that charming snuff-box, and anything else he would like in the way of pictures or furniture, and all you got for your kindness was the information that his wife would throw it into the street! He said himself that the book was of no value, so why worry?"

"Sentimental value," murmured Elfrida.

"Pshaw!" exclaimed Mr. Sandford in disgust. "I disliked the fellow in the old days and he hasn't improved. Put the whole thing out of your head, Elfrida. That's my advice."

It was good advice, but Elfrida was unable to take it, for Mrs. Chowne was a persevering woman; she had made up her mind to find "the red book" and she continued her search for days. Elfrida would discover her diving head-first into disused cupboards or hunting amongst piles of rubbish which had been banished to the cellars. Mrs. Chowne found quite a number of queer things during her search: amongst them a large crystal ball on an ebony stand; a copper preserving pan with a hole in the bottom; one Wellington boot; the model of a sailing-ship in a glass bottle; a warming pan; an ivory fan with broken sticks; two books of sermons; a box containing a cocked hat; a pair of duelling pistols, exceedingly rusty and, last but by no means least, a very amateur water-colour painting of an unknown mountain with snow on the top and with white clouds, which looked like handfuls of cotton-wool, floating in a pale blue sky. Mrs. Chowne was enchanted with this and when Elfrida refused to have it in the parlour asked permission to "borrow it" and hung it proudly over the chimney-piece in her sitting-room.

All these unrelated objects were discovered by Mrs. Chowne, but she did not find "the red book" and presently gave up the quest in despair.

To Elfrida the collection was intriguing for it evoked visions of the past. What had happened to the other Wellington boot or had this belonged to a man with one leg? What member of the family had worn the cocked hat? Had the duelling pistols ever been used in anger? The crystal ball was the best of the bunch in Elfrida's estimation; she cleaned it carefully and put it on the top of the bureau in the parlour, where it stood reflecting the colours of the room. Who had owned it and why had it been wrapped up in an old linen towel and stowed away in the cupboard under the stairs?

These unanswerable questions sent Elfrida to the photograph albums; she brought them into the parlour and studied them with care, beginning with the oldest in which slightly yellowed photographs of ladies with leg-of-mutton sleeves and tiny waists leant against sundials. Sometimes they were accompanied by gentlemen in formal attire with curiously-shaped silk hats on their heads and silver-topped canes in their hands. Who were they? It seemed sad that Mountain Cross (which presumably had been their home) had come into the possession of a girl who did not even know their names.

The more recent albums were more interesting; instead of formal portraits they contained snaps. . . . Snaps of Marjory as a baby; as a small girl in a sunbonnet; as a girl of fifteen or so with a pigtail; as a "grown-up" girl in a frilly frock and a cart-wheel hat. Elfrida searched for the picture of Walt and discovered a youth in long white trousers with the same unattractive features as Cousin Walt and an expression which quite definitely was glum.

The most interesting was a group of three, posed upon the steps which led down from the side door of Mountain Cross. It was very small, but quite clear when examined with a magnifying glass, and consisted of a middle-aged lady, whom Elfrida took to be her grandmother; a young man, who most certainly was Robert Sandford—his eyebrows alone would have identified him—and a very pretty girl with fair hair, which was Marjory, of course.

Mr. Ware had taken these snaps with his "lovely Kodak" and Marjory appeared in nearly all of them. How young she looked, how happy and healthy and carefree! These old photographs, examined with so much interest, had a curious effect upon Elfrida. From the very first day of her arrival at Mountain Cross, Elfrida had been conscious of her mother's presence . . . but now it was not the worn-out, sick woman who was at her side, but the young happy Marjory of long ago. Elfrida had begun to think of her as "Marjory"—as an elder sister rather than a mother—as the beautiful girl of the portrait which hung on the wall in Mrs. Ware's bedroom.

Elfrida often went and looked at the portrait; she toyed with the idea of taking it down and hanging it in the parlour which she used as her sitting-room, but for some reason she was reluctant to move it.

The days slid by with amazing speed; there was so much to do at Mountain Cross, so many new experiences to savour: the sea, constantly changing; the salty breezes; the green buds opening in the hedges. Marjory had talked of it all during her last illness—and Elfrida had listened—but hearing is not seeing.

The seagulls were especially interesting to Elfrida and she never tired of watching them soaring in the blue sky and diving into the sea. They were playful creatures and enjoyed aerobatics, allowing themselves to be carried upwards by the lift of air which occurred when the sea breeze struck the cliff . . . then they would hover for a few moments and swerve and bank and glide gracefully away.

Mrs. Chowne was fond of the seagulls and every night when she and Chowne had finished their tea she came out onto the top of the cliff with a basketful of scraps. The seagulls knew the exact moment when she would appear and were always ready, waiting for her. They screamed loudly and darted at the scraps, sometimes catching them in mid-air, sometimes squabbling for them on the ground.

Elfrida never missed this performance; she watched from the parlour window and laughed inordinately.

The sunshine and fresh air and good country food were doing wonders for Elfrida; she had recovered from her bad time in London and was putting on weight . . . better still the complete change of environment and the various interests of her new life had helped her to recover from Glen Siddons. She had "worked him out of her system," as Miss Martineau had advised, and when she thought of him—which was seldom—she could think of him calmly and wonder at herself for being such an idiot.

One day Elfrida walked up to the copse to see how Mr. Cobley was getting on; she found him hard at work. He had two assistants with him: the burly Tom Parkins and an even larger and heftier young man.

Mr. Cobley welcomed her with his usual cordiality and explained that "Ernie was busy with the garden and suchlike" so he had engaged Ned Bouch in his place. "It'll be done all the sooner," said Mr. Cobley; adding hastily, "And it won't cost you nothing."

"The place is in an awful mess," she murmured unhappily.

"You wait till we've finished! We'll tidy it up and it'll be lovely. You can 'ave picnics 'ere. It'll be lovely, won't it, Tom?"

Tom Parkins said, "That's right," and spitting on his hands seized an axe and laid on with a will.

This incident reminded Elfrida of the secret understanding between Mr. Cobley and Chowne about the "pens" (there had been so much to think of lately that if it had vanished from her mind) and she went home determined to get to the bottom of the matter.

The best way of getting information from Mrs. Chowne was to approach her obliquely—Elfrida had learned this from experience—so when Mrs. Chowne brought in her tea she opened the subject in a round-about way.

"Those barns have been empty for a long time," said Elfrida.

"You're telling me!" exclaimed Mrs. Chowne. "Those big barns standing empty got on Ernie's nerves. He can't bear waste—neither can I, really. Things come in useful if you keep them long enough, put away carefully in moth-balls. I said that to Ernie and he said he couldn't put the barns in moth-balls . . . but he did, in a way. He's kept them clean and weathertight all these years and now you're going to use them, so I was right."

Elfrida was silent. She had no idea how she was going to use them, but Mrs. Chowne would tell her if she waited.

"There's money in pigs," continued Mrs. Chowne. "Ernie likes pigs—he asked Mr. Ware, but Mr. Ware wouldn't hear of it. Ernie says he told you about it, Miss Elfrida."

"Pens," murmured Elfrida.

"Yes," agreed Mrs. Chowne. "Ernie'll make pens with some of the wood that Charlie Cobley doesn't want. You've got to have properly-made pens. Pigs don't thrive unless you treat them right. You buy them young and feed them up and then you sell them . . . you can make them streaky for bacon or let them gorge themselves into heavy hogs. Ernie knows.

"But I haven't any money to buy pigs!"

"You could buy a few to start with, couldn't you? They don't cost much when they're young . . . and we thought," said Mrs. Chowne twisting the corner of her apron in an embarrassed manner, "we thought . . . perhaps . . . you wouldn't mind if Ernie bought some too. You see, Miss Elfrida, we've got a little money saved up in the post office and there's plenty of room in those big barns. It would make Ernie so happy," added Mrs. Chowne in wheedling tones.

"I see," said Elfrida thoughtfully. "Well I don't mind if he wants to have pigs . . . as long as he looks after them properly and keeps them clean."

"Oh, he will!" cried Mrs. Chowne joyfully.

"But I don't think I can afford to buy any."

"Just a few, Miss Elfrida. Just a few to start with. Ernie will buy them for you at the market in Cherleigh—you won't have any bother—Ernie will look after them, he knows about pigs. When he was with Sir Henry—before I married him—there were hundreds of pigs."

Elfrida hesitated. She thought of the two hundred pounds which Mr. Sandford had put in the bank for her to "tide her over" until her grandmother's affairs had been settled. "Perhaps I could buy a few if they aren't very expensive——" she began in doubtful tones.

"Of course you could," Mrs. Chowne assured her. "Ernie'll watch the market; the price of pigs goes up and down."

There was a good deal more talk about the matter, but Chowne was so cheerful at the prospect of keeping pigs that Elfrida had not the heart to disappoint him . . . besides the Chownes were very kind, and she was not paying them anything, so if they could make a little money by keeping pigs, it was all to the good.

The pens were constructed in the smaller barn (a friend of the Chownes' came up from the village and lent a hand) and before many days had passed Elfrida was the owner of ten small pigs. They were unexpectedly attractive; they frisked about playfully in their nice clean pen, ate large quantities of food and snuggled down at night upon their comfortable bed of straw. In the pen next to them were ten little pigs which belonged to Chowne and, beyond that, a very large sow in a pen by herself. She had been a good deal more expensive, but Chowne had lost his heart to her so Elfrida had agreed to "go fifty-fifty" with him in the purchase.

Part Two

16

Spring came to Mountain Cross with dramatic suddenness—or so it seemed to the girl who never before had experienced country life. She had watched spring creep shyly into the city; swell the buds on the trees in the square gardens; awaken drifts of crocuses and fill the flower-shops with flowers and the windows of the big stores with delightful garments . . . this had pleased her because it was a sign that winter was past. Here at Mountain Cross there was nothing surreptitious about spring; it came like an army with banners. All of a sudden the chill east wind had gone and a soft south-wester was blowing (Mr. Cobley called it "the ladies' breeze"). Showers fell gently and, between the slowly moving clouds, there were large expanses of blue, blue sky.

Elfrida was happy. Who would not be happy amongst all these wonders? She was out all day walking through lanes and woods and fields. There was beauty everywhere. The sheltered lane where she had found early primroses and violets was now a mass of may-blossom, so thick and heavy that it looked as though the trees were weighed down with pink and white snow. The scent, confined by the high banks, was so strong that it caught her breath . . . and, from top to bottom, the whole lane was buzzing and humming with thousands of wild bees. In the old garden the fruit trees had burst into blossom and there was a group of lilacs filling the air with fragrance. There were syringas and old gnarled laburnums with golden necklaces which hung down almost touching the ground. The huge blooms on the rhododendrons flaunted their brilliant colours in the sunshine and, at dusk, seemed to glow with an inner light, like lanterns amongst their dark green foliage. In the fields there were ox-eyed daisies, scarlet poppies and a small but very blue variety of cornflower amongst the ripening hay . . . and there were sheets of bluebells, spread beneath the trees, and lily-of-the-valley in shady corners where the ground was moist.

In one place, where a stream wandered through a green meadow, Elfrida found a little backwater with watercress growing in it . . . and a great many other water-plants and flowers which she had never seen before. She knew watercress because Marjory had been fond of it, and occasionally had brought a small basketful of it from the little shop at the corner near their flat, but to Elfrida it had seemed dry and tough and tasteless. This watercress, which she picked and took home with her, was very different; it was delicious. Perhaps, long ago, Marjory had found the streamlet and gathered watercress and taken it home! Perhaps the wretched little basket packed with dried-up salad had reminded her of the delicate flavour and crunchy consistency of these fresh green leaves! Perhaps that was why Marjory had enjoyed it, thought Marjory's daughter sadly.

One day when Elfrida went to pick her salad, she found the backwater hopping with thousands of frogs . . . yes, literally thousands! The whole place seemed alive with the tiny creatures. She had never before seen a real live frog and would not have known what they were if she had not been acquainted with Mr. Jeremy Fisher, depicted by Beatrix Potter in the children's classic . . . but, there was not the slightest doubt about it, here was Mr. Jeremy Fisher at home, with his brothers and sisters and hordes of children! It was an enchanting discovery; Elfrida sat down on the bank and watched them.

Time was no object here; she had all the time in the world at her disposal. She wandered vaguely, half dazed with delight, making new and interesting discoveries wherever she went. Birds flew from the hedges as she approached and she found their nests with blue or brown or speckled eggs lying cosily in beds of woven grass and feathers. There were little animals, too: a field mouse, balancing precariously on a slender stem of flowering grass; a squirrel, sitting on the branch of a tree, chattering with annoyance at being disturbed by a human wanderer; a hedgehog running across the path and curling into a spiky ball at the sound of a human footstep.

At first Elfrida tired easily, not only because she was unused to walking, but because there was so much to see, so many new and exciting sights and sounds and scents, but soon she was able to walk further and found even more to delight her senses. She would take a couple of sandwiches in her pocket and stay out all day, returning at tea-time tired and happy and drowsy with the sweet air, to sit by the log-fire in the parlour and enjoy tea and cakes and read poetry.

Poetry seemed the only kind of reading for this time of blossoming; her grandfather's shelves provided ample fare. At night she drifted into dreamless sleep, lulled by the sound of waves splashing on the rocks beneath her window.

The old house became familiar and friendly, every creak in the wooden stair became known to her; she began to feel as if she had been born and bred in the old house.

For the first time in her life Elfrida was enjoying the peace and security of a settled home in which—wonder of wonders—everything belonged to her. Everything belonged to her; it was an amazing thought! She could not get used to the strange idea. She would pause for a few moments with her hand on a fine old chest of drawers and say to herself in wondering tones, "This belongs to me!"

The drawing-room furniture was swathed in dust-sheets and at first Elfrida had avoided this room, but one very wet afternoon she went in and found a glass-fronted cabinet standing against an inner wall so she pushed aside the sheet and opened the doors. The cabinet was full of treasures: little figurines of shepherds and shepherdesses; tiny Venetian glass vases; a whole set of ivory chessmen, intricately carved, and several china cottages with thatched roofs and china roses growing at their doors. Elfrida took them out one by one and looked at them—they belonged to her! They belonged to Elfrida Jane Ware, who had led a hand-to-mouth existence ever since she could remember, who had never owned anything pretty and utterly useless in all her life, who had had to think twice and count her pennies before she could buy a new blouse and had shed futile tears over a ladder in a new pair of nylon stockings.

Quite often during her wanderings and discoveries Elfrida thought of Ronnie . . . for Ronnie had said, "I do envy you spending spring at Mountain Cross!" Elfrida had not understood at the time—not really understood—but now she realised why he had envied her. She had received a very nice bread-and-butter letter from Ronnie and had answered, thanking him for it. Then, after a while, Ronnie wrote again, asking how she was getting on and whether the arrangement he had made with the Chownes was working out well. He went on to say, "I feel a bit worried about you sometimes, because it was I who encouraged you to go to Mountain Cross. I do hope you are not feeling lonely and missing all your friends. The Senior Partner seems to have enjoyed his visit to you—all except the lunch with Cousin Walt, who must be a very irritating individual! I heard all about what he said and did! London is dry and dusty. I wish I were a farmer in 'the West Countree.'"

It was such a kind friendly letter that Elfrida sat down to answer it at once and this time she had plenty to tell him, so it was quite a long letter all about what she was doing; all about Mr. Cobley's work in the copse and the ten little pigs which Chowne had bought for her at Cherleigh Market. She told him about the cross on the hillock and Mr. Cobley's explanation of its use in bye-gone days and she told him that she was busy and happy and was learning all sorts of interesting things about country life, including the very useful art of milking a cow.

The letter was finished late at night and the next morning she went down to the village to post it.

For some time after her arrival Elfrida had avoided the village which lay at her gates. She was afraid the villagers might resent the presence of the new owner of Mountain Cross but, quite by accident, she had discovered that they were anxious to meet her and eager to be friendly. The older people remembered her mother and invited Elfrida into their cottages and offered her tea . . . and told her stories about "Miss Marjory when she was a girl."

Most of the cottages were old, with small windows and few modern conveniences, but the people who lived in them seemed quite contented with their lot. The largest cottage and most up-to-date was the post office and general store; it had a pillar-box outside the door and a telephone kiosk. Mr. Doubleday, the postmaster, lived here, of course, with his wife and son.

It was in the post office, where she was buying stamps, that Elfrida first saw Lucius Babbington. A tall dark-haired man in grey slacks and a tweed jacket was leaning against the counter chatting to Mr. Doubleday and enjoying a joke with that worthy. Elfrida, being unused to country ways, was not interested in the man and had no idea that he could be interested in her, so she bought her stamps from Mrs. Doubleday and asked how Henry James was getting on at school. Then she stuck a stamp onto Ronnie's letter and went out to post it.

She was just about to slip the letter into the pillar-box when she discovered that the tall, dark-haired stranger had followed her and was waiting to speak to her. "You're Miss Ware of Mountain Cross," he said.

"That sounds very grand!" exclaimed Elfrida, taken by surprise.

He smiled at her. "But it's true, isn't it? I'm Lucius Babbington; we're near neighbours. My sister meant to call on you when you arrived, but she has been laid up with a sprained ankle."

"Oh, I'm sorry!"

"It's a good deal better, but she still can't get about very easily and it's maddening for her. She's a very energetic person, you see. Will you come and have lunch with us one day? She would like to meet you."

Elfrida was not very pleased; she was shy of strangers and

was perfectly happy wandering about the country by herself, but when Mr. Babbington suggested Friday and offered to call for her at twelve-thirty in his car, she could find no reasonable excuse.

"Do you think you're going to like being here?" he asked doubtfully.

"Oh, I'm loving every moment of it!" she replied. "I've never seen anything so beautiful in my life. The flowers are wonderful. Look at that chestnut tree with its pink candles! How could anyone not like it?"

"I'm so glad," he said. "Of course we think this is just about the most beautiful place on earth, but we wondered if you would find it dull."

"Dull?"

"I mean you're used to a gay life in London, aren't you? Lots of parties and—and all that sort of thing."

"I didn't find it—gay," replied Elfrida. There was a lot more she could have said about her life in London, but she did not know Mr. Babbington well enough.

"I'm so glad you feel you can settle down here," declared Mr. Babbington. "Mary will be delighted when I tell her about you; it makes such a difference having congenial neighbours."

17

Mrs. Chowne was quite excited to hear about the luncheon at Winford Hall . . . and burst into a torrent of information. "It will be nice for you to get to know some nice people, Miss Elfrida—you wander about by yourself far too much—and the Babbingtons *are* nice, you'll like them. Mr. Lucius was at Eton—I remember him at church in his Eton jacket and striped trousers, very smart he was! Their parents were great friends of Mrs. Ware and used to come to dinner in the old days when there were big dinner-parties. They're both dead now, so Winford Hall belongs to Mr. Lucius; it's a lovely big place with several farms on the estate. Mr. Lucius farms them himself—and a very good farmer he is! Mr. Lucius and Miss Mary used to come here when they were children; there are some snaps of them in Mr. Ware's album—I could show them to you if you like. Mr. Lucius must be about—about thirty-five now," declared Mrs. Chowne, making hasty calculations. "Miss Mary is a bit younger. I haven't seen them for years, of course; there was no entertaining when Mr. Ware was ill—he was ill off and on for a long time—and after he died Mrs. Ware didn't feel like seeing people. It's been a very quiet house for years, but now that you're here it'll be nice to see some life about the place. You could have a party, couldn't you? We could open up the drawing-room and——"

"I don't know anyone to ask to a party."

"No, but you will. You just need a start-off, that's all. Perhaps there'll be some other people at the luncheon on Friday," she continued hopefully. "None of the people round about are very young, of course—except the Harlows and *they* aren't likely to be at Winford Hall—but Mr. and Mrs. Endicott are nice, everyone likes them, and Colonel and Mrs. Ferrier of Heatherdale Manor are sure to be there. The Colonel is a funny old gentleman with a red face and a white moustache. They've got two sons; one of them is in the Navy and sometimes comes home on leave. Heatherdale Manor is about seven miles from here, but if they ask you to tea—or anything—I can lend you my bicycle."

"I've never ridden a bicycle in my life," said Elfrida shortly. She was getting a little tired of the saga.

"Ernie could teach you," suggested Mrs. Chowne.

Elfrida thanked her, but declined the offer; she knew her limitations and was aware that she did not shine in the company of strangers. She would have to go to the luncheon on Friday, of course; but that would be the end of it as far as her neighbours were concerned.

Seven people had been invited to lunch at Winford Hall and they all came, full of interest and eager to meet the new owner of Mountain Cross. She was reputed to be an actress, so she was not likely to settle down and be a congenial neighbour, but all the same they wanted to see her.

Mrs. Chowne had been correct in her prophecy; Colonel and Mrs. Ferrier were there, so also were Mr. and Mrs. Endicott. There was a Mr. Maldon and his two young daughters, but there were no Harlows.

Elfrida, remembering Miss Martineau's advice, went to the luncheon in tweeds, wearing a string of pearls which she had found in her grandmother's jewel-case. She was interested to observe that all the female members of the party, except the younger Miss Maldon, were similarly attired. She went with reluctance, and at first she was so frightened of all these strangers that she could scarcely speak, but she had not been there long before she began to feel better. They were friendly people; there was nothing the least alarming about them, and although they all knew each other—and she did not know any of them—they were taking trouble to talk to her so that she should not feel out in the cold.

Mr. Endicott was sitting next to Elfrida at luncheon; he asked what she was doing at Mountain Cross, and obviously wanted to know, so she began to tell him about the pigs. She was getting on quite well when suddenly she realised that everyone had stopped talking to listen to her story . . . and her tongue faltered.

"Go on, go on, Miss Ware!" exclaimed Mr. Maldon. "We all want to hear. You've got 'ten little pigs and half a big one'! Please explain."

"Yes, please explain," said Mrs. Endicott.

"Well, Chowne fell in love with her, you see," said Elfrida, smiling. "Unfortunately he hadn't enough money to buy her, so I said I'd go halves with him."

Everyone laughed.

"An excellent arrangement," nodded Mr. Maldon.

"Are there going to be lots of little pigs?" asked Mrs. Ferrier with interest.

"We hope so."

"You'll go halves with them, of course," said Miss Babbington.

Elfrida smiled and nodded.

"What happens if there's an uneven number of little pigs?" enquired Mrs. Ferrier, her bright brown eyes sparkling mischievously.

"They cut one in half—like Solomon," suggested Mr. Maldon.

"Shame on you, Edward!" exclaimed Lucius Babbington. "You ought to know better. Solomon didn't cut the baby in half, nor had he any intention of doing so. It was a clever ruse to discover the mother of the child . . ."

"Let's hear what Miss Ware proposes to do with the eleventh piglet," Colonel Ferrier suggested.

"Oh, I couldn't bear to cut it in half!" cried Elfrida in horrified tones.

Mr. Maldon laughed. "That's extremely interesting. If you follow the matter to a logical conclusion it would seem to prove——"

"Miss Ware and Chowne will toss for it," interrupted Mrs. Endicott.

"Much the best way," agreed Mrs. Ferrier, nodding.

"How is dear Mrs. Chowne?" asked Lucius Babbington. "Mary and I loved her when we were children; she made the most delicious cheese-cakes."

"She still does; they melt in the mouth," Elfrida told him. "You must come to tea one day and sample them, Mr. Babbington."

"Me, too!" exclaimed Mary.

Elfrida nodded at her across the table, "Any day you like."

"I remember the Chownes," said Mrs. Ferrier. "They've been at Mountain Cross for years and years. Does she still talk all the time without stopping to breathe?"

"She doesn't often stop to breathe," replied Elfrida seriously.

Again they all laughed.

By this time Elfrida had lost all her shyness and was feeling happy and comfortable . . . for these were her sort of people and, wonder of wonders, they seemed to like her.

"Tell us about your garden, Miss Ware," said Mrs. Ferrier.

"Oh, yes!" exclaimed Mrs. Endicott. "The garden at Mountain Cross used to be a dream of loveliness."

"The garden has gone wild," replied its owner sadly. "Chowne does what he can—he's very hard-working—but it's much too big for one man."

"I remember the lily-pool," said Mrs. Endicott.

"Oh, so do I," declared the elder Miss Maldon. "There were goldfish swimming about in it."

"It's choked with weeds," Elfrida replied. "But I'm going to clean it out one of these days when I have time."

"Not with your own hands, I hope," objected Colonel Ferrier. "It's no job for a lady."

"I can give you some water-lily roots," put in Lucius Babbington. "Just let me know when you're ready for them."

"How kind of you!" exclaimed Elfrida.

They urged her on to tell them more and listened with interest. They all wanted to know what the new owner of Mountain Cross was doing with her property; they all wanted to help.

"That little copse on the hill is in bad shape," said Mr. Maldon. "Nothing has been done to it for years."

"Charlie Cobley is the man for that," said Mr. Endicott.

"If you can get him!" cried several people in chorus.

"I've got him," Elfrida told them. "He's working there now."

"My goodness!" exclaimed Colonel Ferrier, throwing himself back in his chair and raising his eyes to the ceiling. "I've been waiting since this time last year for the fellow!"

"But you aren't young and pretty, Ned," said Mr. Endicott.

Shouts of laughter greeted this statement.

"How did you get him, Miss Ware?" asked Mr. Maldon.

"I don't know," admitted Elfrida. "He just walked in one evening and said he'd come about the copse. I'd been out all day and was half asleep and I thought for a moment that he had something to do with Scotland Yard."

There was more laughter.

"But why Scotland Yard? I don't see it," said Mrs. Endicott. "Am I too stupid?"

"No, only too highbrow, Netta," chuckled Lucius Babbington.

It was not very sparkling conversation, but it was great fun. Elfrida was enjoying herself and for the first time in her life she was a social success.

After lunch they all went into the garden, except Mary Babbington, who was still very lame, and Elfrida received quite a number of invitations from her neighbours (the Ferriers asked her to lunch, the Maldons were having a cocktail-party, the Endicotts wanted her to come to dinner); but although she had enjoyed the Babbington's luncheon she did not want to be swept into a social round. Fortunately it was easy to refuse all these invitations gracefully, and without giving offence, for she had no means of transport.

"Oh well, you'll be getting a car soon, of course," said Mrs. Ferrier. "You must come and see us when you get your car and by that time Richard may be home on leave."

"More interesting for Miss Ware when Richard is home," agreed the Colonel. "Not much fun for her to come to lunch with a couple of old fogeys."

"Let me know when you want a car," said Mr. Endicott. "I could give you some useful tips."

"Yes, he's the man to advise you about cars," declared Lucius Babbington.

Elfrida had never thought of owning a car; she could not drive and she had no money to spend upon inessentials, but she smiled and thanked Mr. Endicott and promised to remember his offer.

The Babbingtons were the only neighbours within reasonable distance of Mountain Cross; there was a foot-path over the hill, which made a pleasant afternoon's walk. Elfrida was sorry for Mary, who was still unable to get about in her usual energetic fashion, so she went over to see her and take her a book. Her visit was such a success that she was urged to come again—as often as she could—so she soon became friendly with the brother and sister. She could drop in at Winford Hall to tea and be sure of a warm welcome . . . and when Mary's ankle was better she and Lucius came to lunch at Mountain Cross and renewed their acquaintance with Mrs. Chowne.

Mrs. Ferrier and Mrs. Endicott both called on their new neighbour. Elfrida was out when Mrs. Endicott called, but Mrs. Ferrier was more fortunate and was entertained to tea.

"I wanted to have a chat with you because I knew your

mother," explained Mrs. Ferrier, accepting a cheese-cake. "I didn't mention it the other day at the Babbingtons because I thought it might embarrass you to speak of her—and you were terrified enough as it was! Did you think we would bite you or something?"

"I was terrified at first," admitted Elfrida. "But you were all so nice to me that I soon began to enjoy myself."

"Why shouldn't we be nice to you?" asked Mrs. Ferrier in surprise.

This was difficult to answer. Elfrida might have said that when she went to parties in London she was usually ignored by her companions, pushed out into the cold; she might have said that, at the Babbington's party, all the others knew each other—and she was a stranger—but she realised that these people had a different code of manners. It was just because she was a stranger that they had taken the trouble to make her feel at home. This was impossible to explain so after a short pause she said, "I'm not very good at parties."

"Well, you were very good indeed at the Babbington's party," declared Mrs. Ferrier, laughing. "You were a howling success. As a matter of fact, between you and me and the gatepost, we were all a little bit frightened of you. We knew you were on the stage and we thought you would be frightfully smart and sophisticated—bored stiff with us—so it was a great relief to discover you were one of ourselves. You're like your mother, of course. I knew her long ago; she was a good deal younger than I was, but we were great friends and saw quite a lot of each other. Marjory often came and played with my little boys, she loved children. I used to think Marjory was the happiest person in the world; she was full of joy—if you know what I mean."

Elfrida nodded.

"Then she met Frederick Thistlewood," continued Mrs. Ferrier. "He persuaded her to marry him and make a career on the stage. The Wares were against it and to my mind they behaved rather foolishly; the whole thing might have fizzled out if they had let Marjory have him to stay as often as she wanted, but instead of that Mr. Ware put his foot down and wouldn't listen to anything Marjory said. Marjory was miserable about it and Mr. Thistlewood kept on writing to her. . . . She used to come to Heatherdale and tell me her troubles, so I wasn't really surprised when I heard she had run away. She had promised to write to me, but she never did, and I often thought of her and wondered how she had got on. We never heard any more about her; she simply . . . disappeared." Mrs. Ferrier sighed and added, "I used to look for her name in the theatrical news but perhaps she changed her name."

"She couldn't act," said Elfrida in a low voice.

"Couldn't act!" exclaimed Mrs. Ferrier in astonishment. "But Mr. Thistlewood was sure she would make her name on the stage! She was so pretty and graceful and so full of personality! Mr. Thistlewood told me himself that all Marjory needed was a little coaching. I must say I believed him. Of course Marjory was thrilled at the idea—what girl of eighteen wouldn't be thrilled at the prospect of being a star?"

"She tried hard—and she had quite a lot of coaching—but it wasn't any good."

"Oh, poor Marjory, she must have been terribly disappointed!" exclaimed Mrs. Ferrier in distress.

"I suppose she must have been," said Elfrida in thoughtful tones. "I don't remember, really—I was just a child. Children take things for granted, don't they? I just took it for granted that Mother couldn't act . . . she got odd jobs behind the scenes, helping the wardrobe mistress and mending the costumes."

"Oh, poor Marjory!"

"You said you knew Father, didn't you, Mrs. Ferrier?"

"I only saw him once."

Elfrida would have liked to hear more about her father, but Mrs. Ferrier changed the subject rather abruptly. She began to talk about her sons. "Edward is in business in London," she said. "Richard is in the Navy; he has been in the Far East for years, but he's hoping for leave in October. It's a long time off, but it's something to look forward to. You must come over to Heatherdale while he's here. If you haven't got a car by that time Richard can easily come and fetch you; it will be nice for him to see some young people and there aren't many youngsters in this part of the world. The Maldon girls are young, of course, but they're terribly dull, poor things."

"I thought they were very pretty."

"Pretty isn't enough," replied Mrs. Ferrier. "At least it won't be enough for Richard."

Elfrida laughed. She liked Mrs. Ferrier.

It was nearly six o'clock when Mrs. Ferrier rose to go away. She said, "Goodness, look at the time! I meant to stay for twenty minutes. Goodbye, my dear. I'm going to call you Elfrida."

"Please do," said Elfrida, smiling.

Elfrida went out to the drive to speed her departing guest and, after the car had disappeared, she stood for some time lost in thought. Miss Martineau had told her that she was unlike other girls, "made of different stuff," and Elfrida had felt this to be true, but now she had discovered that she was not a freak. Her new friends were made of the same stuff as herself (Mrs. Ferrier had said, "it was a great relief to discover that you were one of ourselves. You're like your mother, of course." She could have said nothing nicer!). If Dolly Garden were here—or Clarissa or Daphne or any other members of "the gang"—they would have been the freaks.

Elfrida sighed happily; she had found her place in the world.

18

June was the month of roses. There were roses everywhere; climbing over the cottages in the village, blooming in every garden. Mrs. Perrimont, the vicar's wife, was very proud of her rose garden; she pruned her roses skillfully and often won prizes for them at the Cherleigh Show. In the garden at Mountain Cross the roses rioted madly, the bushes were huge and straggly, many of them had reverted to briars.

Having seen the vicarage-garden, Elfrida decided that she must learn about roses so that she could prune her own roses and try to bring order out of chaos. Meanwhile it was definitely not a garden to be proud of.

Lucius Babbington dropped in one morning to bring Elfrida a book which he had promised to lend her. He had a large bouquet of roses, which he proffered rather diffidently, saying that he expected she had plenty of roses in her own garden, but these were "rather special" and Mary thought she would like them.

"They're lovely," declared Elfrida, accepting the offering with delight. She added, "My garden is a jungle."

"A jungle?"

"Yes, I wouldn't be surprised to meet a tiger in it."

"I'd like to see your jungle," said Lucius, smiling.

"You can if you like, but I'm rather ashamed of it, Lucius." She was all the more reluctant to show Lucius her jungle because at Winford Hall the garden was kept in perfect order.

"You needn't be ashamed," he told her. "Mother Nature enjoys luxuriance; sometimes I think we're a bit too strict with her—we put her in a strait jacket—she gets her own way if she's left alone."

However in spite of the warning Lucius was rather horrified when his hostess opened the green door and disclosed the work of Mother Nature. He noticed that the fruit-trees and the vegetable-garden had been carefully tended, but the remainder of the garden was in a frightful state. Elfrida had not exaggerated when she called it a jungle.

"It's awful, isn't it?" said Elfrida with a sigh. "I want to get the place cleared up, but I don't know where to begin."

"My dear girl, you can't possibly do it yourself! I can give you the names of a couple of chaps in the village who might be able to come and do it, but you'll have to wait until the autumn."

Elfrida was silent. She could not afford to engage men for the work . . . so she might as well put it out of her head.

"Are you successful with cucumbers?" asked Lucius after a short silence. "Ours are a complete failure this year."

"Oh, I have a few," replied Elfrida, smiling mischievously. "I'll show you, Lucius."

He followed her along a path which was so overgrown with nettles and brambles that it had almost disappeared . . . and stopped suddenly in astonishment at the sight that met his eyes: in the farthest corner of the garden there was a tumble-down greenhouse, it's woodwork was rotten, its glass panes broken or cracked, but the whole ruin was a mass of green vegetation amongst which there were dozens of cucumbers, some large, some small.

"Good heavens!" exclaimed Lucius. "How did you do it?"

"I didn't do anything; Mother Nature did it all by herself."

He burst out laughing.

"How many would you like?" asked Elfrida.

Chowne had found time to mend the path down the cliff,

making steps in the worst places and driving in iron stanchions for a strong hand-rail, so now at last it was possible for Elfrida to go down to the bay and bathe.

She chose a particularly warm day for her first attempt and went down with her swim-suit and a towel. There was a sheltered corner at the west end of the bay which made a convenent dressing-room. Elfrida undressed, and ran down to the edge of the water.

The sea was calm, gleaming in the morning sunshine; tiny wavelets were lapping gently on the shore and retreating invitingly . . . but in spite of this she hesitated. Years ago, when she was a child, she had learnt to swim in an indoor swimming-bath but this was different; the sea looked so very large!

Perhaps I should wait, she thought. It would be rather nice to have someone with me for my first bathe in the sea . . . Mary might like to come.

But Marjory had bathed in this little bay and enjoyed it; there were several delightful snaps of Marjory splashing about in the water.

Elfrida plucked up her courage and went in. The sea was a good deal colder than she had expected, but she persevered and tried a few swimming strokes; at first tentatively with one foot on the ground, and then with increasing confidence. Swimming is an accomplishment one never forgets, so after a minute or two Elfrida began to feel at ease in the clear cool water . . . it was soft as velvet against her skin. She swam with a long slow breast-stroke, as she had been taught, then she turned on her back and floated, gazing up at the pale blue sky.

It was blissful—she was enjoying herself immensely—when suddenly she noticed that she was getting further away from the shore every moment. At first the pull of the current was gentle—so gentle that she could not understand what was happening—then it became stronger and she realised she was being carried out to sea.

It was alarming! It was terrifying! She was so frightened that she turned over on her face and, forgetting to swim, found herself sinking . . . a mouthful of salt water brought her to her senses! She struggled and splashed and swam desperately and at last managed to seize hold of a bunch of brown sea-weed and pull herself onto a flat rock at the west side of the bay.

For a few minutes Elfrida lay there, breathless and exhausted, too upset by her horrible experience to move. Then she rose and made her way over the rocks, back to the shore.

Never again! Never, never, never! thought Elfrida looking at the smooth water in horror.

A few days later Elfrida was talking to Mr. Cobley who was still at work in the copse. By this time Mr. Cobley had become a trusted friend, so it was natural that she should tell him of her experience and of her determination never, never, never to bathe again.

"Gracious, goodness, you must 'av gone in on the ebb!" he exclaimed. "That's dangerous, that is!"

"On the ebb?" asked Elfrida in puzzled tones.

Mr. Cobley took a stick and drawing a diagram on the ground explained the matter carefully. " 'Ere's the promontory, Miss Ware. It sticks out on the west side of the bay—sticks out into the sea like this . . . that's why the bay's so nice and sheltered."

"Yes, I know."

"Well, there's a current flows past the outside of the bay—like this, you see—and when the tide's on the ebb—going out, that is—the current draws the water out of the bay. If you bathe when the tide's going out you'll be drawn out and swept out to sea, which was what very nearly 'appened. See what I mean? Lucky for you it was a calm day; if the waves 'ad been rough you'd 'ave been done for."

"Yes, I see," said Elfrida. "But my mother used to bathe in that little bay, so why——"

"I dessay she did when the tide was flowing—coming in, that is—it's quite safe then."

"Really safe?"

"Safe as the Bank of England. You've got to watch the tide, that's all."

Elfrida had such absolute confidence in Mr. Cobley that she

bathed safely and with enjoyment, sometimes before breakfast and sometimes later in the day, depending upon the state of the tide.

She spent many hours in the little bay. If she could not bathe, she could always sun-bathe in the sheltered corner and it was too warm to walk far. The lanes with their high banks were airless and baking hot; the sun shone brilliantly in a cloudless sky . . . a sky that no longer was blue but almost white with heat.

Elfrida had now become strong and brown, her eyes were clear and her hair, which had been stringy and lifeless, was glossy and full of golden lights. She had never felt so fit in all her life, so there was no longer any excuse for idleness. The rose-garden was hopeless (as she had said to Lucius she did not know where to begin), but she worked in the vegetable-garden every evening after tea—it was cooler then. Chowne supervised her labours and found her an apt pupil; he had come out of his shell and talked to her occasionally in a queer laconic manner accompanied by expressive gestures of his large hands . . . or sometimes he would take a hoe and show her how he wanted the earth gently loosened and the weeds turned over to wither in the sun.

There was a great deal of hoeing done in the vegetable-garden at Mountain Cross.

Chowne had promised, through his interpreter, to do "light work on the farm," but in addition to looking after all the animals and keeping them clean he worked early and late in the garden. Elfrida was worried about him; she was aware that he was subject to "black-outs" if he were tired or upset, so quite often when he was digging or carrying heavy cans of water, she approached him and told him to go and sit down in the shade. It was useless, in fact it was worse than useless, for Chowne only smiled and shook his head and worked all the harder.

Chowne's smile was somewhat alarming; it split his lean brown face in half from ear to ear and displayed a double row of enormous white teeth.

Part Three

19

One evening after tea when Elfrida was working in the garden as usual (weeding a row of beans very carefully by hand so as not to disturb the roots) she heard someone calling her and looked up to see Mrs. Chowne trotting down the path.

"Quick, Miss Elfrida!" cried Mrs. Chowne, in breathless excitement. "Quick, it's a visitor! Oh dear, what a mess you're in!"

"You can't weed a garden without getting in a mess," declared Elfrida, sitting back on her heels and laughing.

"It's a visitor," repeated Mrs. Chowne. "He's a great friend of yours—such a nice friendly gentleman! If you'd told me he was coming I could have had a lovely dinner for him."

"But I didn't know! Who is he? Do you mean he intends to stay to dinner? We haven't enough food!"

A voice from behind her said, "Don't worry, Elfie! Bread and cheese will do."

Elfrida leapt to her feet—and turned—and saw him standing there, smiling at her in the old way "as if there were nobody else in the world." She was speechless with astonishment.

"Here's a wanderer," he said. "Here's a stranger within your gates, come to beg for a night's lodging."

"Glen! Oh, Glen! Yes, of course you must stay! Where have you come from? Why didn't you let me know?"

"Because I didn't know myself," said Glen, laughing. "I had to come down to this part of the world on business—"

"On business?"

"Yes, I had business in Morchester—it's only about twenty miles from here—so I thought I'd look in and see how you were getting on. I couldn't go back to London without a glimpse of you, Elfie. You aren't cross with me, are you?"

"Why should I be cross?"

"No reason at all," replied Glen cheerfully. "I rang up that number you gave me, but the woman said you had gone to Mountain Cross. I meant to write to you, of course, but I've been so terribly busy—and worried. How are things going, Elfie? Are the ducks behaving properly? I've been thinking about you so much. . . ."

He went on talking; he had taken her hands and was holding them. Elfrida was too upset to listen properly; she had imagined herself "cured," but his voice and his smile were as charming as ever and she was falling under the spell.

"Oh Glen," she cried. "You must stay as long as you like! It's a lovely surprise."

Mrs. Chowne murmured something about dinner and beds and hastened away.

"A few days, perhaps," said Glen. "This is a beautiful place—and so peaceful. If you could bear to have us for a few days, it would be delightful. I've been having rather a difficult time—one way and another. We'll help, of course; we shan't cause any trouble. You mustn't put yourself out——"

"We?" she asked.

"The boy is with me. I left him in the car until I saw if you could have us."

"What boy?"

"My little son," explained Glen. "You knew I had been married, didn't you?"

"Yes. At least someone said——"

"Let's sit down on that seat over there and I'll tell you about it," said Glen.

She followed him to the wooden seat near the lily-pool. Like everything else in this part of the garden the lily-pool was weedy and neglected.

"I'm going to clean it out when I have time," said Elfrida apologetically. "One of my neighbours has promised me some water-lilies. This part of the garden is a disgrace."

"It's a Sleeping Beauty Garden," declared Glen, looking round in delight. "What a wonderful set for a ballet!"

She smiled at this unusual reaction to her jungle.

"I said I'd tell you about my marriage," continued Glen, as he sat down beside her on the seat. "It all happened so long ago that I feel as if it had happened to someone else. I met Bridget in Dublin when I was playing Lorenzo in *The Merchant*—I was very young at the time. Bridget was even younger; she was a lovely creature with dark hair and a rose-leaf skin and Irish eyes. We fell in love madly and (as neither of us had any relations) there was nothing to prevent our marriage. I had a little money which had been left to me by an old aunt, so we rented a cottage and stayed there together, living the simple life. We stayed there until there was no money left . . . not very wise, you'll say, but it seemed to us that nobody had ever been young and in love before so we gathered our rosebuds while they were in bloom. Then, when the money was all gone, she went to the nuns to have the child and I went back to the stage." Glen paused for a few moments and then continued in a low voice. "There was no 'sweet sorrow' about our parting—it was agony to both of us—but you can't live on air. I think I said that to you, Elfie. I've tried it, you see. It doesn't work."

"I'm sorry, Glen," she said sadly.

"It all happened a long time ago."

For a few moments there was silence . . . absolute silence except for a bird twittering gently in one of the straggly bushes.

"How quiet it is!" said Glen. "I'd forgotten what silence was like. I haven't known real silence since that time in Ireland with Bridget. The cottage where we lived was in the depths of the

Irish country-side—a beautiful place but very small and not very civilised."

"How old is your child, Glen?"

"I suppose he must be seven or eight," Glen replied vaguely. "Time passes so quickly, doesn't it? His name is Patrick; the nuns christened him when he was born. Bridget was terribly ill, so they wired for me and I flew over, but she was dead when I got there. They showed me my child."

Glen paused . . . but Elfrida could find nothing to say.

"It gave me a frightful shock," he continued. "I had expected to see a baby—a chubby little cherub—not a wizened little creature like a monkey. They told me he was all right, but I didn't believe them. He's still like a monkey . . . which seems odd (Bridget was so lovely and I'm not exactly an ogre); but he's a good, quiet child which is something to be thankful for. I left him with the nuns—what else could I do?—and went to New York with a Gilbert and Sullivan opera."

"You said he was here."

"Yes, he's here. The nuns couldn't keep him after he was four years old, so I had to make other arrangements. I found a place for him in London, but that didn't work, so I moved him again, this time to Morchester, and he has been there ever since."

"That's what you were doing in Morchester!"

"Yes, I came to fetch the boy. Mrs. Landor is a widow—a nice kindly woman—but she wrote and said she was getting too old to cope with a child, so I must make some other arrangement." Glen sighed and added, "I've promised to have him with me for a time; I shall take him to Brittany for a holiday. Now you know the whole story so we needn't talk about it any more."

"But, Glen——"

"I mean it," he said earnestly. "It hurts me to speak of it. I've told you because you're so sympathetic and kind; I don't talk about it to other people. Tell me about you. How are things going? Are you tired of your moated grange? Are you ready to come back to civilisation?"

"No."

"Not yet?"

"Not ever," she declared vehemently. "This kind of life is right for me. I'm happy."

He looked at her critically. "I believe it's true! You have become exceedingly pretty . . . twice as pretty!"

"Fresh air and hard work suits me."

"It wouldn't suit me. Your moated grange is certainly very beautiful—delightful for a holiday—but after a bit I should want a fuller life, and so will you."

She shook her head. "I belong here, Glen. I'm the sort of person who needs a home. Look at this handful of earth! It's mine. That satisfies something inside me. Don't you understand?"

Glen smiled at her. "Not really . . . but I'm interested. You'll have to teach me, Elfie."

Their conversation was interrupted by the clamour of a large hand-bell with which Mrs. Chowne was wont to summon Elfrida to meals. It was being rung even more energetically than usual.

"Good lord! Is the house on fire?" exclaimed Glen.

"Only supper . . . I think," replied Elfrida, leaping up.

The ringing continued until Elfrida and Glen left the garden and hastened up the path to the house . . . a small boy in long red pants and a blue pullover was standing at the back door, ringing the bell with all his might. Glen sprinted up the path and seized the bell out of his hands.

Elfrida, following more slowly, heard the child say, "But, Glen, she said I was to ring it *hard*. Supper's nearly ready. I helped her to lay the table."

"That was very kind of you," said Elfrida. "You're Patrick, aren't you?"

He glanced at his father and then nodded, "The nuns called me Patrick."

"I call him Jacko," said Glen, laughing.

Mrs. Chowne had managed to produce a very satisfactory supper in record time. It was a cheerful meal for, although Elfrida had left the stage and had no intention of returning, she was interested to hear all the gossip—and Glen could make a good story out of the most unpromising material. *The Motor Car* had died a lingering death and the cast was scattered: Clarissa was going to America; Dolly Garden was in Spain with a friend—she had said she wanted a long holiday—several of "the gang" had managed to get parts in a new play which was even sillier than *The Motor Car* . . . and so on and so forth.

Presently Elfrida said, "And what about you, Glen? You told me you had heard of something good."

"Oh, that fell through! Jacko and I are going to Brittany together."

Patrick had been silent. He had enjoyed the meal and was now indulging in strawberries and cream; but he put down his spoon and looked at his father sadly.

"What's the matter, Jacko?" asked Glen.

"Nothing," replied Patrick. "Except—well—except that I'd like to see you acting. You said before that I wasn't old enough, but I'm eight now—and I wouldn't be a nuisance."

"Don't you want a holiday in Brittany?"

"If you're going for a holiday, I want to come . . . and if you're going to act in a play, I want to see you acting."

Glen looked at him in surprise. "Well, you seem to know what you want."

"Yes, I know what I want," said the child gravely.

It was a curious little exchange. Elfrida did not understand what it meant, but she had a feeling that it was important. What a strange little boy he was! She knew very little about children but it seemed to her that he was too "quiet." He was not attractive in appearance: his dark hair was long and straggled over his forehead; his brown eyes were too large for his thin white face and, when in repose, his face wore an anxious expression which was very unchildlike. This anxious expression gave Patrick a fleeting resemblance to a monkey (Elfrida had seen monkeys at the zoo with exactly that same worried look upon their poor little wizened faces), but all the same it was not right for Glen to call him 'Jacko' . . . nor did she approve of the child calling his father "Glen."

I suppose I'm old-fashioned, she thought. Anyhow it's none of my business.

20

It was a lovely mild evening so, after Patrick had been sent to bed, his elders went out and sat in an old summer-house which Elfrida had discovered on the edge of the cliff. Mrs. Chowne had told her that it had been put there for Mrs. Ware, who loved looking at the sea and watching the seagulls.

Although Elfrida had seen a great deal of Glen, had been in his company every day for weeks, she had never been alone with him before—not really alone, thought Elfrida—they had always been surrounded by a crowd. All the talks they had had were hurried and uneasy; a few hasty words at rehearsals or between scenes or when Glen was on his way to one of the innumerable parties. There was no hurry here, no interruptions; there was time for little silences which were more revealing than words. At the moment the little silence told Elfrida that Glen was happy and comfortable.

Presently, however, he began to talk; he had travelled widely, on tour with repertory companies, and had had many amusing experiences.

"What a lot you've seen and done!" exclaimed Elfrida. "You've had a pretty hard life, one way and another—I never realised that before—but now you've arrived, haven't you?"

He laughed and replied, "I'm still ambitious. I want to play Hamlet. That's what every actor wants, isn't it?"

"Why shouldn't you?"

"Because, my dear Elfie, I'm on the wrong road."

"Yes, I see what you mean; you've made your name by playing in Musicals and Drawing-room Comedies. Still, I don't see why you shouldn't——"

"And anyhow," interrupted Glen. "I should want to play Hamlet quite differently. I have a feeling that nobody has ever got to the bottom of Hamlet."

"How would you play him?"

"Oh, that's too long a story—too serious a story for a summer's evening:

> "In such a night,
> Troilus, methinks, mounted the Trojan walls,
> And sigh'd his soul toward the Grecian tents,
> Where Cressid lay that night."

Fortunately Elfrida knew The Merchant of Venice pretty well—it was her favourite—so she replied:

> "In such a night
> Did Thisbe fearfully o'er trip the dew,
> And saw the lion's shadow ere himself,
> And ran dismay'd away."

Glen looked at her in astonishment. He had not expected this! He said:

> "In such a night
> Stood Dido with a willow in her hand
> Upon the wild sea-banks, and wav'd her love
> To come again to Carthage."

Elfrida continued:

> "In such a night
> Medea gather'd the enchanted herbs
> That did renew old Aeson."

Glen went on:

> "In such a night
> Did Jessica steal from the wealthy Jew
> And, with an unthrift love, did run from Venice
> As far as Belmont."

Elfrida hesitated for a moment and then said:

> "I would out-night you, did nobody come . . ."

"Here!" exclaimed Glen. "You've missed your cue . . . and we were getting on so nicely!"

She had missed her cue because she could not bring herself to say that in such a night Lorenzo had stolen her heart "with many vows of faith." It might have been possible on the stage, where she could have imagined herself speaking to Lorenzo, but here, in the summer-house at Mountain Cross, this was Glen and she was "Elfie."

Glen did not press her. Perhaps he understood, for he smiled and said, "You surprised me. I had no idea you were interested in Jessica."

"I'm not interested in Jessica!"

"Perhaps you're interested in Portia?"

"Yes. Silly, isn't it? I believe I could play Portia; I understand her. She's a real person—one of the few real flesh-and-blood women in Shakespeare's plays."

"Oh, poor Elfie! You're interested in Portia and you were given Mrs. Carruthers!"

Elfrida's eyes flashed. "I hated that woman! I tried to understand her, but there was nothing to understand. She was supposed to be a society woman, silly and decadent, but she wasn't even that. Mrs. Carruthers was a doll, stuffed with sawdust and—and leaking at the seams!"

Glen roared with laughter.

"It's true," she declared. "You know it's true, Glen."

"She was a mess," he admitted. "Dolly made an even worse mess of her than you did. Dolly made her coy; it was rather disgusting. You've changed," he added. "It isn't only that you're twice as pretty, you're twice as interesting. Why have you changed? Tell me seriously."

She thought about it. "I've become a whole person," she said.

"Yes. But why?"

"Because I belong here."

"Is that all?"

"Isn't it enough? Some people love the stage—they're in their element—but I couldn't understand the fascination."

"Your father was an actor."

"Yes, but I'm like Mother. This was her home; she loved Mountain Cross and longed to come back. Now, at last, I've come back—it feels like that."

"I should have thought that your mother might have been attracted by the glamour——"

"She wasn't the stuff that actresses are made of," interrupted Elfrida. "Father couldn't understand it; he was sure she could learn if she tried; he wanted to make her a star! She was very intelligent, she was beautiful and graceful and had a lovely figure, but that isn't enough, is it?"

"No, I suppose not," said Glen thoughtfully. "Well, well, Thistlewood failed in his endeavour to make his wife a star, so *that* was the reason he deserted her and went off to Australia!"

Elfrida was dumb with astonishment. This aspect of her father's behaviour had never occurred to her before . . . and how did Glen know?

"Elfie!" exclaimed Glen, looking at her in alarm. "Didn't you know he had deserted her? No, I can see I've given you a shock; how stupid of me! I never met your parents—it all happened before my time—but everyone talked of it. Everyone liked her and thought he'd behaved very badly (you know the way gossip goes round in the theatre), so I thought you knew the whole story."

"No, I just thought . . . I mean Mother told me he had—had died in Australia. She never said——"

"She wouldn't, of course! You were a child at the time and she wanted you to remember your father with pride and affection. I've been very silly," said Glen remorsefully.

"It doesn't matter, Glen. I'd rather . . . know . . . really. It's a long time ago and I scarcely remember him." She hesitated and then added thoughtfully. "Mr. Sandford thought it was madness not to make enquiries about him . . . but, of course, that was the reason. Poor Mother!"

Glen put his arm round her shoulders. "Forgive me, Elfie. I wouldn't have distressed you for worlds."

"There's nothing—to forgive."

For a few moments they were silent.

"Was she really beautiful?" asked Glen at last.

"I'll show you her portrait," replied Elfrida in a breathless whisper. It had been lovely talking to Glen, he was so kind and understanding, but his arm round her shoulders was more than she could bear—her heart was beating so loudly that she was afraid he would hear it—she was glad of the excuse to move. She disengaged herself gently and rose, "I'll show it to you," she repeated.

"Need we go in?" asked Glen. "I can see the portrait tomorrow morning, can't I? It's such a lovely evening and it's quite early."

"Early for you, but not for me; I'm usually in bed and asleep by this time."

He got up with reluctance. He had been enjoying himself; he could have spent hours talking to this new Elfie, who was not only twice as pretty as before but twice as interesting.

It was dark by this time—or nearly dark—so when they came to the side-door Elfrida ran up the steps and put on the light for Glen to see his way. She stood in the doorway with the light above her head, looking down and waiting for him.

Three times as pretty, thought Glen, gazing at her in admiration: the sun-tan made her eyes more blue; her light-brown hair was wavy and golden; her lips, innocent of rouge, were fresh and pink . . . best of all there was a glow of radiant health in this new Elfie; she was warmly alive. London had been stuffy and airless, everyone was pale and strained and tired, so it was natural that Glen should feel the attraction of health and beauty. All the same he was surprised at himself for, since his youthful marriage, he had been attracted by sophisticated women. Clarissa Downes with her pale face, scarlet lips and langorous drawl had moved him profoundly; his *affaire* with her had been passionate and completely satisfying. What has happened to me? he wondered.

Elfrida took him upstairs to Mrs. Ware's bedroom and showed him the portrait. "There, Glen! Isn't she lovely?"

"Yes," said Glen. "Yes, you were right; she's a lovely creature. You know, Elfie, it might almost be a portrait of you."

"Almost, but not quite," said Elfrida, smiling. "I've got the same colouring, but I haven't her regular features."

"You're very like her, Elfie."

"I know I'm like her . . . but there's a difference. I expect you kissed the Blarney Stone when you were in Ireland."

"Well, as a matter of fact I did," he admitted, turning and smiling at her. "It's the thing to do, you know, but the Blarney Stone has nothing to do with the case. You're every bit as lovely as your mother—and you're alive!"

He had taken her hand as he spoke, but Elfrida turned away and released herself. She said, "You're interested in furniture, aren't you? Come and look at this chest of drawers, Glen. Tell me what you think of it."

At the moment he was not particularly interested in the chest of drawers, but he agreed that it was a very fine piece of furniture and beautifully polished.

"I polish it myself," she told him. "I like polishing it. I've never had beautiful things before—of my very own. Sometimes I just can't believe it all belongs to me."

"This is a beautiful room," he said, looking round at the rest of the furniture. "Is it your room, Elfie?"

"No, it was Grandmother's room. I could use it if I liked, of course, but I prefer Mother's room which is at the end of the passage; it has a lovely view of the sea and the sound of the waves breaking on the shore sends me to sleep."

"It would keep me awake," Glen told her. He added a trifle irritably. "Are there no snags, Elfie? Isn't there a snake in your Garden of Eden?"

"No snags and no snakes," she replied, smiling happily.

They were still standing in Mrs. Ware's bedroom when the door opened very quietly and Mrs. Chowne appeared.

"Goodness!" exclaimed Elfrida. "Why aren't you in bed, Mrs. Chowne? It's frightfully late."

"Yes, it's late," agreed Mrs. Chowne, nodding.

"Is something the matter?"

"Well, it is . . . and it isn't," replied Mrs. Chowne cryptically. "Could I speak to you a minute, Miss Elfrida?"

Elfrida was alarmed. "All right, I'll come," she said. "You can wait for me in my bedroom. I'll just make sure that Mr. Siddons has everything he wants."

21

It did not take long for Elfrida to escort her guest to his room and make sure he had all the necessary creature-comforts. She said goodnight and hastened back to her bedroom where Mrs. Chowne was awaiting her.

"Miss Elfrida, could I speak to you for a minute?" repeated Mrs. Chowne.

The request was a curious one, considering the fact that Mrs. Chowne spoke all the time—in and out of season—but apparently there was something very important to be said, so Elfrida gave the required permission.

"Well, I don't know what you'll say, Miss Elfrida," declared Mrs. Chowne, starting off at a tremendous rate. "It's a big thing to ask—I know that and Ernie knows it too. If it hadn't been for the parent getting in a state and sending the message, he needn't have gone. I told you about the parent, didn't I? Ernie says I ought to know better at my age, but you do hear of funny things happening, don't you? In the papers, I mean. It won't be much trouble to you, Miss Elfrida—I'll take your things down myself—and Judy's room is very comfortable with a good bed and all. I wouldn't ask it else. Ernie was a bit doubtful about going—but I told you about the parent, didn't I?" She stopped to breathe.

Elfrida had become fairly skilful at disentangling Mrs. Chowne's circumlocutions. This was a little more difficult than usual because the speaker was embarrassed.

"You mean," said Elfrida slowly. "You mean Chowne had to go over to Cherleigh to see his father and you want me to come downstairs and sleep in Judy's room?"

"I know it's a lot to ask."

"Of course I will," said Elfrida smiling at her. "It will be rather fun."

"Oh, it *is* kind of you!" exclaimed Mrs. Chowne, heaving a sigh of relief. "I was quite ashamed of asking you to do it. You can undress here and come down in your dressing-gown—it's a warm night so you won't get a chill. I'll take your tooth-brush and sponges and your towel and run down to get everything ready. You can wash in our bathroom, can't you?"

Elfrida agreed.

"Oh, it *is* a relief to my mind," declared Mrs. Chowne.

It was not until Mrs. Chowne had gone and Elfrida began to undress that she realised it would have been much easier and more sensible for Mrs. Chowne to have moved upstairs to the small spare room. When Mrs. Chowne was talking, she absorbed one's whole attention and it was only afterwards when one had time to think that one was able to see flaws in her plans. Anyhow it was too late now to alter the arrangement; Mrs. Chowne was enchanted at the idea of having her to sleep in Judy's room and it would be unkind to disappoint her.

Chowne's parent had "got in a state" before, on several occasions, and the Chownes had been obliged to drop whatever they happened to be doing and rush over to Cherleigh on their bicycles, but that had been in the day time. It was to be hoped that he would not make a practise of getting in a state at night.

Elfrida had heard a lot more about the parent and was aware that, although he was over ninety, he still had eleven teeth and was looked after by a widow-woman who lived next door and came in and did for him. It *had* just crossed her mind that the widow-woman might be even more dangerous to the Chownes' expectation than the cats, but she had refrained from saying so.

By this time Elfrida had brushed her hair and pinned it into a net. As she put on her blue silk dressing-gown she glanced at her own bed with the blue aertex blanket and the smooth white sheet turned back . . . how inviting it looked!

Oh, what a bother! thought Elfrida. Who would have thought that Mrs. Chowne suffered from nervous fears? Sane, sensible, practical Mrs. Chowne! It's almost incredible! Why did I say I'd do it?

However she had said she would do it, so she put out her bedroom light and went across the landing to the stairs. Patrick's room was dark, of course, but there was still a band of light beneath Glen's door; he was probably reading in bed.

Half-way down the stairs Elfrida paused with her hand on the smooth mahogany banister-rail. It belongs to me, she thought. All of this is mine. The panelled hall, the stairs, the banisters, the old mahogany chest, carved and polished, the rug which had faded with the passing years were all her very own. This was not a new thought, of course, she had thought it often and often, but it always took her breath away for a few moments.

When her breath returned, she went on down the stairs, across the hall and through the red baize door into the kitchen. The door of the Chowne's sitting-room was ajar; she pushed it open and here she was.

Mrs. Chowne welcomed her as if they had been parted for weeks—pulling forward the most comfortable chair and arranging a cushion behind her back. "This *is* nice," said Mrs. Chowne happily. "The kettle's boiling, so we'll have a cup of tea."

Although Elfrida was not in the habit of drinking tea at this hour, she did not refuse so they sat down and had it together, hob-nobbing in a friendly manner.

"This *is* nice," repeated Mrs. Chowne. "Ernie is all very well in his way but it's lovely to have someone like you to talk to. Miss Marjory used to come in sometimes and have a chat like this. You're like her, you know, Miss Elfrida . . . but there's a difference. I'm not clever enough to explain it properly, but it's the difference between a plant that's been cossetted in a greenhouse and a plant that's been grown out-of-doors and had to bear all sorts of weather."

Elfrida nodded.

"When I first came to Mountain Cross, I was very small beer," continued Mrs. Chowne. "I didn't have much to do with Miss Marjory, but she'd give me a smile when we met on the stairs and ask how I was getting on . . . and she'd ask properly and listen to the answer as if she really cared."

"She did care. She always cared about people."

"Yes," said Mrs. Chowne thoughtfully. "She cared about people—even a raw under-housemaid like I was in those days. I was as raw as a turnip, but Alice was good at teaching and she never grudged the time. She was a good sort," added Mrs. Chowne, nodding. "Then one day Mrs. Ware sent for me and said, 'You've done well, Emma, and I'd give you Alice's place when she gets married if you could learn to talk nicely.' I was Somerset, you see, and very broad. I said I'd learn—and I meant it—but it wasn't easy. Still I managed it and I got Alice's job. You see, Miss Elfrida, in those days you were Somebody if you were head-housemaid at a place like Mountain Cross. Soon after that I met Ernie at Cherleigh Flower Show; I was wearing a new hat and it was a fine day and I felt on top of the world . . . anyhow we just—sort of—clicked."

Elfrida looked at her and tried to imagine the scene . . . but it was impossible to imagine!

"So Ernie and I walked out for a bit," continued Mrs. Chowne. "Then we got married and Mr. and Mrs. Ware both came to the church—very kind, they were. They gave us a dinner-set, which we're still using to this very day (I've been so careful that scarcely any of it has got broken). They gave us our flat and Ernie left Sir Henry Champion and came here to live and to look after the cars and the garden. He had two men under him in those days. We've been here ever since except when Ernie went to the war and got blown up in his tank . . .

but he came back when he got out of hospital. Mr. Ware liked Ernie and said it didn't matter about Ernie not being able to talk; he could do the work all the better because he didn't waste time talking . . . not like me! After the war things were different. All the big families were having to tighten their purse-strings and a lot of gardeners and housemaids got the sack. It couldn't be helped, of course, it was the war that upset everything. We were lucky to be here in our nice little flat—and we both knew it.

"Well, you see I've been here a long time, Miss Elfrida, so that's why Mrs. Ware talked to me and told me her troubles. She knew I'd understand."

"What troubles?" asked Elfrida.

"Miss Marjory, of course. She longed for Miss Marjory. Often and often she said it to me: 'Oh, Emma, if I could just see her! If I just knew where she was and what she was doing! Do you think she's happy?' I could have cried sometimes. I used to think: What would I feel if Judy had gone away with some man and I didn't know where she was or what had happened to her? I used to say, 'Why don't you ask Mr. Ware to find her?' She did ask him. She asked him again and again, but he put her off. It was difficult for him to forgive Miss Marjory because he'd been so proud of her; he thought the world of her; nothing was too good for her."

"Did you ever see my father?"

Mrs. Chowne nodded. "Miss Marjory met him when she was in London and asked him to come and stay at Mountain Cross—she could ask anyone she liked, of course—so he came for a week and stayed longer. Well, I won't say anything; he was your father, wasn't he?—but he just didn't fit. He was different from the people here. I don't say he was better or worse, just different . . . so there was trouble when he said he wanted to marry Miss Marjory."

"But she ran away and married him."

"Not just at once. She was miserable when Mr. Ware said she wasn't to marry Mr. Thistlewood, so Mrs. Ware thought it would be good for her to have a change of air and arranged for her to go and stay with a schoolfriend at Guildford. Miss Marjory seemed pleased at the idea so off she went . . . and the next thing we heard she was married."

"So that was how it happened," said Elfrida sadly.

"Yes, that was how it happened. She went away from her home and never came back. She didn't mean it, you know."

"Didn't mean what?"

"Never to come back," explained Mrs. Chowne. "I'm sure she thought they'd forgive her and be friends. I'm certain sure of it. You see she'd always had her own way; they'd never gone against her in anything, so she couldn't believe they'd go against her marriage. Oh dear, it was dreadful," said Mrs. Chowne in distress. "Miss Marjory was so pretty and so sweet that you couldn't help loving her—nobody could help loving her; she could have married anyone. I always thought Sir Henry Champion of Meston Park was sweet on Miss Marjory—they'd have been pleased if she'd married him—and there were others as well . . ."

Mrs. Chowne paused.

"Yes, I see," said Elfrida thoughtfully. Here was another new light on Marjory . . . and a new light on Marjory's mother.

"It wasn't quite so bad while Mr. Ware was alive," continued Mrs. Chowne. "But after he died, Mrs. Ware was all alone, so she wanted Miss Marjory more than ever."

"She sent for Mr. Sandford, didn't she?"

"It was me that asked him to come. He was here a lot in the old days, so I knew him quite well. Then, after his father died, he took over Mr. Ware's business affairs, so he used to come about that . . . and he came for Mr. Ware's funeral, of course. There was nobody else I could think of to ask what to do and I was worried to death. When I rang him up and said Mrs. Ware was ill and would like to see him, he came at once and he was as kind as kind—nobody could have been kinder. Mrs. Ware told him she was longing to see Miss Marjory and he said he would try his best to find her. Well, he tried his best, but he couldn't find her anyhow."

Mrs. Chowne sighed and added, "I was almost sorry I'd got Mr. Sandford to come."

"Why were you sorry?"

"Because it made her hopeful and she kept on asking. Every time the telephone rang she used to ask. At first she'd say it: 'Any news, Emma?' and then, when the days went by and there was no news, she'd ask me with her eyes. I couldn't bear her asking me, so I'd come into her room and say quickly, 'That was the butcher; he's got lambs' sweetbreads today, so I told him to send them up. You'll enjoy them for your dinner, won't you?'—or whatever it happened to be."

"Oh, dear, how sad!" said Elfrida mournfully. "If only we had known . . ."

"Would she have come, Miss Elfrida?"

"Of course she would have come if she had known her mother wanted her. She was longing to come to Mountain Cross."

There was a little silence. Then Mrs. Chowne took out her handkerchief and blew her nose violently. "I'm an old silly, keeping you talking till all hours and making you miserable," she said.

22

Elfrida was very sleepy next morning—she was not used to late hours—but she felt better when she had had her bath and she was ready for breakfast at nine. Glen was late; he came down looking rather cross. Actors are never at their best in the morning, so Elfrida was not surprised; she told him to help himself to grapefruit or bacon and eggs or whatever he would like and did not bother him. There was no sign of Patrick.

Presently Glen said, "I thought that was your room at the end of the passage, Elfie."

"Yes, it is."

"But you weren't there last night. I had a touch of neuralgia and went along to see if you had some aspirin."

"Oh, I'm sleeping downstairs just now. I'm so sorry about the neuralgia, Glen. Is it better this morning? There's a bottle of aspirin in the bathroom cupboard. Shall I get it for you?"

"You're sleeping downstairs?"

"With Mrs. Chowne," explained Elfrida. "Here's your coffee, Glen. Just help yourself to sugar."

"I don't like sugar in my coffee. What's the idea of sleeping with Mrs. Thingamybob?"

"Her husband had to go and see his father at Cherleigh and she's nervous of being alone on the ground floor."

"What an extraordinary arrangement! Couldn't the woman have come into the house?"

"She could, I suppose," admitted Elfrida . . . and left it at that. After all it was not Glen's business and if he had been up and about late at night and had wandered into her room—looking for aspirin—perhaps it was just as well that she had moved downstairs to the Chowne's flat.

At this moment Patrick appeared. He slid into his chair and said, "Sorry, Glen! I woke up early and went out to look at the sea. It was gorgeous!"

"You should apologise to your hostess for being late."

He turned at once. "I'm sorry, Miss Ware. I didn't mean to be late—but it really was simply gorgeous."

"It doesn't matter," replied Elfrida, smiling at him. "Mrs. Chowne is keeping your breakfast hot. Do you think you could find your way to the kitchen and fetch it?"

"You bet! I can smell bacon!" cried Patrick and was off like a rocket.

He appeared a few moments later, carrying the plate very carefully. "It's sausage *and* bacon *and* egg—gorgeous!" he said and putting it on the table fell to with a will.

" 'Gorgeous'!" said Glen irritably. "Is that the only word you know? If you use it to describe the sea, it's unsuitable for a plate of bacon and egg."

Patrick stopped eating and looked at his father in alarm.

"What about 'delicious'?" suggested Elfrida smiling at the child.

"Dilishuss," said Patrick, grinning. "Yes, that's a good word. I'm having a dilishuss breakfast. This is a dilishuss house . . . everything here is dilishuss and——"

"Oh, shut up!" exclaimed Glen, rising and walking out of the room.

"Glen's cross with me," said Patrick and his lip quivered.

"I shouldn't worry if I were you," Elfrida told him. "People are often a little cross in the morning, especially actors like Glen." She hesitated, looking at Patrick and wondering whether he was old enough to understand what she wanted to say—she knew so little about children—but perhaps it was worth trying.

"Glen wasn't really cross with you," she said. "He was just cross."

Patrick looked at her with a worried frown.

"There's a lot of difference," Elfrida told him. "If people are just cross, you needn't worry. It's only when they're cross with you that it matters. Remember that when you go with Glen to Brittany . . . and remember not to chat to him at breakfast. Now, finish up your bacon and egg before it gets cold and then we can go out. There's a cow up at the farm—you'd like to see her, wouldn't you?—and I've got some pigs too."

"Oh, how gor—I mean how nice," said Patrick.

Elfrida found Glen in the parlour reading the paper. He had recovered from his ill-humour and when she told him she was going to take Patrick up to the farm, he said he would like to come with them.

"I'm interested in those ducks," declared Glen, putting down the paper and rising.

"It's pigs," said Elfrida. "Pigs and a cow called Pansy. She's a darling and she knows me quite well. I didn't get ducks because there isn't a suitable pond."

"Oh dear, I was looking forward to seeing the ducks!" exclaimed Glen, registering a ludicrous expression of disappointment.

Elfrida laughed. She was not surprised to find that the thunder-cloud had passed so quickly; she had spent most of her life rubbing shoulders with actors so "the artistic temperament" was nothing new. People like Glen who could move thousands to laughter or tears, people like Glen who had the Gift, were liable to blow up suddenly and explode with a resounding bang and then forget all about it. You could not judge them by ordinary standards because they were not ordinary people. Elfrida was all the more willing to make allowances for Glen because she admired him so much . . . and because she had a pretty shrewd idea what it was that had upset him.

They spent some time walking round the farm and looking at the animals. The pigs were growing bigger and fatter every day in a most satisfactory manner . . . but Glen was not really interested in pigs; he became rather bored and said he would go home and ring up his agent in London—if Elfie didn't mind—and wandered off by himself.

Just beyond Pansy's paddock there was a seven-acre field which originally had been part of the Mountain Cross estate, but which had been sold some years ago to a neighbouring farmer. It was Elfrida's 'Naboth's Vineyard'; she always looked at it when she visited Pansy and wished that her grandfather had not sold it—or that she had enough money to buy it back! The love of land is hereditary; it was strong in Elfrida, but apparently it had had no lodging in the heart of the late Mr. Ware.

Elfrida took Patrick to the gate and they stood and looked at the field. She had watched the hay grow and ripen in the sunshine; she had seen it being cut; today she saw that the swaths of dry hay were being gathered by a machine towed by a tractor. It was a very clever machine, for it picked up the loose swaths of hay and transformed them into neat bales. . . and then threw them out.

"How does it do it?" asked Patrick when they had watched the process for a minute or two.

Elfrida could not tell him; she had been wondering exactly the same thing herself.

Presently the man who was driving the tractor stopped at the gate and asked if the little lad would like a ride. He smiled kindly and added that he had a little lad of his own who liked riding on the tractor.

Patrick was charmed with the idea; he climbed up nimbly and off they went. Elfrida could see that he was enjoying himself immensely. They went round and round the field, gathering up the hay; every time they passed the gate Patrick waved joyously and Elfrida waved back.

This went on for some time and there was still a great deal of hay to be gathered and baled. Elfrida was beginning to wonder how she would be able to tear him away from the entrancing entertainment when the tractor stopped and Patrick came running back to her across the field.

"It's Joe's dinner-time," he announced breathlessly. "That man is called Joe and he has four children. He said he would take me for another ride whenever I liked. He said I mustn't tell anyone because it's against the law."

"Against the law?"

"That's what he said, but it's all right if I don't tell anyone. I like secrets, don't you, Miss Ware?"

Elfrida did not really believe it was "against the law," but she promised to keep the secret.

All the way home Patrick prattled excitedly: he was going to be a farmer when he grew up; he was going to have pigs, and a cow just like Pansy; he was going to have a huge hay-field with lots of white daisies and blue cornflowers growing in it; he was going to have a tractor and a baler to fit on to it—just like Joe.

"I thought you were going to be an actor, like Glen," objected Elfrida. "That's what you said last night."

"No, I've changed my mind. Joe says it's grand to be a farmer. He said if I was bigger, he would take me on as a farm-hand. I wonder how big I would have to be . . ."

Elfrida listened in amusement; it was a new experience for her to be in close contact with a child. Patrick had been a little shy at first, but now quite suddenly he had become friendly and the anxious look, which had seemed so unchildlike, had completely vanished. Elfrida was pleased about this; she was even more pleased when she felt a small, hot, grubby hand slide into hers in a confiding manner.

23

In the afternoon Elfrida took her guests down to the bay, to her favourite nook in the shelter of the rocky promontory. It was so warm and sunny that she and Glen were able to lie on rugs and sun-bathe while Patrick pottered about on the shore.

"It's warm enough to bathe," said Glen after a short silence.

"You'd find it pretty cold," replied Elfrida, smiling at the idea of Glen, the hot-house plant, splashing in the sea. She added, "Besides there's a strong back-wash at ebb-tide."

"Please enlighten the landlubber."

"Mr. Cobley explained it to me; he knows all about tides." She sat up as she spoke and proceeded to draw Mr. Cobley's diagram on the sand. "Look, Glen, here's the promontory running out into the sea. A current flows past the entrance to our bay and when the tide is going out the current sucks the water out of the bay."

"Why?" asked Glen, who had been following the explanation with interest.

"I don't know why . . . but I know it does. I had a horrid experience one day when I was bathing, so now I never bathe unless the tide is coming in."

"What happened, Elfie?"

"I found I was being carried out to sea. Fortunately it was a very calm day, so I managed to swim to a rock . . . if the sea had been rough I wouldn't have had a chance."

Glen said no more about the matter . . . and she was glad, for she disliked speaking of it. She had tried hard to forget all about those horrible moments when she had struggled against the pull of the tide, but she still dreamt about it sometimes and awakened bathed in perspiration.

"Tuppence for your thoughts, Elfie," said Glen suddenly.

"They aren't worth the money."

"I'll tell you mine for nothing."

She looked at him and saw that he was lying back with his hands behind his head . . . and was smiling at her. Glen's smile had always charmed her; yes, "charmed" was the word. There was magic in Glen's smile.

"I was thinking about you," he said. "You're a golden girl, Elfie."

"I'm very sunburnt," she agreed.

"Golden," said Glen in a thoughtful voice. "Gold all over from head to foot . . . your feet are beautiful. It's a joy to see beautiful feet! So few women have beautiful feet! No, don't hide them under the rug; I want to look at them."

"Patrick is—enjoying himself," said Elfrida with a little gasp. "Look at him, Glen!"

"I don't want to look at the little monkey; I want to look at you. There are a lot of very interesting things about you, Elfie. Perhaps the most interesting of all is the way you glow . . . it's a sort of radiance, as if you had a light inside."

"Nonsense, Glen!"

"It isn't nonsense. I'm sure you would shine in the dark. We must make an experiment—a scientific experiment—and see if I'm right. We shall have to do it at night, of course. It would be no use in the day-time."

"I don't like scientific experiments."

"But this would be so interesting, Elfie."

She shook her head.

"Why not?" asked Glen. "All I want is to try a scientific experiment. What's the harm in that?"

"It might go off with a bang," replied Elfrida, trying to speak lightly. She had few illusions about Glen and was aware that he could no more help flirting with a reasonably good-looking young woman than he could help breathing. To Glen it was a game . . . but unfortunately this particular reasonably good-looking young woman was not an adept at the game; besides her emotions were too deeply involved. There was a curious magnetism in Glen which affected her profoundly.

The magnetism was very real; it was Glen's chief attribute as an actor, but he had other attractions as well. There was magic in his slow lazy smile; the musical cadences of his voice had enraptured thousands; his hands were long-fingered and shapely —and he used them with easy grace. In addition to all his natural endowments Glen Siddons had cultivated an engaging manner and gave the impression that the woman to whom he happened to be speaking was the only woman in the world.

"This is a delightful place," said Glen, after a little silence. "The house has a strong atmosphere of byegone days. This morning, when I came back from the farm, I sat in your little parlour for quite a time and I felt as if I were drifting back into the days of long ago. I could have gone back quite easily—and how interesting it would have been to see the people who used to live here!"

"I know what you mean," said Elfrida eagerly. "I've felt it often. The people of long ago are quite near and friendly."

"They were your ancestors, I suppose?"

"Yes, of course! They loved Mountain Cross and I love it too—more and more every day."

"You'll get tired of it, Elfie."

"No, never!" she exclaimed. "This is my home."

"You will," Glen told her. "This is a marvellous place for a holiday; it's very kind of you to have us and I'm enjoying every moment, but a week of it would be enough for me. After that I should begin to long for the bright lights of London, the stir and the bustle and the chat. I should long to be in the middle of things with something interesting going on all the time . . . even the quarrels are exhilarating! You're out of the world here and the mere idea of settling down and living here forever and ever gives me the pip . . . I couldn't bear it!"

"Could you bear to live anywhere forever and ever?"

"Clever Elfie!" he exclaimed, smiling at her. "No, of course I couldn't. I'm a nomad. I'd like to be a Bedouin, riding on a camel from one oasis to another, sleeping under the stars."

"Forever and ever?"

"Well, perhaps not," he admitted. "One might get bored with the desert after a bit. Do you think I'd make a good Bedouin Sheik?"

She looked at him critically . . . not that she knew much about Bedouins except that they had dark hair and hawk-like eyes.

He was laughing. "Oh, I shall have to be made-up a good deal, but that won't be difficult——"

"Oh, Glen!" she cried. "Are you going to play the part of a Bedouin Sheik? How exciting! When and where? Do tell me about it!"

"My dear Elfie, you do jump to conclusions, don't you? I said I'd like to be a Bedouin, riding on a camel and sleeping under the stars . . . and I added that I should have to be made-up a good deal to play the part. If you thought for a moment, you would realise that a Bedouin Sheik isn't my line of country."

"No, of course it isn't," she agreed. She saw now that she had been rather silly; Glen's line of country was to play the part of a prince of romance. "You were wonderful in *The Beggar King*," she added. "I wish you could find another play like that."

"I'm tired," declared Glen. "What I want is a nice long holiday. That wretched *Motor Car* took a lot out of me; we rehearsed it for weeks and then, after all the trouble, the damn thing was a flop. Clarissa is an absolute wreck—you found it exhausting, yourself!—so what about me? I had the heaviest part of the burden."

"Oh, I know!" she exclaimed. "I used to feel sorry for you,

Glen. You deserve a long holiday . . . besides you promised Patrick to take him to Brittany."

Glen nodded. "I haven't seen much of the child; I've been too busy—and you can't drag a child about all over the place when you're working—but it's time we got to know each other better."

"Yes, of course."

"What are we going to do tomorrow?" asked Glen, rolling over on the rug and exposing his back to the warm sunshine.

Elfrida had made no plans for entertaining her guest; she had no idea how long he intended to stay. He had said "a few days," but that might mean anything.

"We'll go out to lunch," he suggested.

"A picnic?"

"Heaven forbid! There are few entertainments I dislike more. I'll take you to The Grand Hotel at Morchester. The food is eatable and it will do you good to return to civilisation."

"Have I become a savage?"

"Slightly uncivilised," said Glen teasingly. "You don't even put a dab of powder on your nice little nose! But, not to worry, we'll go to Morchester tomorrow and you'll see the world and his wife."

"What about me?" asked Patrick, who had approached while they were talking and had overheard the last few words.

"You can come too. Won't that be 'gorgeous'?" said Glen, laughing.

"Super gorgeous!" cried Patrick joyfully.

24

Elfrida spent another night in Judy's room. She had asked Mrs. Chowne's permission and Mrs. Chowne had replied in her usual sensible way, "Yes, do, Miss Elfrida. It's such a waste when sheets are only used once; it doesn't seem worth the trouble washing them. You had better dirty them out."

Elfrida had realised that this was an invitation to spend several nights in Judy's bed—a week if she liked—and had thanked her hostess suitably.

When she went in to breakfast, she found a letter from Ronnie lying on the table and opened it with a smile of pleasant anticipation; Ronnie's letters were always entertaining . . .

The letter was an answer to her own long letter, telling him about the luncheon party at Winford Hall and about her plans for the garden, and about the delights of swimming in the bay. She had not told him of her alarming experience because she was afraid it would worry him, but had merely said that Mr. Cobley had warned her about the curious phenomenon at ebb-tide, so she bathed when the tide was coming in.

Ronnie commented on all this in an amusing manner and then went on, "There's a big case pending and I am doing a good deal of work for Uncle Bob. It would be easier if there were not so many parties; there is some sort of party nearly every night and Mother likes me to go with her and take part in the fun. She says 'all work and no play makes Jack a dull boy,' but working and playing all the time is making this Jack a very tired boy. It is hot in London—hot and stuffy and dusty—I have to put on a clean collar three times a day. Perhaps this information is not very interesting to a girl! I am afraid this letter is not very interesting, but Jack feels dull in spite of the parties. I have read your letter several times; it is like a breath of fresh air. Write me another letter soon, dear Elfrida Jane. . . .

Elfrida felt a little worried when she had read Ronnie's letter. The first part was amusing, of course, but the second part was "not like Ronnie." He was usually so full of life and health and strength, bubbling over with vigour. Perhaps he needed a holiday. . . perhaps he could get a few days off and come to Mountain Cross? She decided to write and suggest this; it would be delightful to see Ronnie again.

She was still standing there, reading Ronnie's letter for the second time, when Glen and Patrick came in.

"It's a lovely day for our expedition," said Glen cheerfully, as he helped himself to half a grapefruit.

"Yes, lovely," Elfrida agreed.

"You're taking me, aren't you?" asked Patrick anxiously.

"I said I would take you, didn't I?"

"Yes, but . . ."

"But what?"

"Sometimes you say things and don't mean them."

Elfrida had a moment of alarm, but it was needless for Glen was in a very good humour this morning.

"Don't worry, Jacko," he said laughing. "You're more like a monkey than ever when you put on that worried frown."

"What time are we starting?" asked Elfrida.

"We shall have to start about eleven," Glen replied. "The child wants bathing pants and a spade to dig on the beach. I expect we shall be able to get sea-side equipment for the young in Morchester."

Patrick said nothing, but his worried frown vanished like magic; his face had become pink and his eyes were shining with delight.

Elfrida was almost as excited as Patrick at the prospect of the expedition. She had decided that she must "dress up" for the occasion; tweeds and a string of pearls were the correct wear when visiting her neighbours but definitely not correct for an outing with Glen. Her London clothes were hanging in her wardrobe—she had not worn them for months. She must look for something very pretty, something that would show Glen she was not a savage . . . and she would find her Beauty Box and make up a little. That would show him!

Elfrida was surprised to discover that most of her London clothes were much too tight (Mrs. Chowne's bread-and-butter puddings were responsible), but she managed to get into a silk frock, patterned with blue flowers and she found a little black straw hat which Marjory had said was becoming. It was bonnet-shape with a blue flower beneath the brim. Foundation cream, powder, lipstick and a carefully-applied touch of eye-shadow was all she needed from the Beauty Box. She found suitable gloves and a small black hand-bag and stood for a few moments surveying herself critically in the full-length mirror.

Not bad, she thought, nodding at the picture of the London Girl.

Glen and Patrick were waiting for her when she went downstairs (the metamorphosis had taken a little longer than she had expected). Glen was arrayed in a light grey suit; the boy in corduroy trousers and a shabby green pullover.

Glen's eyes took her in at a glance. He smiled, and opening the door of his car, said, "Get in, beautiful lady! You've kept us waiting for ten minutes . . . but patience has its rewards. Unfortunately Jacko has nothing fit to wear."

"He's all right like that, Glen!"

"He doesn't match," objected Glen.

She was too happy to continue the argument: Glen was pleased with her appearance; the sun was shining; she was sitting beside Glen in his comfortable car, gliding smoothly through beautiful country. There were woods and fields and little rivers, their waters sparkling in the sunshine; there were churches standing boldly upon hillocks, or nestling shyly among trees.

This was a new part of the country to Elfrida, she had no idea where they were going, but Glen seemed familiar with the district; he pointed out various objects of interest and stopped the car in a village on the banks of a river near a hog-backed bridge where there was a row of half-timbered cottages.

"Look at them, Elfie!" he said.

Certainly they were worth seeing; they were old—probably they had been standing here beside the hog-backed bridge when Drake was a boy—some of them were adorned with climbing roses, others with clematis or ceanothus, and all their little gardens were full of summer flowers.

A voice from the back of the car exclaimed, "Oo, how pretty! can I get out and look at the flowers properly?"

"No time to spare if you want that spade," replied Glen.

Until now Patrick had been very quiet, but as they approached Morchester he began to chatter:

"This is where I lived with Mrs. Landor," he said. "I wonder if we'll see Mrs. Landor . . . or perhaps Mrs. Fulbright and her baby——"

"You won't see anyone you know at The Grand Hotel," said Glen.

"But we might see them when we're buying my spade; Mrs. Landor always does her shopping in the morning. Oh, look, Miss Ware! That's my school!"

"It isn't your school any more," said Glen.

"Will I be going to school in Brittany?"

"No," said Glen.

"You're going there for a holiday," put in Elfrida.

"But where will I be going to school afterwards?"

"Oh, shut up, Jacko," said Glen. "We've heard enough from you."

"I just wondered . . ." murmured Patrick and relapsed into silence.

Elfrida was surprised to see that Morchester was such a large town; there were fine buildings, wide streets and shops with summer frocks and hats displayed in their plate-glass windows. There was a great deal of traffic in the main thoroughfare, so Glen was unable to stop; he drove on until he came to the car park belonging to The Grand Hotel.

"This is where we lunch," he said. "Jacko and I have some shopping to do, but we'll be as quick as we can. If you want anything you'll find the shops quite good . . . or you can wait for us in the garden of the hotel."

The shops had looked tempting but Elfrida decided not to be tempted; she had spent more than she intended upon pigs and the two hundred pounds—which had seemed riches—was dwindling in a somewhat alarming manner. She strolled round the corner of the hotel and found herself in a very pleasant garden with wide lawns and shady trees and flower-beds full of roses. They were beautiful roses; she wandered round looking at them and admiring them and memorising the names on the tickets . . . perhaps someday she would be able to get her own garden cleared and have some really good roses.

Having looked at the roses carefully, she sat down upon a seat beneath a tree and watched the people.

It had always amused Elfrida to watch people—and wonder about them—and she had been "out of the world" for so long that it was very entertaining indeed. She saw what was obviously a honeymoon couple wander past, so absorbed in one another that they had no eyes for anyone or anything else; two young men in tennis kit with racquets under their arms hurried by, talking earnestly. There was a young mother with a child of about five-years-old who wanted to pick some roses and screamed when her mother would not let her.

Presently an elderly gentleman and a beautifully-dressed lady with blue hair came and sat down on the seat beside Elfrida; they were in the middle of a serious conversation.

"She's most unsuitable," declared the lady.

"She's a pretty creature," objected the gentleman.

"She uses cheap scent."

"Perhaps you could give her a hint——"

"Oh, it isn't the perfume! It shows a lack of refinement which is most undesirable. A woman who uses cheap scent could do anything," declared the lady didactically.

"Would it be a good plan to give her a bottle of Chanel?"

"No."

"Why not? I'm quite willing to——"

"You don't understand."

Silence fell. The gentleman began to poke holes in the lawn with his stick.

Elfrida felt sorry for them; it seemed a pity that they could not understand each other when she saw both points of view so clearly. She also felt sorry for the pretty creature who used cheap scent. Perhaps she could not afford to buy good scent and would have been delighted to receive a bottle of Chanel; possibly it might have weaned her from her undesirable habit.

Glen and Patrick were away for over an hour (which seemed more than ample time to buy bathing pants and a spade), but Elfrida was so interested in "the world and his wife" that she did not mind waiting. Presently, she saw Glen approaching followed by a small boy in grey flannel shorts, a white shirt and a blue blazer . . . she did not recognise Patrick until he ran to her across the grass!

"Are you surprised?" he asked excitedly. "Do you like me? Am I your sort of boy now?"

"You're simply gorgeous," declared Elfrida taking him in her arms and hugging him.

"I had my hair cut, Miss Ware. That's what took so long——"

Glen was smiling. "What a difference clothes make!" he said. "We're all of a piece now. Let's go and have lunch."

They were "all of a piece" and they made an entrance. The large, luxurious dining-room was full of people, but the head-waiter saw them at once and hurried forward to meet them and led them to a table in the bow-window. Glen had that effect upon head-waiters; he was never neglected, never offered an inconvenient table near the service-door. Glen looked like Somebody (and, of course, he is Somebody, in his own particular line, thought Elfrida). As she followed the waiter across the room she became conscious of observation and realised that many of the diners were interested in the almost regal progress. What were they thinking? Probably that she was Glen's wife and the boy was their child!

Glen seemed to have got the same idea for when they were seated he leant forward and said, "I'm proud of my family."

Elfrida's eyes twinkled. "They recognise Glen Siddons."

"I doubt it. We're a long way from London. No, they're all thinking how fortunate I am to have such a charming wife and a son at Beechings."

"A son at Beechings?" she asked in surprise.

"It's a well-known prep school not far from here. The boys wear blue blazers . . . but of course they haven't the sole right to wear blue blazers," added Glen, chuckling.

"I suppose not," said Elfrida doubtfully. She saw now that the blazer had a crest embroidered on the pocket; the device appertaining to Beechings, of course!

Elfrida felt unhappy about it; not because she was in any doubt as to Glen's right to buy a blue blazer for his son—even with a device on the pocket—but because Glen had wanted to do so. It showed a strange lack in Glen, a lack of good taste. (This same lack of good taste was shown by a man who bought and wore an Old Etonian tie when he had never set foot within the portals of the famous and venerable college).

Elfrida thought of Lucius Babbington. What would Lucius say to the purchase of the blue blazer? It was an involuntary thought and not a happy one.

"What's the matter, Elfie?" asked Glen.

"Nothing—really," she replied, trying to smile. She added, "This is a beautiful hotel, Glen. It's very kind of you to bring me here and give me such a marvellous lunch. Have you been here before?"

"Once or twice," said Glen. "It's the best place to stay in this part of the world and a place where you can be sure of seeing interesting people. I like the look of that party near the door. There's a pretty woman in a red hat and an older woman who looks like a duchess. I wonder who they are."

Elfrida glanced at the party and agreed that they looked interesting.

No more was said at the time but afterwards, when Elfrida and Glen and Patrick were having coffee in the lounge, the interesting party came in and settled down in a far-off corner.

"I'm sure I know that woman," said Glen suddenly. "I've seen her before, somewhere or other, and she looked at me as if she knew me."

"The one in the red hat?" asked Elfrida.

"Yes. Perhaps I had better go and speak to her." He rose without more ado and made his way across the big room.

Elfrida could not hear what was being said, but she saw explanations and introductions taking place and after a few moments another chair was found and Glen was invited to sit down. It had been a cheerful party before, but now it was gay . . . Glen was charming them, he had them all laughing merrily. A girl of about twelve-years-old produced a little book and Glen took out his pen and wrote in it. The book was handed round and they all looked at it—and laughed.

Elfrida was watching the little scene and smiling to herself in amusement.

Patrick had been watching, too. Suddenly he said, "Glen is acting, isn't he, Miss Ware?"

She turned and looked at the child in astonishment. "Acting?" she said. "What makes you say that, Patrick?"

"Well, he isn't Glen, really. What did he write in that girl's book?"

"I don't know," she replied. Somehow the child's remark had given her a little shock.

Presently the "interesting party" began to make a move.

They stood up, still talking and laughing, and collected their belongings—gloves and hand-bags—and went away.

Glen returned to Elfrida and Patrick, "Nice people," he said as he sat down. "The older woman is Lady Winterton; she saw me as Ralph de Coverley in *Silver Bells*. It's amazing how many people have seen me in one thing or another. I would have introduced you, Elfie, but they were in a hurry. I hope you didn't think it rude of me."

"Of course not! I was much happier sitting here with Patrick. I'm not good with strangers; you told me yourself I wasn't very good value socially . . . and it was Glen Siddons they wanted to see."

He smiled and agreed, adding, "Lady Winterton asked who you were and when I told her she said she had heard about you from some friends of hers who live quite near you. She would have liked to meet you, but they are going to a wedding and didn't want to be late."

"Who were the friends?"

"I think Barrington was the name. She said he had been to Eton with her son."

"The Babbingtons," said Elfrida nodding.

"You never told me you knew any people in this part of the world."

"Oh, I know quite a lot of people."

"I'd like to meet some of your neighbours, Elfie."

"We must arrange it," she said . . . but somehow she was not very happy about the idea. This was strange for Glen was so charming and was such a success with everyone!

"You could throw a party, couldn't you?" suggested Glen. 'Tell them it's 'to meet Glen Siddons.' "

Elfrida was looking a little doubtful.

"Don't worry, Elfie," said Glen laughing. "The party will go with a bang—I promise you that. Meanwhile what would you like to do this afternoon? There's a very good film at The Picture House; Miss Brookes told me about it."

Elfrida looked at him in astonishment; she had heard him

say more than once that "the silver screen" was a very poor form of entertainment and the ruination of the theatre.

"You'd like to see it, wouldn't you?" asked Glen.

"Do you want to see it, Glen?"

"It would be good fun," he replied. "We had better get moving, Elfie. We don't want to miss the beginning, do we?"

It was late when they got home to Mountain Cross and Elfrida was very tired. The film had been quite unsuitable for Patrick, but Glen had insisted on staying until the end.

As she got into Judy's bed, and snuggled down thankfully, Elfrida reviewed the events of the day and was surprised to discover that she had not enjoyed the outing with Glen as much as she had expected.

25

The south-westerly wind had blown all night, but the sound of it had not disturbed Elfrida, for the Chownes' quarters were situated at the east end of the house and therefore were much more sheltered than her own room. This was the third night she had spent in Judy's bed and now all her daily requirements had been moved downstairs, so she had her bath in the Chownes' bathroom and was fully dressed when she emerged from the red baize door.

Glen was coming downstairs and they met in the hall. "Still sleeping with the Chownes, Elfie?" he enquired, raising his eyebrows. "They must be more attractive than they look."

"My room is so noisy in a west wind," she replied. This was perfectly true, but all the same she felt herself blushing.

Patrick was waiting for them in the dining-room; he was standing at the table with a postcard in his hand. He looked up, smiling cheerfully and said good-morning. Already, after three days at Mountain Cross, he was beginning to look less pinched and there was a little colour in his thin cheeks.

"Hullo, Jacko! Has one of your pals sent you a card?" asked Glen.

"It's for Miss Ware," replied Patrick, putting it down on the table. "It's a picture of people sun-bathing in Spain. It looks a gorgeous place."

"You took Miss Ware's card—and read it?"

"Not read it, exactly. I was just looking at the picture."

"You must have read it, or you wouldn't have known it was for Miss Ware. I suppose it's too much to ask that my son should behave like a gentleman?"

Patrick looked at his father anxiously.

"Gentlemen are not in the habit of examining other people's correspondence," explained Glen.

"I wasn't . . ." began the child in a trembling voice.

"You were examining the card, weren't you?"

"I was just . . . just looking at the p-picture. Such a lovely bright p-picture of people sitting on the shore and . . . and flowers. Besides it's just . . . just a postcard. I mean the p-postman . . . or anyone . . . could read it."

"You are not a postman."

"No, but I mean——"

"You are my son and therefore you are expected to behave in a manner befitting a gentleman."

Elfrida had been silent, she had felt it was not her business to interfere, but the child had become as white as a ghost and the agonised look on his face was more than she could bear. "It's all right, Glen," she said quickly. "He was just looking at the picture. The card is from Dolly—you told me she was in Spain, didn't you? She just says she's having a wonderful time, that's all."

Elfrida held out the card to Glen, but he waved it away.

"Please accept my apologies, Elfrida," he said formally. "I shall not ask the boy to apologise, because——"

"Of course not!" cried Elfrida. "There's no need for any apologies."

"I was about to say because it is my fault. Yes, my fault for not having seen that the child was being properly brought up. My only excuse is that I am a widower, Elfrida. The child has never known a mother's care."

"It's all right," she repeated breathlessly. "Please, Glen——"

"It is very far from 'all right.' My son has put me to shame."

Patrick burst into tears and blundered out of the room.

"Oh, Glen!" cried Elfrida. "Oh, Glen, how could you! He's only a child! You've upset him dreadfully."

"He has upset me dreadfully."

"What nonsense! He was doing no harm——"

"He has upset me—dreadfully," repeated Glen with a heavy sigh. "I feel quite shattered."

"Really, Glen, you're making——"

"Quite shattered . . . but I shall have to pull myself together and deal with the matter as calmly as I can. The child must be punished, of course. I shall have to——"

"Glen, you mustn't! Patrick has been punished enough already—far too heavily punished! Didn't you see his poor little face? It was tragic."

Glen hesitated.

"It was tragic," she repeated. "He was heartbroken. Oh, how could you be so cruel!"

"But, Elfrida, he must learn——"

"No!" she cried. "I shall never forgive you if you say another word about it."

There was a moment of silence.

"Oh, well," said Glen. "If you put it like that . . ." He threw out his hands in a gesture of renunciation and sank gracefully into a chair.

"Promise me," said Elfrida earnestly. "Promise me that you won't say another word about it."

"I promise," he murmured in a trembling voice. "Yes, I give you my solemn promise."

Elfrida left him, sitting at the table in a dejected pose, and hurried upstairs to find Patrick. He was lying on his bed with his face buried in the pillow weeping bitterly.

"Oh, Patrick!" exclaimed Elfrida. "Patrick, darling, don't cry like that!"

"Glen was angry," croaked the muffled voice. "He said . . . he said he was . . . ashamed of me."

She hesitated, wondering how to deal with this; then she sat down beside him on the bed and took his hand.

"Patrick, listen! It was all a mistake," she said.

"I didn't mean to be naughty," he wailed. "I didn't—really. I didn't know . . . it was naughty to—to look at the p-picture."

"It was a mistake," repeated Elfrida.

"What was . . . a mistake?"

"Glen didn't understand. He thought you had read the post-card, but——"

"I didn't!"

"I know. You were just looking at the picture, that's all. I explained it to Glen and he understands."

"He's angry—with me," sobbed Patrick. "He's t-terribly angry. You said—you said it didn't matter—if people were cross—as long as they weren't—*cross with me*. Glen's angry—*with me*."

"Not now," declared Elfrida earnestly. "He isn't angry with you, Patrick. He isn't angry at all. I explained it to him so he understands." She gave his hot little hand a firm squeeze and added, "It's all right, now, Patrick. It's all over. Glen isn't angry any more."

It was some time before she could get him quietened . . . but she repeated the same words over and over again: it had all been a mistake; she had explained it to Glen and he had understood; he wasn't angry any more; it was all right now.

At last the storm of tears was over. Patrick sat up and let her hug him and dry his eyes. She sat on the bed, holding the child in her arms and stroking his hair. (How thin he was! Elfrida could feel every bone in his little body! She wondered if that woman had given him enough to eat!) Then she helped him to sponge his face in tepid water and they came downstairs hand in hand.

Fortunately Glen had finished his breakfast and gone away, so they sat down at the table together. Neither of them wanted much to eat, but Mrs. Chowne heated up the coffee and brought in a rack of fresh toast. She looked at the child compassionately, but Elfrida signed to her not to speak.

The storm had upset Elfrida almost as badly as Patrick—but for a different reason. She had realised that Glen was a fraud.

Elfrida had known that Glen was an actor—and not only an actor when he was on the stage—there was studied grace in his every gesture and in every pose of his body, but this had been part of his charm. There had been nothing charming in the scene which had taken place this morning!

That was what it was, thought Elfrida. It was a scene. She had known at the time that it was not real; she had known all the time that Glen was not in the least distressed . . . and now, looking back and thinking about it, she realised that he had been revelling in his own performance, a performance in which the incomparable Glen Siddons was a widowed father 'dreadfully upset' over the behaviour of his motherless son. It was a performance which would have brought lumps into the throats of his fans—how they would have enjoyed it!—but Elfrida had been one of the actors in the scene and had not enjoyed it. In fact she was of the opinion that the incomparable Glen Siddons had overplayed his part.

Patrick, the third actor in the scene, had certainly not enjoyed it. He had been sacrificed . . . yes, sacrificed was the word. It was cruel; it was a wicked thing to have rent the heart of a little boy! Let Glen put on his performances for grown-up people, thought Elfrida, as she glanced at Patrick's puffy face and swollen eyes and watched him trying to swallow a piece of toast.

She discovered, when she tried to pour out a cup of coffee, that her hand was shaking with rage.

Goodness! she thought. I must try to calm down. For Patrick's sake I must put the whole thing out of my mind and behave as if nothing had happened. The performance is over . . . Glen has probably forgotten all about it.

Two cups of strong hot coffee helped to steady her nerves and presently she got up from the table and went in search of Glen.

Elfrida found Glen in the parlour, sitting at Mrs. Ware's bureau in the window, writing a letter. She saw at once that she had been correct in her surmise; he had forgotten all about it.

He looked up with his usual charming smile. "I hope you don't mind, Elfie. I ought to have asked your permission . . . but I didn't know where you'd gone and I want to get this letter off by the mid-day post if possible. I found some writing-paper in the desk, but there aren't any envelopes."

"I'll get you some envelopes," said Elfrida. "If you want your letter to catch the post to London, I can send Chowne over to Cherleigh on his bicycle. It's no good posting it here."

"We can go in the car," said Glen. "It will be a nice run—we can take Jacko with us—and I want some petrol."

Elfrida hesitated. Could she bear to spend the morning sitting beside Glen in his car? And what about Patrick?

"Don't you want to come?" asked Glen in surprise.

"I really ought to go up to the farm this morning," she replied. "I'll take Patrick with me, if you don't mind. He likes seeing the pigs."

"Goodness, Elfie!" exclaimed Glen, laughing. "Don't look so tragic about it! You can do as you like, of course. I'll nip over to Cherleigh myself."

26

Glen had said he disliked picnics, but it was such a fine sunny afternoon that Elfrida managed to persuade him to have tea on the beach. Patrick was delighted, of course; he had asked several times if they could have a picnic. Burdened with rugs and vacuum flasks and a basketful of cakes and sandwiches they made their way down the cliff-path and stood for a minute or two watching the waves.

The south-west wind had been blowing for two days and nights so the waves were coming in from the Atlantic in long green rollers, hurling themselves upon the rocks of the promontory and throwing up clouds of spray; they were rolling into the bay and breaking into foam on the steeply-shelved beach.

"It's a fine sight," said Glen. "But it will be too windy to have tea on the beach."

"It won't be windy in the sheltered corner," Elfrida replied, leading the way to her favourite nook.

They spread the rugs and sat down. It was not warm enough for sun-bathing today, but all the same it was very pleasant; even Glen did not complain. He began to talk, reminding Elfrida that she had promised to throw a party so that he could meet her neighbours and suggesting that she should ring them up tonight after dinner and fix a day.

Elfrida had not promised to throw a party and was even less pleased with the idea than before. She said, "Quite honestly,

Glen, I couldn't afford it. I told you I wouldn't have much money, didn't I?"

"We'll have a cocktail-party," said Glen cheerfully. "I'll provide the drink . . . you needn't worry about anything. All you've got to do is to ring up your pals."

"It's very kind of you . . . I'll think about it," she told him.

"Think about it soon," he said. "I shall have to be on the move one of these days."

Elfrida unpacked the basket and poured out tea. She was glad to see that Patrick had quite recovered from the "scene" and was natural and cheerful. Unfortunately Elfrida had not recovered; she felt neither natural nor cheerful. Quite suddenly her eyes had been opened and she saw Glen Siddons clearly . . . there was no more magic in him as far as she was concerned. His manly beauty and grace—the very charms which had attracted her—were exposed as fraudulent, and repelled her so forcibly that she could scarcely bear to be near him.

"You were right, Elfie," said Glen as he helped himself to a sandwich. "This really is delightful. Oh, how wonderful to be able to rest in peace with no sound except the splash of the waves! No rehearsals, no worries, no arguments, no leading lady getting into tantrums and clamouring for limelight!"

"I thought you enjoyed all that sort of thing," said Elfrida coldly.

"You misunderstood me," said Glen plaintively. "I don't enjoy it, Elfie. It's my *métier*. One has to work, you see. No work, no bread-and-butter! But I often wish I had chosen a different trade. One gets so tired of it all, so tired of being 'on the stage' all the time . . . there's no privacy for Glen Siddons. You saw that yesterday when we were having lunch at the hotel, didn't you, Elfie? Instead of the quiet, peaceful meal we had planned I was besieged by people . . . people asking silly questions, children producing autograph books and clamouring for my signature!" He sighed and added, "Here, in these beautiful peaceful surroundings I can relax and be myself."

But he was not being himself, thought Elfrida. He was playing the part of a leading actor relaxing and being himself. . . .

Patrick had been silent, eating steadily, but now he could eat no more. He said suddenly, "Can I take off my shoes and socks? I want to paddle, Glen."

"Go ahead, old chap," said Glen lazily.

"Glen, he mustn't paddle!" exclaimed Elfrida. "The tide has turned and the beach shelves very steeply. We'll come down in the morning if he wants to paddle."

"It won't hurt him if he falls in and gets a wetting; one shouldn't keep children in cotton-wool."

"It's dangerous—really!"

"Oh, well, it's for you to say. Come on, Jacko, your aged father will help you to build a sand-castle—the biggest ever!" Glen rose and added, "Or we can play 'retrievers.' "

"What's retrievers?"

"It's a game I used to play when I was your age."

"Yes, but what is it?"

"What a lot of things you don't know! Never mind, Jacko! Someday I'll give you a dog of your very own; a retriever with long ears and a silky coat. You'll have to train him to run after a ball and fetch it back to you."

"When can I have him?" asked Patrick eagerly.

"Someday . . . when my ship comes home," replied Glen, laughing. "Meanwhile we'll build a great big sand-castle. Where's your spade?"

They went off together and began to build a sand-castle; Elfrida watched them for a few minutes—Patrick digging industriously and Glen looking on—then she lay back and rested. She felt tired and miserable; it is not a happy experience to see an idol, lying broken at one's feet.

Why have I begun to think that everything Glen does is acting? thought Elfrida, as she lay and looked up at the sky. Isn't there anything real about Glen? He was acting that frightful scene this morning; he's acting *now*—acting the part of a father playing on the beach with his son—he was acting a few minutes ago when he pretended he was tired of being Glen Siddons . . . as for yesterday, at the hotel, it was nonsense to say he was "beseiged by people"; he walked the whole length of the room and thrust himself upon that wedding-party! They were pleased, of course, they welcomed him and surrendered to his charm . . . as everyone does.

One thought led to another. Elfrida decided quite definitely that she would not ask her neighbours "to meet Glen Siddons." Her neighbours might like him—or might not!—but she would know that his beautiful manners were insincere; it would be just another performance by the incomparable Glen Siddons . . . and she would not be able to bear it. Somehow or other she must make Glen understand that there was to be no party at Mountain Cross.

He can't *make* me do it, thought Elfrida, setting her mouth in a firm line.

Having reached this decision, she sat up to see how the sand-castle was getting on. She hoped Glen was taking his turn at digging; it was too hot and exhausting for the child.

There was little sign of a sand-castle, the work had been abandoned and Glen and Patrick had gone down to the edge of the sea.

At first Elfrida could not make out what they were doing, but when she shaded her eyes from the glare she realised that they were playing "retrievers." Glen was throwing sticks into the sea and Patrick was dodging between the waves and "fetching" them.

It was a foolish game—foolish and dangerous!—she leapt to her feet and shouted, but they were so near the sea that the sound of the waves drowned her voice. She had begun to run down the beach to warn them when she saw it happen . . . Glen threw a stick further into the sea and the boy hesitated.

"Go on, Jacko! Fetch it, good dog!" cried Glen waving his arm and laughing excitedly.

Patrick dashed after the stick, seized it and turned . . . he was too late. The wave broke over his head and knocked him down; the backwash swept him seawards; he rolled over and over and disappeared from view.

Elfrida ran, as she had never run before, down the beach and straight into the sea. A huge wave curled over her head . . . she saw the child's leg and seized hold of his ankle. The next moment she was engulfed in broken swirling water, lifted up like a cork and flung face downwards on the pebbles.

The wave retreated, the back-wash tore at her—it was terrifying! Her clothes, wet and clinging held her down; the pebbles were sucked from beneath her with a loud rattling noise—she was deafened and blinded, gasping for breath—she felt herself slipping backwards, pulled backwards by an irresistible force.

She was still gripping the child's ankle, but her left hand was free . . . she clutched desperately at the shifting pebbles and, finding a small ledge of solid rock, dug in her fingers and clung to it with all her might. When the suction passed, she crawled forwards on her hands and knees, dragging the child with her . . . the next wave broke over them both and tumbled them onto the beach.

Now Elfrida was able to crawl a few feet further, out of reach of the sea, and for a few moments she lay there, exhausted but unutterably thankful for her escape. She was safe . . . and the boy was safe . . . nothing else mattered.

When she was able to sit up, she discovered to her surprise that except for a grazed and bleeding arm and a bruised knee she was undamaged. Patrick had struggled onto his hands and knees, he was coughing and gasping for breath . . . then he was violently sick.

Elfrida loosened her grip on his ankle and put her arms round him, holding him tightly. She tried to speak to him, but her voice was little more than a husky whisper. It was not until he had recovered and lay back to rest that Elfrida remembered Glen. What on earth had Glen been doing?

Glen was standing on the beach a little way off, but now he approached and said, "That was very spectacular, Elfie."

"Spectacular? We were nearly drowned!"

"There was no real danger."

"Why didn't—you help me?"

"It wasn't necessary."

"We were both nearly drowned . . . and you stood there watching!"

"I can't swim," explained Glen. "And as I said before there was no real danger. The waves were washing you onto the shore."

"The waves were washing us out!"

"You were washed up onto the shore," he pointed out. "And anyhow, what could I have done?"

He went on arguing and explaining, but she took no more notice. What was the use of arguing with him? She rose and took Patrick's hand and tried to help him up.

"Come on, Patrick," she said. "You're better now. We must go and change."

"I can't," he whispered, beginning to sob.

"Come on, darling. You mustn't lie here in your wet clothes. You can get up, can't you?"

He struggled onto his feet and stood, shaking all over.

"That's right," she said encouragingly. "Come on, Patrick. I'll help you. We must go and get dry clothes."

By support and encouragement she managed to get him to come a few yards further up the beach . . . but how was she to get him up the steep cliff path? Her own legs felt weak and trembly—as if they did not belong to her—so it would be impossible for her to carry Patrick. Glen must carry him . . . but Glen had turned and was walking away and she was so furious with Glen that she did not want to call him.

Elfrida stood there, shivering in her wet clothes, and wondered what to do. Then she heard a shout and, looking up, saw Chowne and Mr. Cobley coming down the path to help her.

27

Elfrida awoke at eight o'clock next morning. She lay still for a few moments wondering why she was stiff all over and why she was wrapped in blankets . . . then she remembered.

She remembered her battle with the waves; she remembered the two men coming to her aid; she remembered that Mr. Cobley had helped her up the steep path and Chowne had followed carrying Patrick in his arms. She remembered that somehow or other they had dragged her upstairs to her own room and that Mrs. Chowne had peeled off her wet clothes and rubbed her with warm towels and put her to bed surrounded with hot water bottles. She remembered drinking a cup of hot sweet tea and swallowing a small pink tablet; she remembered no more.

She wondered if she should get up and see what had happened to Patrick when she saw the door opening very slowly and quietly.

"Is that you, Mrs. Chowne?" she asked.

"Oh, you're awake!" said Mrs. Chowne, coming in and drawing back the curtains. "I've looked in several times; you've had a nice long sleep. I expect it was that pink tablet. The doctor gave them to me for Mrs. Ware and I had a few over so I gave one to you and half a one to Pat."

"How is he?" asked Elfrida anxiously.

"Perfectly all right," replied Mrs. Chowne in cheerful tones. "He slept like a top and he's getting up now. I don't think he remembers a thing about it; he was surprised to find himself in Judy's bed. We put him in Judy's bed last night so that we could keep an eye on him."

"Are you sure he hasn't been injured?" asked Elfrida incredulously.

Mrs. Chowne nodded. "He's as right as rain except for a bruise on his ankle. Charlie Cobley says it's because he's so light—as light as a feather. That's why he didn't get hurt. How are you feeling, Miss Elfrida? Shall I bring up your breakfast? If you'd like a rest Pat can have his in the kitchen with Ernie and me."

"I'll get up and have a hot bath," replied Elfrida. She yawned and added, "That tablet must have been very strong; I still feel sleepy . . . and frightfully stiff. I feel as if I'd been battered all over."

"It's a wonder you're alive!"

Elfrida nodded. She realised that she had had a very narrow escape. If it had not been for that little ledge of rock . . .

"I saw it all happen," continued Mrs. Chowne. "Charlie Cobley was having tea with us last night and I'd just gone out onto the cliff to feed the seagulls—like I always do—so I saw the whole thing. I saw that man throwing sticks into the sea and making Pat fetch them. Did he want to drown the boy?"

"No, of course not! It was just a game."

"It was the silliest game I ever saw, I never was so frightened in a my life! When I saw the boy go under I screamed and screamed—I thought he was done for. If you hadn't gone after him, he would have been done for; there isn't a doubt of that. You're a heroine, that's what you are, Miss Elfrida. I'm saying it now and I'll say it to everyone in the place."

"Please don't!" exclaimed Elfrida in alarm. "It was nothing; anyone would have done it!"

"You ought to get the Victoria Cross."

"Nonsense! That's just for soldiers."

"Well, I think——"

"Is Mr. Siddons up yet?" interrupted Elfrida, changing the subject.

"He's gone out this morning."

"Gone out?"

"Well, he wasn't in his room when I went to call him, so he must have gone out."

"How funny!" said Elfrida, yawning again.

"Are you quite sure you want to get up?" asked Mrs. Chowne anxiously.

"Yes, it will do me good to have a hot bath. I'm just a bit stiff, that's all."

It was a curious thing for Glen to do, thought Elfrida, as she lay soaking in a very hot bath. Glen was not the sort of person who enjoys rising with the lark. Then she thought of last night and tried to remember what she had said to him . . . but it was all rather hazy in her mind. He had been neglected, of course. He had been left standing on the beach while she and Patrick had been fussed over and taken up the cliff . . . and Glen did not like being neglected. Glen liked to be in the limelight so it was quite "in character" that he should have wakened early and gone for a walk by himself. He would soon recover—he always did—and would return in a cheerful frame of mind. She must remember to tell Mrs. Chowne to have his breakfast ready for him.

Patrick was waiting for Elfrida in the dining-room so they sat down to breakfast. He said nothing about last night's misadventure, but he ate so little and looked so miserable that Elfrida was worried. He had no visible injury except the bruise on his ankle (she had gripped it so tightly that her fingers had left blue marks), but perhaps she ought to send for the doctor and make sure that he had not sustained an internal injury. It was difficult to know what to do, for she did not want to frighten the child.

At last she said, "Have you got a pain, Patrick?"

"No."

"What's the matter? Why don't you want any breakfast?"

"He's gone."

"He has just gone out for a walk, that's all."

"His car is gone. I went to look—and it's gone."

"He'll be back soon. I expect he'll come back to lunch."

"He won't."

Elfrida looked at the child in astonishment; he was shaking all over and his face was puckered up as if he were going to cry, but instead of crying he banged on the table and shouted, "Glen has gone away. He isn't coming back."

"No, no, Patrick," said Elfrida, trying to pacify him. "Glen has just gone for a spin in his car. I expect he woke early and——"

"He's gone, I tell you!"

"How do you know?"

"I know."

"You don't mean he has gone to Brittany?"

"I don't know where he's gone."

Elfrida tried to speak calmly and sensibly. "Listen, Patrick. Glen told you that he was going to take you to Brittany for a holiday. You know that, don't you?"

"I knew he wasn't going to take me."

"But he said——"

"I knew all the time." Patrick choked back a sob and added, "I can always—guess—what he's thinking but I thought—I thought he'd take me back to Mrs. Landor—before he went away."

"But he wouldn't go away without you."

"Why don't you believe what I say?" shouted Patrick.

She was silent for a few moments, half convinced. Could it be true? Could he have gone off like that without a word to anyone? At last she said, "Well, we shall have to wait and see. I must speak to Mrs. Chowne for a minute and then you and I will go up to the farm together. You'd like to do that, wouldn't you?"

Patrick did not reply so, after hesitating for a few moments and wondering if there was anything else she should say, she left him and went to look for Mrs. Chowne.

28

When Elfrida went into the kitchen, she found Mrs. Chowne sitting with her elbow on the table and her head leaning upon her hand. This was such an extraordinary sight that Elfrida was considerably alarmed. "Mrs. Chowne, are you ill?" she asked anxiously.

"No," said Mrs. Chowne.

"What's the matter?"

"Ernie says I must tell you all about it."

"Tell me about what?"

"About last night, of course. He wasn't very pleased, Miss Elfrida."

"Who wasn't pleased?"

"Mr. Siddons wasn't pleased. He's taken the huff; that's why he's gone away."

Elfrida was beginning to see light. She said, "Has he really gone away?"

"He's taken all his things. I didn't notice when I went to call him, because the room was dark and he doesn't like me drawing back the curtains, but I went up a few minutes ago and all his things have gone: his brushes and combs and sponges and his electric razor have gone and the wardrobe and all the drawers are empty. He must have packed his things in the night and carried down his suitcases. We never heard him."

"How amazing!" exclaimed Elfrida, sitting down suddenly upon a kitchen chair. "I can't believe he would go away like that without a word."

"He wasn't very pleased last night," repeated Mrs. Chowne in a shaky voice. "His dinner was late by the time I'd got you to bed and everything—and to tell you the truth I was feeling a bit upset—so when he said there wasn't any need for all the fuss I lost my temper. I don't like Mr. Siddons at the best of times—he isn't a proper gentleman—so that was the last straw. You know what I'm like when I lose my temper, Miss Elfrida. I don't often lose my temper, but I'd been so frightened, you see. I thought you were both drowned and done for."

She stopped for a moment to breathe and then continued, "Charlie Cobley has just been here (he came to ask how you were, this morning) and he said you knew all about the current being dangerous. He said it was one of the bravest things he ever saw in all his life—you going after the boy like that, straight in without stopping. He said you ought to get a life-saving medal because it's a miracle you're alive. Oh well, you *are* alive, that's the main thing. Last night when I went and looked at you and Pat and saw you sleeping safely in your beds I knelt down on the kitchen floor and said my thanks to God."

"I'm thankful too," said Elfrida softly.

There was a short silence.

"Mrs. Chowne," said Elfrida at last. "You haven't told me——"

"I wish you'd call me Emma," interrupted Emma Chowne. "I *wish* you would, Miss Elfrida."

"Of course I will," said Elfrida, patting the work-worn hand which was lying beside her on the table. "Of course I will, Emma. You've been terribly good to me and I'm not likely to forget it. I was going to say you haven't told me what you said to Mr. Siddons."

"I was a bit upset."

"I know you were. Everything was upset."

Emma sighed heavily. "I didn't want to tell you what I said, but Ernie says I must . . . so I suppose I'd better. I just told Mr. Siddons he ought to stick to films and get other people to "stand in" for the dangerous bits. I told him camels were dangerous, that's all. It wasn't much to say—not really—when he'd stood like a dummy and watched you drowning and never raised a finger to help. Mr. Siddons didn't answer, or say a word, but he was annoyed with me for saying it. I could see he didn't like it."

He wouldn't like it, thought Elfrida. Glen had to be Everybody's Hero . . . so he had packed up in the night and fled from Mountain Cross. Elfrida could understand Glen's feelings; she could understand his being ashamed of the part he had played—it was not a heroic part!—she could even feel rather sorry for him.

"Are you angry with me, Miss Elfrida?" asked Emma.

"No, of course not. It was natural that you should have been upset . . . but why did you tell him that camels were dangerous?"

"Because they are, of course! Camels have got a poisonous bite."

"What has that got to do with Mr. Siddons?" asked Elfrida in bewilderment.

"Well, because there's going to be a lot of camels in that film. It says so in my paper."

Elfrida was looking even more bewildered so Emma Chowne got up and fetched her paper and, licking her thumb, turned over the pages until she found the right place. Then she put the paper on the table and said, "There, Miss Elfrida! That tells you all about it. Of course I thought he'd be sure to have told you or I'd have shown it to you before."

THE ELEPHANT FILM COMPANY INC. will commence screening its NEW PICTURE next week. A spokesman of the company informs us that although the ELEPHANT is renowned for the magnitude of its productions this will be the BIGGEST EVER.

The Sheik's Dilemma is a soul-stirring drama packed with hair-raising thrills, passionate love scenes and agonising suspense. It is to cost the colossal sum of a Million Dollars. The action takes place in the Colorado Desert where a camp has been prepared to house three hundred people and twenty camels. (Turn to page 45 for a description of the camel and its habits).

Our representative was permitted to inspect the camp which resembles a small town with tents and wooden huts and bungalows. There are kitchens and dining-rooms, a club with a dancing floor and a cocktail bar.

The cast includes a galaxy of Stars: Glen Siddons in the title-rôle, Clarissa Downes as the beautiful young Englishwoman who is kidnapped from her luxurious home by the fierce, hawk-eyed Bedouin Chief . . . and a fine supporting team.

Pictures and further news of this Sensational Production in next week's issue of your favourite paper!

Elfrida read it and then pushed the paper aside. "Oh, poor Glen!" she said sadly.

"Poor?" exclaimed Emma. "He'll get thousands of pounds for acting in the film!"

"I didn't mean that."

"What did you mean?"

" 'There is no truth in him,' " said Elfrida. She added under her breath, "Shouldn't we be sorry for people like that?"

"Aren't you angry with him?"

"No, just sorry."

Emma Chowne gazed at her in amazement. "But he's behaved terribly badly!"

"Yes, that's why I'm sorry for him."

This was beyond Emma's comprehension. She said anxiously, "He isn't your sort, Miss Elfrida."

"No."

"So you needn't bother about him any more."

"No."

"Mr. Lucius is your sort of gentleman. You like him, don't you?'

"Yes."

Emma was puzzled; she was also very worried (Miss Elfrida was not a bit like herself) however there was nothing she could do. So, after a few moment's pause for reflection she said, "And what about Pat? I suppose he's going back to that lady at Morchester?"

"No, she's getting too old to cope with a child . . . but perhaps that was another lie."

"Oh dear, it's an awful business! What are we to tell the boy? He asked if he could read my paper and I said he could. Then, when I saw about the Sheik, I pretended I'd lost it because I could tell by the things he said that he didn't know his father was going to America . . . but he'll have to know, of course. I mean he's bound to hear about it."

"Yes, sooner or later, but perhaps his father will come back to say goodbye before he goes."

"There isn't much time, is there?"

"No, not much."

Emma took the paper and put it back in the drawer of the dresser under her ironing blanket. She said, "Charlie Cobley told Ernie and me that it's all a fake. Colorado isn't the right desert for Sheiks and camels."

"Mr. Cobley is right—as usual," said Elfrida with a sad little smile.

29

When Elfrida went out, she found Patrick sitting on the step waiting for her. There was a pathetic droop in his thin little shoulders and his eyes were dull and lifeless. He got up when he saw her and followed her without speaking.

Elfrida stopped and looked back. "Are you tired?" she asked.

"Awfully tired."

"Perhaps you had better not come up to the farm. Would you like to go to bed or would you rather sit here and wait for me?"

"It's inside tiredness."

"Because you're disappointed?" she suggested.

"Not disappointed; I knew he wasn't going to take me. It's because I don't know what I'm going to do," said Patrick in a low voice—so low that it was scarcely audible. "Before, when he went away, he left me—somewhere. I stayed with the nuns when I was a baby and then I stayed with some people in London . . . and then I stayed with Mrs. Landor. But this time he's just—just gone away without—without bothering. If I was older I could work on a farm or—or something, but nobody wants a boy of eight."

Elfrida put her arm round him and they sat down on the bank. "You can stay here," she said. "That was what he meant you to do. He knew you'd be all right with me."

Patrick shook his head. "It's no good. Mrs. Chowne says you're very poor."

"Not as poor as all that! It won't cost much to feed you."

"There's clothes, too. That's what bothered Mrs. Landor. You see clothes wear out and get too small. That's why I hadn't any nice clothes to wear when we went to the hotel. Mrs. Landor did her best, but she hadn't got enough money to buy clothes for me . . ."

Now that he had begun to talk he went on and on in a monotonous voice; he talked about Mrs. Landor and her troubles; sometimes she had not enough money to pay the rent and had to borrow from Mrs. Fulbright. Patrick had gone to school every day except when Mrs. Landor was "very miserable" and did not like being alone in the flat. Sometimes Mrs. Fulbright came in and cooked a chop for Patrick, but it was a nuisance for her because she had a baby and Mrs. Landor couldn't pay her anything . . .

Elfrida thought it was good for the child to talk so she listened until she could bear it no longer, then she said, "You'd like to stay here with me, wouldn't you?"

"Yes, but you don't want me."

"I do," she declared, giving him a little squeeze. "Of course I want you, Patrick."

"I'd be a nuisance. I was a nuisance to Mrs. Landor."

"You won't be a nuisance to me. We'll have fun together. You can help Chowne with the pigs; you'll be very, very useful."

"It's no good pretending."

"What do you mean?"

"Well, I expect you think Glen will send money for me. He promised Mrs. Landor to send money—but he never did. He just—just forgets or something. So you see it's no good pretending. I'm not a baby, Miss Ware. I'd rather—have it—plain."

For a few moments Elfrida hesitated (she had been thinking) then she took his hand and held it tightly. "All right,

Patrick, we'll have it plain. Your father has gone away and left you with me because he thinks you'll be happy here . . . and you will be happy, won't you? It will be much more fun than staying with Mrs. Landor. There's lots to do here, isn't there? Mr. Cobley has finished clearing up the wood and I've sent for some little plants which like growing under trees; I want you to help me to put them in."

"I'd like that!"

"I was sure you'd help me."

"But Mrs. Chowne says you're very poor so you couldn't——"

"Listen," she said. "Listen, Patrick. We're having this plain, aren't we? It's quite true that I haven't much money, but Glen can easily afford to pay for your food and clothes."

"Yes, but he won't!"

"He will," declared Elfrida with conviction. "It will be quite easy to get the money from Glen because I shall ask my lawyer to get it. There, that's plain," she added, smiling at him.

"Oh no!" exclaimed Patrick in alarm. "Oh no, you can't do that. He doesn't like lawyers—it would make him angry."

"My lawyer will write him a nice, polite letter and there will be no more trouble."

Patrick was frowning anxiously. "Why?" he asked. "Why will the lawyer be able to get the money without any trouble?"

Elfrida had no intention of answering that question plainly, so she just said, "Oh, people have got to do what lawyers tell them. Now, don't you think it would be fun to go up to the hay-field and see if Joe is there?"

Patrick's face brightened. "Oh, yes!" he exclaimed. "But I thought you were going to the farm."

"I'll go later," she told him. "I want to talk to Mrs. Chowne about something . . . but you can go up to the hay-field by yourself."

"Can I really go by myself?" asked Patrick eagerly.

"Yes, of course! You're eight, aren't you?"

He jumped up, his troubles forgotten, and began to run up the hill.

"Come home when Joe goes for his dinner!" shouted Elfrida. He turned and waved cheerfully.

Emma Chowne was in the spare bedroom; Elfrida traced her by the sound of the vacuum cleaner and opened the door.

"Oh, it's you, Miss Elfrida!" exclaimed Emma, turning off the machine.

"Yes, I want to speak to you about something."

"I thought you'd gone up to the farm. I'm giving this room a thorough turn-out because it smells of that scent he put on his hair; besides it's good for me. I feel all upset, Miss Elfrida. I can't help thinking about that poor little boy. What he'll say when he hears his father has gone off to America without so much as saying goodbye, I can't imagine."

"Patrick is all right. He has gone up to the hay-field to find Joe."

"Joe Thorne," said Emma, nodding. "He's a very nice chap and he has children of his own . . . but Pat isn't 'all right.' I'm miserable about him; he isn't like a proper child at all. He hasn't had a child's life. That Mrs. Landor unloaded all her troubles onto Pat. It wasn't right of the woman."

"I know," agreed Elfrida. "And I don't think she fed him properly either, so——"

"She starved him; he's as thin as a rake!"

"Yes, terribly thin. Anyhow he can't go back to the woman, so I thought it would be a good plan to——"

"Pat worries about things," interrupted Emma. "Children didn't ought to worry; it isn't natural. I can't bear to see that anxious frown he puts on when he's worried. He worries about everything; he even worries about his clothes. There was a hole in the elbow of his pullover and he was quite upset about it. He kept on saying he was sorry all the time I was mending it for him. I'd like to see Henry James bothering his head about a hole in his pullover! I've seen him come in for his dinner as dirty as a tinker, and nearly as ragged, and all Judy does is laugh and give him a hug.

"Oh, dear!" cried Mrs. Chowne. "Oh, dear, when I think of all the love and care Henry James has had ever since he was born I could sit down and cry! I could—really. It doesn't seem fair that one child should have so much and another child nothing. He's never had any love all his life——"

"Listen, Emma!" said Elfrida loudly. "You needn't sit down and cry; you'll be able to give Patrick all the love and care he needs because he's going to stay here, at Mountain Cross."

"We're keeping Pat!" exclaimed Emma in delight. "Oh, Miss Elfrida, what a lovely idea!"

"You'll help me with him, won't you? I don't know much about children so——"

"Of course I'll help you—and so will Ernie—Pat won't be a bit of bother. He's such a good little boy; he's far too good. We must try to make him naughty; it's natural for children to be a little naughty sometimes. Now let's see," continued Emma, screwing up her eyes in a thoughtful manner. Pat had better go on sleeping in Judy's bed so that we can keep an eye on him and give him his breakfast early. He'll be going to school next term, of course—he can go with Henry James until he gets into the way of it. Henry James is a bit of a pickle, but he's very kind-hearted. And I always take Henry James to the Children's Service on Sunday afternoons, so Pat can come with us. I don't know if you've noticed, Miss Elfrida, but Pat hasn't learnt to say his prayers. That woman at Morchester must have been a heathen! But we can teach him, of course, and he'll learn a lot from Mr. Perrimont, who is very good with children in spite of not having any himself. There's another thing, Miss Elfrida; we shall have to do something about Pat's clothes. His clothes are a disgrace. I don't know what that woman was thinking of to let him go about looking like a—a refugee or something. Next time Ernie and I go over to Cherleigh we can take Pat with us; he can sit on the carrier on the back of Ernie's bike. There's a very good shop in Cherleigh where Judy gets things for Henry James. It isn't an expensive shop—you don't want expensive clothes for children because they outgrow them before they're worn out. I always say to Judy it's better to have . . ."

Elfrida was laughing so heartily that she was obliged to sit down on the bed. Perhaps her laughter was a trifle hysterical; she had had a good deal to bear this morning, one way and another.

"What's the joke, Miss Elfrida?" asked Emma, pausing and looking at her in surprise.

"Just that I was—worried—in case you—wouldn't be—pleased," gasped Elfrida.

Emma smiled, "Of course I'm pleased! It will be lovely to have a child in the house. We must give him lots to eat and fatten him up."

"You're very good at fattening people up! I've had to let out all my waist-belts."

"Yes, but it suits you," said Emma, nodding in approval. "You've improved a lot since you've been here; you're very nearly as pretty as Miss Marjory was . . . but I've never been able to fatten up Ernie. I've tried for twenty-seven years." She switched on the vacuum cleaner and proceeded with her work.

As Elfrida went downstairs she heard, mingling with the hum of the cleaner, the loud humming of Emma Chowne. It was "The Voice That Breathed O'er Eden" and, as usual, slightly out of tune.

Lucius Babbington was standing in the hall; he had rung the front-door bell three times and, on receiving no answer, had come in and was looking about him and frowning anxiously.

"Hullo, Lucius!" said Elfrida. "I didn't know you were here; I was upstairs talking to Emma Chowne. Would you like another book? I've just been reading——"

"Elfrida!" he exclaimed, coming forward and taking her hand. "I came to enquire . . . I thought you would be in bed!"

"You thought I would be in bed?" asked Elfrida in surprise.

"Yes, of course! Are you all right? Mary and I were terribly worried."

She still looked surprised so he added, "We heard you had

rescued a boy from drowning and had been swept out to sea by the current."

"Oh yes," said Elfrida nodding. "As a matter of fact such a lot has happened since the accident that I had forgotten about it for the moment."

"But it only happened last night!"

"Was it only last night?" said Elfrida vaguely. "It seems like a week."

"My dear girl!" exclaimed Lucius in alarm. "Are you feeling all right? Perhaps you've got concussion or—or something. Why don't you go to bed and send for the doctor?"

She smiled. "I'm all right, Lucius. It feels a long time ago because so much has happened this morning. I'm sorry you and Mary were worried."

"Of course we were terribly worried!"

"How on earth did you hear about it?"

"The fish-boy told us."

"The fish-boy?"

"Yes, he was full of it. I came over at once to see how you were and when I stopped at the garage for petrol the men were all talking about you."

"Talking about me?" asked Elfrida in astonishment.

"Saying it was a very brave act," explained Lucius. "So it was. . . very brave indeed. You might have been drowned. It was rough yesterday so the back-wash must have been fierce . . . and you aren't a strong swimmer, are you? Elfrida, my dear," said Lucius earnestly. "I wish you wouldn't bathe in that bay. It's terribly dangerous."

"But, Lucius, I wasn't bathing . . . and anyhow you seem to have heard a very exaggerated account of the accident."

"Who was the boy and why was he bathing in Mountain Cross Bay?" asked Lucius.

"He wasn't bathing; he was just—just paddling about at the edge of the sea when a wave knocked him over."

Lucius still looked worried so Elfrida added, "Come and sit down and I'll tell you what happened."

As they went into the parlour and sat down Elfrida suddenly remembered Glen's desire to meet her neighbours. It was the sight of Lucius that had reminded her; now that he was before her eyes (clad as usual in his old tweed jacket), she felt more than ever certain that he would not like Glen . . . they would have nothing to say to each other, they did not speak the same language!

Elfrida had been so busy this morning, comforting Patrick and talking to Emma, that she had not had time to realise the relief to herself of Glen's departure. He has gone, she thought. I shan't have to "throw a party to meet Glen Siddons." I shan't have to watch him acting a part; I shan't have to put up with his "temperament." He has gone!

The relief was so great that Elfrida heaved a big sigh.

"I'm sure you aren't well, my dear," said Lucius anxiously. "Don't tell me what happened if you'd rather not."

"Oh, I want to tell you," she replied.

There was a good deal to explain, but the Babbingtons were her friends, so Elfrida felt they had a right to know the story . . . or at least part of the story. When she thought about it, she realised that she could not tell Lucius the whole story. She would have to water it down considerably if she did not want to set everyone in the neighbourhood talking about her.

She began by telling Lucius that she had known Glen Siddons in London (she was somewhat surprised to discover that Lucius had never heard of him) and went on to say that he and his little son were staying with her for a few days and she had taken them down to the beach for a picnic-tea. She explained the accident by saying that Glen Siddons was a Londoner, a stranger in this part of the world, and could not be expected to know about the peculiarities of the bay at Mountain Cross, so he had allowed the boy to paddle. This explanation was not quite true—and it sounded thin to Elfrida—but she hoped Lucius would believe it.

Unfortunately Lucius did not. He said, "Tom Parkins told me rather a different story."

"Tom Parkins wasn't there . . . and I was," Elfrida pointed out. "We had finished tea and I was sitting on the beach. I had just got up to go and warn Glen that it wasn't safe when I saw the wave break over the child's head and knock him down. I ran down the beach as quickly as I could and pulled him out of the water. He's small and thin and very light which made it easier."

"That isn't what I heard," objected Lucius.

"Well, it's true—more or less—and I do hope that if you and Mary hear any garbled accounts of the accident, you'll deny them."

Lucius still looked doubtful; there were several details which he could not understand. For instance why hadn't Elfrida warned Siddons that it was unsafe for his child to paddle? And if Siddons was there, on the spot, why hadn't he pulled his child out of the water himself? Why leave it to Elfrida? It all seemed rather queer.

Elfrida had been watching his face; she said earnestly, "You'll deny any garbled accounts of the accident, won't you, Lucius?"

"Oh, yes, we'll play it down—if that's what you want—but I don't think it will make much difference what we say; the story is all over the district by this time and you're the heroine of the hour."

"What nonsense, Lucius!" exclaimed Elfrida, laughing.

Part Four

30

RIGGS, SANDFORD AND WILKINS,
22 - 23 - 24 WINTER STREET,
WESTMINSTER.

My dear Elfrida Jane,

Your letters are always welcome as the flowers in spring and always interesting. Your last was particularly interesting. First: I must apologise for the slight delay in answering (your problem required careful consideration). Second: let me say I am honoured by your request that I will 'be your lawyer' and will do my best to carry out your instructions faithfully.

You are right, of course. It would NOT be good publicity for the wonderful Glen Siddons if it became known that he had abandoned his child. Matinée idols are allowed a certain amount of latitude as regards women, but children are in a different category. The Great Warm-Hearted British Public would be dismayed to learn that its idol was in the habit of dumping his one and only son upon comparative strangers without so much as "by your leave" and omitting to pay for his board and lodging. You ask if we could take the case to court and "make him pay." The answer is, yes, a father is responsible for the maintenance of his child. It would be a scrumptious case (think of the headlines in the Sunday Press), but as you have pointed out it is unlikely to come to court; the risk of adverse publicity would be too great. How much better and wiser to accede gracefully to your modest request for three pounds a week! He must be earning thousands by acting in that film, so you could ask a great deal more, but I gather you are averse to blackmail.

You suggested I should consult the senior partner and I did so. He has a great deal of experience and often comes up with wily ideas . . . but your problem is somewhat unusual. As a matter of fact Glen Siddons had suddenly become NEWS (everyone is talking about the Million Dollar Film which is being shot in the Colorado Desert), so when I informed the senior partner that Mr. Glen Siddons had been staying at Mountain Cross he was considerably startled; his eyebrows nearly disappeared into his hair when he learnt that the aforesaid Mr. G. S. had packed up during the night and departed to Colorado leaving you to hold the baby! His first reaction was that the baby should be returned to its parent forthwith—"because Elfrida cannot afford to add to her liabilities"—but after some argument I managed to convince him that you were extremely anxious to keep the baby and merely wanted a small weekly payment to cover expenses.

I was glad to find that the senior partner agreed with my findings. After some thought he said that "under the circumstances" we must insist on a banker's order for four pounds a week.

To cut a long story short we put our heads together and drafted a letter to Mr. Glen Siddons. It was a little difficult because the senior partner was annoyed with the man! I was obliged to repeat several times that you wanted the letter to be "polite" and you did not want it to be "nasty." Having got this understood we proceeded with the task, endeavouring to steer a course between the Scylla of weakness and the Charybdis of nastiness . . . and I think we succeeded none too badly.

So much for business, Elfrida Jane. Now I must answer the personal side of your letter. It is kind of you to be anxious about my health. I admit I was feeling rather jaded when I wrote to you, but I am better now. I told Uncle Bob about the tiresome parties and he spoke to Mother and said it was essential for me to have "plenty of sleep." I do not know what else he said, but he put the wind up properly, so now Mother chases me off to bed at ten o'clock and goes out to parties with some other escort. I read for a bit—do you enjoy reading in bed, Elfrida Jane?—and then go peacefully to sleep. It is extremely kind of you to suggest that I should come to Mountain Cross for a little holiday and there is nothing I should like better. Perhaps I might ask Uncle Bob for a few days off . . . but I shall have to be tactful about it. You see I am the junior partner and very unimportant; even Peter Riggs, "that egregious ass" (Uncle Bob's latest name for him), is senior to me. If I can possibly manage to wangle a few days off, I will certainly let you know . . . but it will not be until after next week.

No more at present as I must type the letter to Mr. Glen Siddons. This is somewhat beneath my dignity as a partner, but Uncle Bob is unwilling to disclose its contents to his secretary. As I told you before Glen Siddons is NEWS . . . so the letter might cause an undesirable flutter in the dovecotes!

Please write again soon, Elfrida Jane.

Yours Ronnie.

P.S. I was hard at work typing the aforesaid letter to the aforesaid G.S. when the senior partner came in and said "you had better go and see her and show it to her before sending it." So, if that's all right, I shall be with you for dinner on Saturday night. Hurrah!

Great haste,

R.M.L.

"Tomorrow!" exclaimed Elfrida joyfully.

"What's tomorrow?" asked Patrick, pausing in the middle of a large plateful of bacon and egg.

"A friend of mine is coming to stay."

"Is it a girl?"

"A girl? Oh, I see! No, it's—it's a man."

"What sort of a man?"

"A very nice man; you'll like him," said Elfrida. She

crammed the letter into the pocket of her cardigan and hurried away to find Emma and speak to her about food for the prospective guest.

When Elfrida awoke the following morning she was dismayed to find everything shrouded in thick mist; however Emma assured her that it would clear later and Mr. Cobley, who came in at ten-thirty to have his elevenses with the Chownes, endorsed her opinion.

They were right of course. By twelve o'clock the mist had lifted and the sun was shining brightly in a cloudless sky . . . so Ronnie would have a good day for his run after all.

As he was not expected to arrive until dinner-time Elfrida took Patrick to spend the afternoon on the beach and have a picnic-tea. They had not been to the beach since the accident, but had spent most of their time in the copse, which had now been tidied up and was beginning to look less battle-scarred. Elfrida and Patrick had been busy planting bulbs and bluebells and lily-of-the-valley; Patrick was happy when he was doing something useful. He had been told that his father was acting in a film in America and had taken the news remarkably well. He had never mentioned the accident—either to Elfrida or to the Chownes—so they felt certain that he did not remember anything about it.

Elfrida had avoided the beach, partly for her own sake and partly because she was afraid it might awaken Patrick's memory, but now the horrible experience had begun to fade from her mind and she decided she must be sensible about it.

Fortunately the incident seemed to be fading from other people's minds as well. It had been "a nine days' wonder" and a very uncomfortable time for Elfrida; the news of the rescue had spread like a prairie fire and Lucius had been the first of a string of visitors. All Elfrida's neighbours were anxious to know the truth of the matter, to enquire whether she had survived her ghastly experience without serious injury, and to congratulate her upon her courage and presence of mind. When they heard she was planting in the little wood, they deluged her with every kind of plant which would thrive beneath trees.

Emma Chowne enjoyed the coming and going; it was she who was left to answer the enquiries and she answered them at length, explaining that she had seen it all happen with her own eyes and had never been so frightened in her life.

Perhaps it was a little unwise of Elfrida to give Emma Chowne a free rein, but what else could she do? She certainly did not want to see the visitors herself . . . she escaped to the wood with Patrick whenever possible, but she was unable to escape from Colonel Ferrier. He caught her on the doorstep just as she was going out and shook her by the hand, telling her that it was "a very good show—by Jove, it was!" and he was proud to know her.

"It was nothing," murmured Elfrida. "I mean anyone would have done it . . . what else could I do?"

This was bad enough, but Mr. Cobley was even more difficult to cope with. Mr. Cobley was determined to write to The Royal Life-Saving Society and "put up the case" so that she would be awarded a medal. It took all Elfrida's powers of persuasion to convince her champion that this was the last thing she desired.

The fuss was inconvenient in other ways as well: Elfrida was obliged to avoid the village; it was impossible to go to church and when she heard a car drive up to the front door she hid herself in the cellar. She felt as if she were living in a beleaguered garrison.

Elfrida thought of all this as she went down the cliff-path with Patrick, and rejoiced in the idea that it was over now . . . or nearly over.

The sea was calm this afternoon and the tide was rising, but all the same she did not go near the water and she forbade Patrick to paddle. They spent the afternoon digging an immense sand-castle and then sat down in the usual corner to have tea.

"Miss Ware," said Patrick, "Tom Parkins says you rescued me from the jaws of death."

"Tom Parkins is a very silly man."

"He doesn't look silly," objected Patrick. "He says you ought to get a medal."

"He's a very silly man," Elfrida repeated. "You fell into the water and I pulled you out, that's all. We both got rather wet, of course, but you aren't given a medal for that."

"You're given a medal for being brave. Are you brave, Miss Ware?"

"No, I'm often terribly frightened."

"You said I fell into the water, but I don't remember anything about it. Why don't I remember?" asked Patrick, looking at her with the anxious expression very much in evidence.

"I expect you bumped your head on a rock," replied Elfrida in a matter-of-fact tone. "Sometimes when people bump their heads, it makes them forget things. Why don't you go and finish the castle?"

"It's finished."

"No, it isn't. You must decorate it all over with little shells and pieces of coloured seaweed."

"Yes, that's a gorgeous idea!" cried Patrick jumping up. "I'll do it now and you mustn't look till it's ready!"

He stood, smiling at her happily, and than ran off to complete the job.

"Thank you, God!" whispered Elfrida, for this was the answer to her prayer that she might be helped to understand the poor little waif who had come to her in such an unceremonious manner. She had been dreading this moment; it had seemed to her that sooner or later some foolish person would be certain to speak to Patrick about the accident and he would be frightened. Now the moment was past; she had been given the right words to say and Patrick had accepted the explanation . . . so she could breathe freely.

31

As Elfrida sat on the shore, taking care not to look in the direction of the sand-castle, she realised that she was very fortunate. She had so much to make her happy: Ronnie was coming, he was her friend and it would be delightful to see him again; the "nine days' wonder" was nearly over and she would be able to go about and meet people without embarrassment; last but not least she would be able to keep Patrick. She had come to love Patrick dearly and was extremely anxious to keep him, but it might have been difficult to make ends meet without financial assistance.

She was thinking about all this when she heard a rattle of falling stones and looked up to see Ronnie coming down the cliff. He hastened towards her across the beach and flung himself down beside her on the rug.

"Ronnie!" she exclaimed. "How lovely! I wasn't expecting you so early!"

"I drove 'too fast,' " he explained.

"Wicked!" said Elfrida, smiling at him.

"I wanted to see you frightfully much, Elfrida Jane. Goodness, how lovely it is to be here! It seems years since I saw you . . . and you're simply splendid. This life seems to suit you."

"It suits me down to the ground. Fresh air and good plain food, lots of exercise and early to bed!"

"You're looking simply splendid," he repeated, gazing at her in delight.

"Have you had tea, Ronnie?"

"Yes, Mrs. Chowne insisted on giving me tea. I had it with her in the kitchen. She seemed quite pleased to see me."

"I'm pleased too. I was very excited when I got your letter saying you could come . . . and I'm glad Mr. Sandford thinks I shall be able to get the money from Glen Siddons, but four pounds a week seems too much."

"Uncle Bob says it isn't a bit too much. He's sure we can get it for you quite easily. I told you that we're insisting on a banker's order, didn't I?"

"What if he refuses?"

"He won't," declared Ronnie. "We're in a strong position, so we can twist his tail. I'll show you the letter, composed very carefully by the senior partner and myself. It's a pretty good letter and——"

"I hope it's polite!"

"Oh, quite polite," Ronnie assured her.

"How long can you stay, Ronnie? I hope this isn't just a flying visit."

"I can stay till Tuesday," he replied. "The senior partner was decent about it. He said I deserved a few days' holiday; I had 'become good value.' That means quite a lot."

"It means an awful lot—from him."

"That's what I think. He doesn't exactly gush, does he? Listen, Elfrida Jane: Mrs. Chowne told me a most amazing story. It isn't true, is it?"

"How do I know unless you tell me what she said?"

"She said a lot, but the main thing was that the boy fell into the sea and you saved his life and were very nearly drowned."

"Emma exaggerates."

"Exaggerates!" exclaimed Ronnie, sitting bolt upright and gazing at her in alarm. "You mean there's some truth in the story? You mean you were nearly drowned? Good heavens, how frightful!"

Elfrida hesitated. Since telling her tale to Lucius, she had told it so often that it rolled off her tongue with the greatest of ease—it was like a gramophone record! But somehow she could not tell it to Ronnie who was sitting up and looking at her with real anxiety in his honest blue eyes.

"Yes, it was frightful," said Elfrida. "I never was so terrified in all my life. I saw the wave break over the child's head and knock him down; the back-wash swept him away and he disappeared completely. I rushed down the beach and into the sea and managed to get hold of his ankle. Then . . . well, then I was hurled about by the waves and dashed down onto the pebbles. I felt myself being sucked backwards by the pull of the tide, the gravel was rattling in my ears . . . I thought we were both done for! If I hadn't happened to find a ledge of solid rock to hold on to we'd both have been swept out to sea."

"How ghastly!" exclaimed Ronnie. "Goodness, what a dreadful experience! What a narrow escape!" He looked at the peaceful waters of the bay and added, "It seems so calm . . . but you must never bathe there any more. Promise me, Elfrida Jane! I can't bear to think of it."

"Don't think of it, Ronnie. I've told you the truth about what happened, because . . . well, because I wanted to. It's over now, so don't worry about it."

"Not worry about you being nearly drowned!"

Elfrida smiled. "But I wasn't drowned and neither of us is any the worse because of the accident."

"Was it an accident?"

"Yes, of course! I don't know what you mean——"

"Mrs. Chowne said it wasn't an accident; Siddons was throwing sticks into the water and making the child fetch them. She said he knew the current in the bay was dangerous."

"Yes, that's true," admitted Elfrida.

"Was he trying to drown his child?"

"No, of course not!"

"What do you mean?" asked Ronnie with a puzzled frown. "Either the man tried to drown his child or else he didn't."

"It's difficult to explain it to you because you're a different sort of person. I'm quite certain that Glen did not mean to drown Patrick—I'm absolutely sure of it, Ronnie—he was just having fun, that's all. He was pleasurably excited by the spice of danger."

"Danger to his child!" exclaimed Ronnie in horrified tones.

"Perhaps he didn't realise . . ." began Elfrida.

"I don't understand," declared Ronnie. He added thoughtfully, "I can understand being excited by danger to myself—risking my own skin—but I can't imagine anyone being 'pleasurably excited' by risking a child's life."

"He enjoyed seeing Patrick dodging the waves. It was a game—they were both enjoying it. Then a bigger wave broke over the child's head and he was gone in a moment."

"Heavens! And you went after him!"

"What else could I do?"

"You couldn't do anything else."

Elfrida smiled at him. He was the only person who had said she couldn't have done anything else. Other people seemed to think she could have stood on the beach and screamed or wrung her hands—or something equally futile—while Patrick was being swept out to sea.

"But what was Siddons doing? asked Ronnie. "He was there, wasn't he? Why didn't he go in after the child himself?"

"He can't swim," she explained.

"Can't swim," growled Ronnie. "I wish I had him here. First I'd beat him to a jelly and then I'd throw him into the sea and watch him drowning."

Elfrida laughed, "And then you'd jump in after him and save his life!"

"No, I wouldn't!"

"Yes, you would, Ronnie."

"Well. . . perhaps," said Ronnie, thoughtfully. "But not until he had come up for the third time. He must be an awful swine."

"You wouldn't like him," said Elfrida, with conviction.

"How could anyone like him!"

She did not answer. Fortunately it was not really a question.

Ronnie was silent for some time; he was thinking. At last he said, "Elfrida Jane, you were—sort of—standing up for the fellow, but I can't see any excuse for him at all. He deliberately put his child into danger and——"

"Not deliberately," objected Elfrida. She hesitated and then added. "I'm just trying to be fair. You see it's difficult for me to be fair to Glen, because . . . because at one time I was silly about him."

Ronnie glanced at her and was astonished to see that her face had become very flushed and she was scraping a hole in the sand.

"You don't mean you were in love with him?" asked Ronnie incredulously.

"I thought I was."

"I suppose . . . I suppose lots of girls admire him?"

"That doesn't make me feel any better about it."

"You were very young, weren't you?" said Ronnie, trying to make excuses. "I mean . . . I mean young girls often get starry-eyed about popular actors."

"I think the right word is 'infatuated,'" murmured Elfrida, scraping away at her hole. "It isn't a nice word, it it? I thought he was wonderful. I used to hang about in the passage outside the door of his dressing-room, hoping he would come out and say 'goodnight' to me before he rushed off to a party."

Ronnie was dumb.

"It was Miss Martineau who brought me to my senses," continued Elfrida. "She made me look at myself and I saw I was being frightfully silly. That was the reason I walked out of *The Motor Car*. You thought I was mad to give up a good part, didn't you? Well, I was running away—running away from Glen. I was determined to get over my silliness—and I did. Mountain Cross cured me. Then he appeared here suddenly, without any warning, and asked if he could stay for a few days . . . and he was so nice, so kind and friendly and charming that it happened all over again. Glen can be delightful when he likes. He's a spell-binder, if you know what I mean. Everyone——"

"But it's over?" interrupted Ronnie, looking at her anxiously. "You said it was over."

"Oh, yes, it was over before the—the accident, or whatever you like to call it."

Ronnie would have liked to call it the attempted murder, but he refrained.

"I saw through him," added Elfrida. "I saw he was a sham. After that I couldn't be fair to him."

"What made you see through him?"

"Several things." She hesitated, searching for something that Ronnie would understand; the postcard scene was dreadful to relate.

"Don't tell me if you'd rather not," said Ronnie, who was watching her face.

"I'll tell you one of the things; it was the first thing that made me. . . well, it made me realise that he wasn't as marvellous as I'd thought . . ." She told him about the lunch at The Grand Hotel and the purchase of the blue blazer.

"Good lord!" Ronnie exclaimed in horrified tones.

"It was a small thing, but——"

"It wasn't a small thing! It would have been pretty low-down if he'd bought a blazer for himself—I mean one that he wasn't entitled to wear—but it was absolutely ghastly to teach deceit to his child. No wonder you were fed up with the fellow!"

Curiously enough this aspect of the case had not occurred to Elfrida. She saw it now and realised that Ronnie was right. "Well, there it is," she said. "I'm glad I've told you about it; you know now what a silly donkey I am."

Ronnie was silent. His face had become quite pale and there was a tenseness in his jaw as if he were clenching his teeth. Perhaps eventually he would have found someting to say, but Elfrida did not wait. She jumped up and called to Patrick, who was giving the finishing touches to his castle, and the conversation was over. Nor was the subject re-opened; there were plenty of other more pleasant subjects to discuss.

Ronnie was anxious to make friends with Patrick, but Patrick was shy and at dinner he scarcely uttered a word. It was a relief when the silent little ghost went off to bed and his companions were left to talk in peace.

"I'm glad you awakened my interest in Sir Francis Drake," said Elfrida. "There are several books about him in the library, and Lucius Babbington lent me a very old book with charts and drawings. It was difficult to read, but it was well worth the trouble. What a wonderful man Drake was!"

"Yes," agreed Ronnie.

"To everyone round about here Drake is the greatest hero of all time. People in the village will tell you stories about Drake and there are songs and rhymes about him which have been handed down from father to son."

"That's interesting. You might make a collection of them."

"I believe I could," said Elfrida thoughtfully. "Perhaps Lucius would help me; it's the sort of thing that would appeal to him."

32

On Sunday morning at breakfast Elfrida asked her visitor if he would like to go to church.

"Yes, I'd like to," he said.

"Can I come too?" asked Patrick. "I haven't been to church since I lived with the nuns."

Elfrida looked doubtful.

"How old were you when you lived with the nuns?" asked Ronnie.

"I'm not sure," replied Patrick. "I don't remember much about it . . . but I remember going to church. Mrs. Landor was too busy to go to church; it made a lot of extra work for her—me being there."

"I wonder——" began Elfrida.

"Of course he can come," interrupted Ronnie. "He's staying with you, so he can go to church with you. I don't suppose his father made any enquiries as to your denomination."

"What's denom . . . that word you said?" asked Patrick.

"There are several different kinds of churches," explained Ronnie. "Some people like one kind and other people like another kind. It depends which kind your father likes."

"Glen doesn't like any church unless it's a wedding."

"That settles the matter satisfactorily," said Ronnie.

Patrick looked a little puzzled, but his elders did not explain further.

They were all ready to go to church in good time.

Patrick had put on his grey flannel shorts and blue blazer. "They're my best clothes," he said proudly. "It's the right thing to put on your best clothes to go to church; Mrs. Chowne said so."

"Yes, you look very nice," said Ronnie. "But we'll have to take that badge off your blazer."

"No," said Patrick. "I like it."

"It's the badge for Beechings School," explained Ronnie. "You wouldn't like people to think you were one of the boys who go to Beechings, would you?"

"Glen said it would be fun to pretend I was."

"Pretending things isn't fun," declared Ronnie.

"Actors pretend things."

"Yes, when they're on the stage. They don't pretend things in real life."

"Glen does," said Glen's son with conviction.

Ronnie was silenced.

While the argument was taking place Elfrida had fetched a small pair of embroidery scissors.

"Oh, you mustn't cut it off!" cxclaimcd Patrick, rctrcating a few steps as he spoke.

"I'll do it very carefully, Patrick."

"No, you mustn't! I don't want you to cut it off! You'll spoil my blazer!" He retreated another step and clasped both hands firmly over his pocket.

All thrcc stood and gazed at each other in silence.

It was very funny. Elfrida realised that; but she was much too surprised and worried to be amused. She was surprised because she had never come to grips with Patrick before and worried because she did not know how to deal with the situation. She realised that this was an important moment, not only because Patrick must be made to understand that 'pretending' was not fun, but also because he must learn to do as he was told. If she began giving in to Patrick, she might have to go on giving in to him. It was wrong to spoil a child.

At last Elfrida said, "But Patrick, you belong to Mountain Cross. You don't belong to Beechings."

"Oh, I see!" said Patrick nodding. "Yes, I belong to Mountain Cross . . . but you'll be very careful, won't you?" He took off his blazer and handed it to her, adding, "It's a pity there isn't a badge to show that I belong to Mountain Cross."

"*Que vous êtes sage, chère* Elfrida Jane!" said Ronnie, smiling.

The operation was skilfully performed and all three set off down the avenue in perfect harmony.

It was a delightful service; the singing was hearty and Mr. Perrimonts' sermon was short and well thought out. It was the sort of service Ronnie liked; in his opinion it compared very favourably with the fashionable church to which his mother belonged where the singing was performed by a trained choir and the congregation listened. Ronnie's companions were not enjoying the service so much. Elfrida had an uncomfortable feeling that everyone was staring at her, and Patrick was puzzled.

Patrick kept on fidgeting and looking round. Presently he whispered to Ronnie, "They've forgotten the scent."

"They don't have scent in this kind of church," whispered Ronnie.

Patrick nodded and settled down, and for the remainder of the service he was good and quiet.

The moment the service was over, and before anyone else had moved, Elfrida seized Patrick's hand and hastened out of the building. Ronnie was surprised and slightly alarmed; he found his hat, which he had put under the seat, and followed. He expected to find Elfrida Jane and the child waiting for him in the churchyard, but there was no sign of them. Ronnie lingered for a few moments, looking for them; he was about to go home when he found the path between the tomb-stones blocked by a small woman with a bright green hat.

"Excuse me," she said. "I saw you with Miss Ware and a little boy."

"Yes. Do you know if they've gone home?" asked Ronnie anxiously.

"I don't know where they are," she replied. "I was hoping to have a few words with Miss Ware . . . is that the little boy she rescued from drowning?"

"Yes."

"He's Glen Siddons' son, isn't he?"

"Yes."

"He isn't a bit like his father, is he?"

"I don't know Glen Siddons."

"Perhaps you could give me some information about the accident."

"I wasn't there," said Ronnie. He tried to sidle past, but the woman in the green hat stood firmly in the middle of the path and without using physical violence it was impossible for him to evade her.

She said, "You're staying with Miss Ware, aren't you? So of course you must have heard all about the accident. I've called at Mountain Cross several times, but Miss Ware was out and the woman didn't seem to know anything. She's rather a foolish woman."

"I think she's very sensible."

"I wouldn't bother about it if it weren't for the connection with Glen Siddons; he's very much in the public eye at the moment, so if you could tell me what part he played in the rescue——"

"I wasn't there."

"But you must *know!* Of course I can get the story from the villagers, but they all tell me something different," said "Green Hat" plaintively.

"They would," said Ronnie, nodding. "That makes a story so much more interesting, doesn't it? Would you mind letting me past? I'm in a hurry——"

"Just a minute! You see it's the true story I want."

"You think you'll get the 'true story' from me?"

"Yes, of course," said "Green Hat" smiling at him.

"And I suppose if I tell you 'the true story,' you'll send it to the editor of your paper?"

"It's the duty of a newspaper to publish news."

"And it's the duty of people like you to snoop about looking for tit-bits."

She laughed as if he had made a good joke. "Oh, you mustn't say that! Don't you believe in the Freedom of the Press?"

"It depends what you mean by the Freedom of the Press," replied Ronnie thoughtfully. "If you mean the Press should have licence to publish the private affairs of a citizen without his—or her—consent then I don't believe in the Freedom of the Press."

"But our readers *like* hearing about people's private affairs!" exclaimed the woman in astonishment. "It's our duty to give them what they want. Besides, it isn't as if this were a scandal. The public ought to be informed of good brave deeds . . . there are so many bad deeds in the world today."

"Yes . . . and one of the worst is lying in wait for people coming out of church and annoying them." Ronnie raised his hat politely, dodged "Green Hat" by leaping over a tomb-stone and made for the gate.

Several other people were hanging about, and looked as if they wanted to speak to him, but Ronnie had a useful turn of speed (he had played rugger for his college) and he ran for his life. He had been worried about Elfrida Jane's hasty departure, but now he knew the reason, so he need not worry any more. He was chuckling to himself as he turned in at the entrance of Mountain Cross avenue.

Sunday afternoon was spent in the copse. Ronnie and Elfrida and Patrick put in some of the plants and bulbs which has been bestowed upon Elfrida by her neighbours and then they had a picnic-tea.

By this time Patrick had lost all his shyness; he and Ronnie had become friends and were chatting and laughing and having fun together as if they had known each other for years.

Patrick finished his tea quickly and went off by himself; he had a secret. Lots of people had given plants to the little wood but, alas, Patrick had nothing to give! Then he had found an acorn. He had found it under an oak-tree in Pansy's paddock and had realised at once that this was the answer to his problem. What could be a better present for the little wood? Acorns grow into oak-trees. He had found a nice open space for the oak-tree to grow and had planted the acorn carefully.

The acorn had now been planted for five days, so it must have begun to grow by this time. Patrick found the place, which he had marked with a stick, and dug it up. He was disappointed to find that it had not begun to grow, it was just exactly as he had planted it . . . rather like a tiny yellowish-brown egg. Birds sit on eggs to hatch them out, so perhaps it would encourage the acorn to hatch out if he held it in his warm hand. He squatted down and nursed the acorn for quite a long time.

Meanwhile his elders were chatting over the remains of the picnic-tea.

"I was caught this morning coming out of church," said Ronnie.

"Oh, goodness, I ought to have warned you! As a matter of fact I thought all that nonsense was dying down until I saw the woman in the green hat and then it was too late. The only thing to do was to take Patrick and run."

"She said she hadn't seen you."

"I hide when I see her coming and leave Emma to cope with her."

"She doesn't seem to have got much out of Emma," said Ronnie thoughtfully. "It's rather strange, really, because Emma is such a talker. I should have thought Emma would have been only too willing to tell her all she wanted to know. Emma revealed the whole story to me without any persuasion."

"The green-hat woman would have got the whole story from Emma if she had gone about it in the right way," explained

Elfrida. "Fortunately she doesn't know Emma so she began by asking questions (Emma doesn't like questions). Then, when Emma showed reluctance, the woman was misguided enough to offer her five pounds for 'the true story.' That absolutely put the lid on it," added Elfrida, smiling.

"It was an insult, I suppose?"

"Worse than an insult! Emma said it was 'thirty pieces of silver.' "

"That's interesting, but all the same I don't see the connection."

"Neither did I," admitted Elfrida. "I think there must be some sort of connection in Emma's mind, but it was no good asking her about it because she couldn't explain."

"I gather you've had rather an uncomfortable time," said Ronnie after a short silence.

"It has been awful. I don't know what I should have done if I hadn't had Emma to ward people off. She doesn't seem to mind saying I'm not at home when she knows perfectly well that I'm hiding in the cellar. You see, Ronnie, it isn't only that I hate all the fuss for myself; I want to clamp down on the whole affair because of Patrick. I hope you didn't tell that green-hat woman anything."

"I told her my views about the Freedom of the Press; then I jumped over a tomb-stone and escaped."

They looked at each other and smiled.

Monday morning was fine and sunny, but there was a stiff breeze. This was unfortunate, for it had been decided that they should take the Wisp and go down to the small fishing village about three miles east of Mountain Cross and hire a boat. Elfrida remembered that in one of his letters Ronnie had said it would be interesting to have a look at the big white cross from the sea.

They went out onto the cliff and looked at the waves.

"Let's go," said Patrick eagerly.

"Not today," said Ronnie, shaking his head. "I wouldn't

mind going myself, but it's too blustry for women and children."

Elfrida agreed with him. There was a fishing-boat anchored off the promontory and it was heaving up and down in a very uncomfortable manner. "The garden will be sheltered," she suggested.

"Supposing we have a go at the lily pool?" said Ronnie. "You want it cleared out, don't you?"

Patrick had been looking rather dejected, but he perked up at the idea of cleaning out the lily pool.

They changed into their oldest clothes and spent the morning raking out the weeds and emptying the stagnant water. It was an arduous job and Elfrida felt somewhat guilty about using her guest like this, but her guest assured her that there was nothing he enjoyed more than grubbing about and getting dirty.

By lunch-time the job was finished; the pool was clean and empty—it could not be filled with water until the lilies were planted.

"You could have goldfish, Elfrida Jane," suggested Ronnie as they stood and surveyed their handiwork.

"Do you think frogs would be happy here?"

"Frogs would be fun!" Ronnie exclaimed. "Why shouldn't they be happy? Where could we get frogs?"

As they walked back to the house Elfrida told him about Mr. Jeremy Fisher and his relations . . . and was pleased to discover that Ronnie's education had not been neglected. Patrick's education had been sadly neglected; he had never heard of Mr. Fisher.

"This must be remedied at once," said Ronnie gravely. "We'll go over to Cherleigh this afternoon and see if we can get some of those little books for you. Fortunately none of us is very fat, so we'll be able to fit into the Wisp quite easily."

The Wisp was a battered little two-seater, which Ronnie had bought second-hand, but Patrick was tucked in between his two companions and all three were very comfortable. They bought as many of the little books as they could find in the book-shops at Cherleigh and then had tea together in a small tea-shop.

33

The days of Ronnie's visit had passed much too quickly. This was his last evening at Mountain Cross, so when Elfrida had said goodnight to Patrick she and Ronnie went out and walked along the top of the cliff to the cross on the hillock. They had been here several times; Ronnie was extremely interested in it and had promised that when he went back to London he would look up a friend who had studied archaeology and see if he could find out when it had been erected.

It was a beautiful evening, the wind had fallen and the sun was declining in a cloudless sky.

"How beautifully peaceful it is!" said Ronnie with a sigh. "This time tomorrow I shall be back in London."

"Must you go early tomorrow?" asked Elfrida. "I feel as if you'd only just arrived."

"I must go after breakfast, I'm afraid."

"I wish you could stay until the afternoon. Lucius is coming tomorrow morning with the lilies and he said he would plant them for me. I'd like you to meet Lucius."

Ronnie did not want to meet Lucius; he had heard too much about the fellow during the last three days. Not that Elfrida Jane had prattled about him; she had just mentioned him several times in the course of conversation. It was Emma Chowne who had prattled about "Mr. Lucius."

"I've got a good deal to do," said Ronnie. "For one thing I

must get hold of Uncle Bob and explain those alterations you want made in the letter to Glen Siddons. The letter must be registered and sent by airmail . . . and the sooner the better."

They turned and strolled back and sat down in the summer-house. Elfrida had not been here since the evening when she and Glen had played part of the little scene at Belmont. So much had happened since then that it seemed a very long time ago. Not only had there been a number of disturbing "outside incidents," but much of a disturbing nature had happened in Elfrida's heart and mind.

"What are you thinking of, Elfrida Jane?" asked Ronnie after a protracted silence.

"I was thinking how queer it is the way Time gets jumbled about."

Ronnie understood at once. One of the nice things about him was his "understandingness"; there was no need to arrange your thoughts before uttering them aloud. "Yes," said Ronnie. "Something that happened months ago seems like yesterday."

"It's the other way round with me," she told him. "Something that happened ten days ago seems as if it had happened last year."

He looked at her and saw that her face was very thoughtful; he would have given a great deal to know her thoughts. Perhaps if he told her what he had been thinking, it would encourage her to speak. "It seems only yesterday—or at the most last week—that we came to Mountain Cross together," said Ronnie. "I remember everything we said and did so clearly that I can scarcely believe it's three whole months . . . and yet, when I first arrived here on Saturday and saw you on the beach, I felt as if I hadn't seen you for years. That's a jumble if you like!"

"Yes," said Elfrida, but still she did not tell him her thoughts.

"You haven't been lonely here, have you?" asked Ronnie.

"Not a bit," she replied. "There's so much to do that I haven't time to feel lonely . . . and even if I hadn't a lot to do I don't believe I should feel lonely at Mountain Cross. It gives me a warm, safe feeling."

Ronnie nodded. "I've felt it too—that warm, safe feeling. You don't get that feeling in a modern house, like Mother's villa, because contemporary houses have been built by men who were paid by the hour; they knocked off work when the clock struck and went home and took their wives to the pictures and forgot all about the job until next morning. Mountain Cross wasn't built like that. The men who built it were interested in the job and proud of it; they put their best work into it."

Elfrida nodded.

"The family who lived in the house loved it," continued Ronnie. "Their children were born in the house and grew up and ran about the place and got to know every yard of it, so when in time it came into their possession it was dear and familiar."

"It has always been a home," said Elfrida.

"Yes, for hundreds of years. That's what makes Mountain Cross feel warm and safe."

"It's a warm safe home to me; I feel as if I had lived here all my life," said Elfrida. She added, "Sometimes I'm quite frightened when I think of the chances that brought me here."

Ronnie wanted to know about the "chances," so she told him: it was chance that Miss Martineau had happened to see the advertisement and had persuaded Elfrida to go and see Mr. Sandford; it was chance that she had met him at the bottom of the steps when she was hesitating whether or not to go in; it was chance that Glen had failed to ring her up until she had left Miss Martineau's. Any of these curious little chances, had they happened differently, might have prevented Elfrida from coming to Mountain Cross.

"It's quite frightening, isn't it?" added Elfrida.

"Yes, if you think of it in that way."

"What other way is there?"

"Perhaps you were meant to come to Mountain Cross."

"Oh, yes!" she cried. "That's a much nicer idea! Thank you, Ronnie."

There was quite a long silence. Obviously Elfrida Jane was thinking about the "much nicer idea," so the author of the idea did not disturb her.

Presently she said, "You're right, of course. Unless we believe that there's some Power with a Great Purpose behind everything life doesn't make sense and we're all floundering about in the dark; that's a dreadful thought."

"But you didn't really think it, did you?"

"Not really," she replied doubtfully. "I'm afraid my brain is rather a rag-bag. I must try to think more clearly, especially now that I've been given such a big responsibility."

"You mean Patrick, of course."

"Yes, God has given him to me to take care of. I do feel that very strongly. I shall do my best to take care of him and make him happy."

"I shouldn't worry too much; he needs love, that's all, and you're giving him love."

She nodded, "I've become very, very fond of Patrick."

"You'll be sorry to part with him when his father wants him back."

"He won't," said Elfrida without hesitation.

"Won't want him back!" exclaimed Ronnie incredulously. "I can scarcely believe a man wouldn't want his son—even a man like Siddons. I thought he had just dumped the child on you temporarily because he had nowhere else to leave him."

"I thought so at first," admitted Elfrida. "I thought Glen had just gone off suddenly, because . . . because he was upset about something; but now that I've had time to think about it I've come to the conclusion that it was all a well-thought-out plan. When he discovered that Mrs. Landor wouldn't keep Patrick any longer, Glen remembered that I lived at Mountain Cross and came here with the deliberate intention of leaving the child with me."

"Good heavens, what makes you think that?"

"I don't know," she said vaguely. "It's just when I look back and remember some of the things he said . . . and did. I may be quite wrong, of course. You can't tell with Glen, because he isn't real."

"Isn't real?"

"Nothing he says or does is real," explained Elfrida.

Ronnie was silent for a few moments. Then he said, "All the same I can't understand how a man could abandon his son."

"Of course you can't," declared Elfrida, turning her head and smiling at Ronnie. "You could never understand Glen Siddons because you're absolutely different in every way."

"I'm real?" asked Ronnie. This seemed the logical conclusion.

"You're real," agreed Elfrida. She hesitated and then added, "I want you to understand that I've got Patrick 'for keeps.' "

"You're sure of that?"

"Perfectly certain. You see Patrick is a nuisance to Glen. Poor Patrick has been a nuisance to everyone all his life . . . but the little ship has come safely into harbour."

"A nice, warm, comfortable harbour," said Ronnie, smiling at her. He added, "Lucky little Patrick."

34

Patrick and Elfrida were standing at the door, saying goodbye to Ronnie; he had expressed his thanks to his hostess and was in his car, ready to start, but he lingered, putting off the evil moment.

"I really must go," said Ronnie at last.

"Come back soon," said his hostess hospitably.

"Junior partners are supposed to work for their livings."

"Don't junior partners ever get proper holidays?"

"They have to take their holidays when it suits their seniors. As a matter of fact Uncle Bob said I could have ten days next month . . . but I don't want to sponge on you, Elfrida Jane."

"Sponge is a horrid word!"

"It's a horrid word for a horrid thing."

"It isn't a word to be used between friends," she told him. "You like Mountain Cross, don't you? So if you have nothing better to do, just let me know."

"Mother is going to Nice with a party, so perhaps——"

"That would be fun for you!"

"It wouldn't be fun," replied Ronnie. "I was going to tell you that Mother is going to Nice with a party, so perhaps I needn't go with her. You see, Mother doesn't like travelling alone, but if she's with a party she'll be quite happy. I'd much rather come to Mountain Cross if you're sure I wouldn't be a nuisance."

"Come," said Elfrida, nodding.

"I'll come," declared Ronnie. "I'll get out of the party somehow. Goodbye, Elfrida Jane . . . and thank you again."

"Goodbye, Ronnie. Take care of yourself and don't drive too fast."

"It depends what you call 'too fast,' doesn't it?"

"Make the Wisp go like the wind!" cried Patrick.

Ronnie smiled and let in the clutch.

The car had begun to move off down the avenue when Chowne came running round the corner of the house with a parcel under his arm. He shouted to Ronnie to stop and opening the left-hand door of the car put the parcel on the passenger's seat.

"What is it, Chowne?" asked Ronnie.

Chowne pointed to the parcel.

"Oh, yes, I see," nodded Ronnie.

Chowne took Ronnie's left hand and placed it upon the parcel.

"All right! I'll give it to him safely. Stand back, Chowne, I'm off!"

Elfrida had seen the parcel put into the car and was smiling to herself; obviously Ronnie had forgotten to pack some of his belongings . . . it was just as well Emma had found it, whatever it was, and had sent Chowne after him!

She watched the little car speed down the avenue and turn the corner, throwing up a spurt of gravel. Ronnie's hand was waving out of the window . . . he shouldn't do that, it wasn't safe!

"He'll come back, won't he?" asked Patrick anxiously.

"I expect so, when he gets his holiday," she replied.

"He said 'next month.' That's a long time, isn't it?"

"Yes, it's a long time," said Elfrida.

Soon after Ronnie's departure Lucius arrived in his car with the lily roots and Elfrida helped him to carry them down to the garden. She wanted to speak to Lucius in private, so she had taken Emma into her confidence and Emma had agreed to "keep Pat out of the way." This was a necessary precaution, for Patrick followed Elfrida everywhere she went.

"Oh, you've cleaned out the pool!" exclaimed Lucius. "Why didn't you wait for me to help you?"

"Ronnie Leighton helped me. He was here for the week-end; I wish you could have met him. We must arrange it next time he comes."

"I think you said he was Mrs. Sandford's partner."

"Yes, he was here on business," explained Elfrida. She added, "I expect you heard I've got little Patrick Siddons staying with me."

"Oh, yes, we heard," admitted Lucius with a smile. "But it wasn't the fish-boy this time. Mary heard about it at the Women's Institute."

"What were they saying?"

"They were saying that Glen Siddons is acting in a film in America and left his child with you."

"Was that all, Lucius? I'd rather know the worst."

"Not quite all," replied Lucius uncomfortably. "They had a wild story that he left here in the middle of the night without troubling to say goodbye. Mary didn't believe it; she said I was to ask you——"

"It's true," interrupted Elfrida. "There isn't any point in denying it."

"He must be mad!"

"Actors are rather temperamental," explained Elfrida, without much conviction.

"It's a curious word, isn't it?" said Lucius. "I've sometimes thought it should be divided into two parts. People who are 'temperamental' have bad tempers and are slightly 'mental.' " He added, "You worry too much about what people say. The grape-vine flourishes in country-places; if you want to keep a secret, you must live in a large town where your neighbours aren't interested in you."

"It isn't exactly a secret; it's because I don't like the feeling that people are talking about me. I suppose I shall get used to it in time."

"Yes, of course you will! What are you going to do with the child?"

"I shall keep him with me. Poor Patrick has had a very miserable life . . . and he's perfectly happy here. He's a dear little boy and a good companion; the Chownes will help me to look after him."

"That sounds a good arrangement. You must bring him over to see us; Mary and I are very fond of children."

"Yes, I'd like to bring him one day."

"We must fix it up," said Lucius, nodding. "By the way, Elfrida, you remember I told you about that man in the village who could come and repair your greenhouse? He's out of a job at the moment, so——"

"I can't afford it," said Elfrida frankly.

"Oh, we're all as poor as church-mice nowadays. The taxes are penal! But all the same it's a pity to let things go to rack and ruin. The man I told you about wouldn't charge very much to put your greenhouse in order . . . and there's another thing, Elfrida. I really think you should get a little car; it would be useful to you, wouldn't it? Chowne is good with cars, he could easily teach you to drive. You're terribly isolated here without any means of transport. It wouldn't be an extravagance," added Lucius earnestly.

"I really can't afford it," she told him. "I simply haven't the money to buy a car. I'm living from hand to mouth."

"You're living from hand to mouth?"

"Yes, literally," replied Elfrida, nodding. "I don't know how much income I shall have until Grandmother's affairs have been settled; Mr. Sandford told me it wouldn't be much."

"But the Wares were very well off!"

"They must have lost money, somehow or other. Mr. Sandford said they were spending capital . . . and nearly all the fields belonging to Mountain Cross have been sold."

"What!" exclaimed Lucius in dismay. "I can't believe it!

Elfrida, are you sure the fields have been sold? I mean are you sure they haven't just been let for grazing?"

"No, they've been sold."

"It's incredible," he declared. "Old Roger Ware was quite crazy about Mountain Cross; he loved every stone of the house and every yard of the land! His family has been here for generations and he regarded the place as a sacred trust. He often spoke to me about it. I should have said he was the last man on earth to whittle away his property . . . and, quite apart from sentiment, you can't run a farm and make it pay without good fields."

"I know," said Elfrida sadly.

"What are you going to do?"

Elfrida did not reply. She had wanted to explain her financial position to Lucius because she was finding things rather difficult. She was unable to subscribe to local charities; she could not hire men to put the garden in order; she could not afford to run a car nor to make any return for the hospitality of her friends. Everyone complained of being badly off (Elfrida had heard one of her neighbours announce that she was "penniless"); but despite their lamentable condition they all had cars and most of them went abroad for their holidays.

"What are you going to do?" repeated Lucius. "You can't live here on half nothing."

Elfrida smiled at his worried face. "I can live quite comfortably on very little. I'm not complaining, Lucius; I just wanted you and Mary to know about it. That's why I've told you. Things are a bit difficult, you see. For instance the other day when Mary was collecting for the Red Cross I could see she was surprised when I gave her five shillings. I don't want people to think I'm mean."

"Nobody thinks that," declared Lucius hastily. "Mary just thought it was all you had at the moment."

"It was all I had," admitted Elfrida. "I've got some more money now—just a little to go on with—from Mr. Sandford, but most of it will be used to pay the butcher's bill."

"I could easily lend you some money."

"It's very kind of you, but I don't want to get into debt. I can just make ends meet if I'm careful."

"I'm terribly sorry," he murmured. "I don't see how you're going to manage."

"Don't worry about me; I'm quite happy," she told him.

It was no good saying any more . . . but Lucius continued to look thoughtful and worried as he unpacked the small hamper which contained the lilies. He had planted the roots in wicker baskets and already they had begun to sprout.

"I've found this the most satisfactory way of growing them," explained Lucius as he bedded down the baskets in the mud at the bottom of the pond. "It gives the lilies a solid bed and the roots aren't disturbed when the pool is filled with water. Would you like some goldfish, Elfrida? I could get some for you at the pet-shop in Cherleigh."

"Thank you, Lucius, but I don't think I want goldfish," she replied. She had a feeling that Lucius would not approve of frogs, so she did not mention Mr. Jeremy Fisher.

The following day—Thursday—was very wet. Elfrida was quite pleased to see the rain, for everything in the garden had been dried up by the hot sun. She spent the day polishing furniture, a task which she enjoyed. Today, however, it seemed less enjoyable than usual and she found herself sitting, duster in hand, and not getting on with the work. The house was very quiet.

At tea-time Patrick asked if he might go out.

"It's still raining," said Elfrida. "I don't think——"

"But not very hard! You said the rain would make things grow, didn't you? I can put on my waterproof and my rubber boots. If I do that it will be all right, won't it?"

"You mustn't go near the cliff."

"No, just up to the wood."

He looked so eager that she agreed. He had been indoors all day; it was boring for him.

Elfrida saw him off at the door. As she turned back into the house, the telephone bell rang so she went into the dining-room and lifted the receiver.

A voice said, "Is that you, Elfrida Jane?"

"Ronnie!" she exclaimed in surprise. She was surprised for several reasons: this was "office hours" and Ronnie never rang her up from the office except on business . . . and if he were ringing up from the office he would not call her "Elfrida Jane." All this went through her mind in a moment and there was scarcely a pause before she added, "Is something the matter?"

"Something the matter?"

"I wondered if you were ringing up from the office."

"Oh, I see what you mean! I'm ringing up from Uncle Bob's room; he's talking to Mr. Riggs. Could you bear to see me tomorrow?"

"Tomorrow? Yes, of course, Ronnie! I told you to come whenever you liked. Are you getting your holiday sooner than you expected?"

"It's business—very important business."

"What is it?"

"I can't explain on the phone; it's much too complicated. Uncle Bob is sending me down to Mountain Cross to tell you about it. I shall leave early so you can expect me soon after lunch. Is that all right?"

"Yes, of course! But, Ronnie——"

"I'm terribly busy getting things fixed up. I'll tell you everything when I see you. G'bye for now, Elfrida Jane."

"But, Ronnie, is it something horrid?" asked Elfrida anxiously.

There was no reply; Ronnie had rung off.

What can it be? wondered Elfrida as she put down the receiver. The only "business" she could think of was the letter to Glen . . . but that was not too complicated to explain on the phone. Perhaps it was something to do with her grandmother's estate . . . but she had a feeling that it was something else. Ronnie's voice had sounded as if he were excited. Oh, what could it be?

35

Ronnie arrived soon after two o'clock on Friday afternoon; he was smiling cheerfully as he walked into the hall—which relieved Elfrida's anxiety—but Patrick was there, hopping with delight, and Chowne had appeared to carry in the visitor's suit-case, so nothing could be said about the mysterious business. It was all the more mysterious because Ronnie had come in Mr. Sandford's big black Jaguar instead of his own little Wisp.

"Oh, why didn't you bring the Wisp?" asked Patrick in disappointed tones. "She's much nicer."

"She was tired," replied Ronnie without hesitation.

When the usual greetings had been exchanged, Ronnie turned to Chowne and said, "I did what you asked me to do. It's all right, Chowne."

Chowne smiled in his usual slightly alarming manner.

Then Ronnie said he would go and unpack. . . and ran upstairs.

Patrick retired to the parlour; he was reading his new little books and, as he was half-way through Benjamin Bunny and was a slow but persevering reader, Elfrida knew he would be settled there for some time. She hesitated for a few moments and then followed Ronnie upstairs and knocked on his door.

"Come in, Elfrida Jane! I hoped you would come; I'm bursting to tell you!"

"It isn't anything horrid, is it?" she asked.

"Were you worrying? I'm sorry," he replied. "I should have told you——"

"I wondered and wondered what it could be."

"It's a long story. You had better sit down on the bed and I'll tell you from the beginning. You remember that, when I was going away on Tuesday, Chowne ran after me with a parcel? You'll never guess what it was."

"I thought it was something you had forgotten to pack."

"Not this time," said Ronnie. "It was a parcel addressed to 'Robert Sandford Esq.' Chowne made me understand that I was to deliver it to him safely by hand, so I said I would. I was in a hurry, so I didn't wait to find out more about it.

"Unfortunately the poor old Wisp didn't behave very well, so it was latish when I got to London. By this time I had examined the parcel; it was heavy and was done up very carefully in brown paper, tied with string and sealed with red wax. It looked important, so instead of waiting to give it to Uncle Bob in the morning I took it straight to his house. To be honest I had become inquisitive about it."

"What was it?" asked Elfrida, who also had become inquisitive.

"Wait a bit," said Ronnie, smiling at her. "Let me tell you the story in my own way. When I got to Uncle Bob's house, he and Aunt Millie were having dinner and I was invited to sit down and share the meal. I accepted with pleasure: I was hungry and they have scrumptious food. I said nothing about the parcel until Aunt Millie retired in the good old-fashioned manner and I was given a glass of port."

"Then you gave him the parcel and he opened it," suggested Elfrida.

"Hold on, you're going too fast! I gave him the parcel, but before opening it, he examined it carefully and pointed out that it was addressed to him in Mr. Ware's writing and——"

"Grandfather's writing!" exclaimed Elfrida in surprise.

"Yes. I didn't know his writing, so I hadn't realised that. It was addressed in Mr. Ware's writing, the seals were intact and the imprints had been made with Mr. Ware's signet. Uncle Bob told me to make a note of these points."

"But, Ronnie, why did he——"

"Because it might have been important to know that nobody had tampered with the parcel."

"Oh, I see!"

"When we had satisfied ourselves that all was well, the parcel was opened and was found to contain a sealed letter and a large red album full of stamps."

"What!" cried Elfrida.

"Yes," said Ronnie, nodding. "It was none other than the famous Red Book."

"But I thought the parcel was valuable!"

"Yes," said Ronnie, nodding again.

"Cousin Walt said the album was of no value!"

"That was just his fun."

Elfrida was speechless.

"Uncle Bob doesn't know much about stamps, neither do I," said Ronnie, continuing his story. "But we were both impressed by the size of the collection. All the sets were beautifully arranged and nearly all were complete. Do you know this," said Ronnie confidentially. "I always thought stamp-collecting was a bit silly, but Mr. Ware's album has made me change my mind. It really is quite fascinating."

"I'd like to see it."

"You must see it before it's sold. Well, where was I? Oh yes! Uncle Bob and I had a look at it and then we decided to pack it up and take it along to Mr. Riggs—his house is about ten minutes walk from Uncle Bob's—Mr. Riggs is an ardent philatelist."

"Yes," nodded Elfrida.

"Do you know Mr. Arnold Riggs?"

"No, but I know he likes stamps."

Ronnie smiled. "He certainly does! Mr. Riggs is a dried-up old stick, but he was thrilled to the marrow when he saw the neat little rows of stamps in Mr. Ware's album. His eyes gleamed and his hair stood on end and he became so red in the face that I was afraid he was going to have a fit."

"Do you mean it's worth a lot of money?" asked Elfrida, somewhat callously.

"Yes."

"Who does it belong to?"

"You."

"Me? Oh Ronnie would there be enough money to buy a field?"

"Several fields . . . and more pigs, if that's what you want."

She gazed at him, wide-eyed. "Ronnie, it can't be true! I don't understand. . . ."

"It's a bit difficult to take in, all of a sudden," admitted Ronnie.

"And where *was* the album?" asked Elfrida in bewilderment. "We looked everywhere for it."

"I know," said Ronnie "I heard an account of the search from the senior partner."

"Where was it, Ronnie?"

"That's one of the things I don't know."

"Well, go on and tell me some of the things you *do* know," said Elfrida impatiently. "How did Grandfather happen to have a valuable book of stamps and why did he hide it—and how did Chowne find it?"

"You had better read this letter," replied Ronnie, producing a typewritten screed from his pocket. "It's a copy of the letter from Mr. Ware which was enclosed in the parcel. Mr. Ware's letter is difficult to read because the writing is very shaky—he was ill when he wrote it—so we made some copies of it. You can keep this one if you like."

"It's very long," said Elfrida, looking at it doubtfully.

"Yes, but it's very interesting. Take your time about it, Elfrida Jane."

Mountain Cross.

My dear Sandford,

As one nears the end of one's life, it becomes difficult to know what to do with one's belongings—at least I find it so. I have no child to come after me, to live in Mountain Cross, to love the dear old house and take care of it as it has been loved and cared for by our family ever since it was built.

As you know, my wife and I made wills in each other's favour. This seemed right at the time but now we are both old—I am gravely ill and my dear wife is not in good health—so our parting will not be for long. For this reason we decided that it would be more sensible for me to bequeath Mountain Cross to my nephew, Walter Whitgreave, and I wrote to him telling him of my illness and asking him to fly over from Canada and see me. He replied vaguely, and not very sympathetically, saying he was in the midst of some business transactions but would try to come later. It is obvious from his letter that Walter is completely absorbed in his own affairs and would never settle down and live in this part of the world.

This being so I shall allow my will to stand; everything will be left to my dear wife to do as she thinks fit. Possibly she will decide to leave Mountain Cross to her brother's only son, Edward Mountjoy, who is a colonel in the Gunners and has two fine sons of his own. This would ensure the future of Mountain Cross which is what we both desire. If she decides upon this, she will make a proviso that the family will adopt the name of Ware . . . but I have no intention of tying her down; she is to have complete freedom of choice in the matter.

For a long time my wife has been anxious for me to try to get in touch with our daughter, Marjory, who left home and eloped with Frederick Thistlewood when she was nineteen years old. It is unnecessary to tell you this, my dear Sandford, I merely want to put it on record. For years I felt I could never forgive Marjory for, what seemed to me, "her treachery"; but gradually I recovered from my resentment. Perrimont helped me—he is a good man, wise and kind—he showed me that my resentment was "a sickness of the spirit." He begged me to forgive Marjory and try to find her.

I took his advice and got in touch with a Private Enquiry Agent in London. The man seemed energetic and competent; he assured me that there would be little difficulty in tracing Marjory (Thistlewood is an uncommon name); but I decided to wait until he had discovered her whereabouts before mentioning the subject to my wife. I realised that Marjory might have died—she was a delicately-nurtured girl, unused to roughing it—and I was anxious that my wife should be spared disappointment. It was as well I said nothing, for Marjory cannot be found. She cannot be found either alive or dead; she seems to have vanished off the face of the earth.

You will wonder why I have re-opened old wounds, but you are the only man I can trust with my confession . . . and the only man who can carry out my last wish.

I am giving this parcel to Ernest Chowne with instructions to keep it safely and to deliver it to you when my wife and I are both dead and the new owner of Mountain Cross—whomsoever he may be—has been in residence for not less than three months. That should be long enough for him—or her—to settle down comfortably in the old house. Chowne will carry out this trust most faithfully, I know; he should be suitably rewarded.

You are not a philatelist, my dear Sandford, but your partner, Arnold Riggs, will be able to give you some idea of the value of this collection. Expert advice will be necessary. I began to collect "the little bits of coloured paper" when I was a schoolboy and continued to add to the collection whenever possible. My stamps have been a great interest to me all my life and a solace in times of trouble. For the last fifteen years I have been in touch with philatelists all over the world and have bought from them with discretion.

You have sometimes wondered why my capital was dwindling! This album will give you the solution to the puzzle. Some men make a success in business; others buy and sell shares to augment their capital; a few invest in diamonds. As I am not a business man, have very little knowledge of the

Stock Exchange and even less of precious stones, these methods of making money were not for me. I have always been interested in philately and have studied the subject seriously, so I have been investing in stamps.

The album can be sold, indeed it must be sold, and the proceeds given to Mountain Cross. By this I mean that the individual who has settled down to live at Mountain Cross is to have the money to spend on the place, to improve its amenities and make it self-supporting.

You may think this arrangement rather strange (I am aware that it would be difficult if not impossible to make a will to this effect); But Mountain Cross has belonged to our family for generations and is very dear to my heart so I should like to think you will do your best to carry out my last wish.

Believe me, my dear Sandford,
Yours sincerely,

Roger Ware

Elfrida read the letter twice; then she looked up and said, "Ronnie, how astonishing! That's what Grandfather was doing with his money! What did Mr. Sandford say about it?"

"He said Mr. Ware must have been mad."

"Mad? Oh, no! He knew exactly what he wanted and he has put it very clearly. He loved Mountain Cross and he hadn't enough money to keep it in proper order, so he increased his capital by investing in stamps. It was the only way he could make money for Mountain Cross. That isn't mad, is it?"

"He knew what he wanted, but he didn't go about it in the right way," explained Ronnie. "The letter isn't sensible from a lawyer's point of view. You see a lawyer is trained to look ahead and safeguard his client's property. To put it simply a lawyer's job is first to understand his client's intentions and then make sure that everything will work out in accordance with his client's intentions. In this case all sorts of things could have happened which would have made the outcome very different from what Mr. Ware intended."

"What sort of things?"

"Mrs. Ware could have left the place to Whitgreave; he would have sold it straight off to the highest bidder."

"Yes, but I don't think she would have left it to him."

"Perhaps not. She might have left it to her nephew, the Colonel, but could he have lived here? Colonels aren't usually well off and by selling the best fields Mr. Ware made it impossible for Mountain Cross to be run as a farm."

"It wasn't very wise to sell the fields," admitted Elfrida.

"He did it because he was obsessed with the idea of getting hold of every penny he could lay his hands on to complete his sets of stamps. When a man is obsessed with an idea he can't see straight. It really is a kind of madness," said Ronnie thoughtfully. "You see Mr. Ware wanted Colonel Mountjoy to come and live here and take the name of Ware, and bring up his family at Mountain Cross, but by running down his estate and selling the fields he made it an impossible proposition. Nobody could live here comfortably unless he had substantial private means."

"That's true."

"So Colonel Mountjoy would probably have sold it," continued Ronnie. "He might have sold it to a man who intended to build on the land and make it into a housing estate—there's a lot of building going on round about Cherleigh—or a syndicate might have bought the house and turned it into a hotel."

"Grandfather wouldn't have liked that!"

Ronnie shook his head. "No, but it was a thing that might easily have happened . . . and supposing it had happened and the hotel-keeper had come to live at Mountain Cross, what then? After he had been settled here for three months, he might have raked in all the money from the sale of Mr. Ware's album. I don't say he *would* have raked in the money, because there are various legal snags; I only say that if Mr. Ware's 'last wish'—as stated in his letter—could have been carried out he would have done so."

"Yes, I see," said Elfrida. "Lucius said much the same thing when I told him the fields had been sold; he said nobody could run the place as a farm and make it pay." She paused and then continued thoughtfully. "I might have sold Mountain Cross. Mr. Sandford wanted me to sell it—and I realised that it was the sensible thing to do—but something prevented me. Something . . . I really don't know what."

"Some Power with a Great Purpose," suggested Ronnie.

Elfrida nodded.

After a few moments silence she said, "You mentioned 'various legal snags.' What are they?"

"There aren't any," replied Ronnie, smiling cheerfully. "As it happens Mr. Ware's 'last wish' can be carried out quite easily . . . but that's more by luck than good guidance. If there had been no letter, you would have been entitled to the proceeds from the sale of the album just the same. The letter makes no difference one way or the other."

"The letter makes a lot of difference to me."

"It makes no difference in law. First, because it isn't a legal document; second, because you inherited Mountain Cross and its contents. The album must have been in the house when you came into possession."

"It wasn't. Emma looked everywhere; she hunted high and low for days on end. There wasn't a nook or cranny that she didn't examine . . . she even took up some of the floor boards which seemed to have been loosened! She found all sorts of extraordinary things but she couldn't find 'the Red Book.' "

"She must have known where it was all the time."

"Known where it was!" cried Elfrida. "I tell you she hunted madly all over the house!"

"Perhaps she was just pretending to——"

Elfrida laughed. "You don't know Emma Chowne! She couldn't keep a secret to save her life."

"Oh . . ." said Ronnie doubtfully. "Perhaps Chowne had put it in the bank or something. I wonder if that would make any difference.

"What difference could it make?"

"I'm not sure. You see the album is valuable and unless it was included specifically in Mr. Ware's bequest to his wife it might be considered as a separate item."

"I don't understand," said Elfrida frankly.

"If a thing is very valuable it ought to be mentioned by name in a person's will."

"Oh, I see! Go on, Ronnie."

"Well, it wasn't specified . . . and, that being so, Whitgreave may think he has a claim to it. I don't think the claim would be valid, but if he thought there was any chance of getting it he might take the case to court . . . which would be unpleasant to say the least of it."

"There's the letter," Elfrida pointed out.

"The letter isn't important."

"It's important to me. I'm so glad to know that Grandfather had forgiven Marjory and had tried to find her and it's good that his last wish can be carried out. He wanted someone to live here and love the place; he wanted Mountain Cross to be 'self-supporting.' The farm can be made to pay if we can buy back some of the fields."

Ronnie nodded. "Yes, everything will be all right if the album was in the house when you came into possession. If not . . . well, it's no good thinking about that until we know. We must ask Chowne what he did with the album; then I can ring up Uncle Bob."

"The Chownes had to go over to Cherleigh this afternoon . . . which reminds me that I promised to milk Pansy and feed the pigs."

"Oh, well, we shall have to wait till he comes back," said Ronnie. He rose and added, "I'll come with you, Elfrida Jane. I can't offer to milk Pansy, but I can help you to feed the pigs."

36

"Is the parent playing up again?" asked Ronnie, as he and Elfrida walked up the hill to the farm.

"Oh, did Emma tell you about him? Yes, he has been rather troublesome lately, poor old thing. I have a feeling that sooner or later he'll have to come and live at Mountain Cross . . . but, never mind that; tell me more about the album. I'm very ignorant, of course, but it seems strange that stamps should be so valuable."

"It's the rare ones—and because there are complete sets—and because some of the stamps are faulty."

"Faulty?"

"If there's a small mistake in the printing or the watermark it makes them much more valuable. Uncle Bob could tell you more about it; he was closeted with Mr. Riggs for hours, going through the album carefully and making notes. He asked me to tell you that he would have come to see you himself, but he had an appointment with an important client this afternoon."

(Uncle Bob had said, "I'm sorry to have to send you down there again, Ronnie; you've just got home and it's a long and tiresome journey, but I can't go myself so I'm afraid there's nothing else for it. You can take my car; it will be less tiring for you than your own little bus. I want you to tell her that the album is valuable, but don't mention any figure—I can't believe Rigg's estimate, it's fantastic, so I'm taking further advice—and for heaven's sake make her understand that she mustn't give the album to Whitgreave! She's quite capable of saying she must keep her promise, but a promise made in ignorance isn't binding. Whitgreave told her that the collection was 'of sentimental value only'. . . and, mark my words, Ronnie; Whitgreave must have known his Uncle's collection was worth hard money."

Ronnie had replied, "I only saw 'Walt' for a few minutes, when he called at the office, but he struck me as being pretty hard-boiled."

"Exactly my own opinion," Uncle Bob had declared. "I would have taken a stronger line with the fellow, but Elfrida didn't want any unpleasantness.")

"Ronnie, wake up! What are you thinking about?" asked Elfrida.

"I was thinking about a conversation I had with Uncle Bob. He said I was to make sure that you didn't intend to give the album to Whitgreave."

"Oh, I couldn't she exclaimed. "When I said I'd give it to him, I thought it belonged to me; but it belongs to Mountain Cross. Grandfather said so in his letter . . . and anyhow, Cousin Walt behaved very deceitfully. He seemed to know a lot about stamps, so he must have known the album was valuable. I thought at the time it was rather queer that he should be so frightfully keen to have it." She hesitated and then added, "As a matter of fact I didn't think it was the album he wanted."

"You didn't think he wanted it? But I thought he spent hours hunting for it," said Ronnie in bewilderment.

"I thought the album was just an excuse," explained Elfrida. "I thought he wanted to have a look round the house to see if he could find Grandfather's will—I mean a later will, leaving Mountain Cross to him."

"That was a very ingenious idea!" declared Ronnie, surprised at her ingenuity. Who would have imagined that Elfrida Jane could have thought of such a dastardly plan?

"Mr. Sandford thought it was a silly idea," said Elfrida smiling. "But, you see, I was so ignorant. It never crossed my mind that stamps could be worth a lot of money. Never for a moment."

Ronnie could not blame her for her ignorance. He had known stamps could be valuable, of course, but it had never crossed *his* mind that they could be worth the fantastic figure which had beeen mentioned with bated breath by Mr. Arnold Riggs.

By this time they had arrived at the farm, so the interesting conversation was over.

Pansy was a beautiful creature and was so quiet and friendly that Elfrida had learnt to milk her without any difficulty. She was standing at the gate of the paddock waiting patiently. She showed signs of pleasure at the blandishments of her owner and allowed her owner's companion to stroke her neck. Then she walked across the yard to her stall and, turning her head, watched the preparations with interest.

"Darling Pansy! She's almost human, isn't she?" said Elfrida, as she found a large white apron and tied it round her waist.

Ronnie agreed. As a matter of fact he had known several "humans" who were not as human as Pansy . . . but the milking had begun and Elfrida Jane was intent upon her task, so he held his peace and watched.

The stall was whitewashed and meticulously clean, there was a large pile of straw in the corner and a rack of hay in the manger. Elfrida Jane sat on a three-legged stool; her head was bent and showed the lovely curve of her neck and one little pink ear; a bright beam of sunshine from the skylight found golden lights in her light-brown hair.

It was a charming picture and Ronnie found it unexpectedly moving, for there was a bond of sympathy and loving-kindness between Elfrida Jane and the little cow. As Ronnie watched, he thought of the long tradition of milking. The task had been performed for hundreds of years in exactly the same way. He had been told by a dairy-farmer that machines were more efficient—and he had seen them working efficiently—but a machine was not beautiful and gentle; a machine did not murmur praise and soft endearments as the creamy milk hissed into the pail.

Something was lost when machines took over this kind of work, thought Ronnie. Something was lost when tractors, instead of fine horses, were used to plough the land. You had to move with the times—this was the machine-age—but something important and beautiful was lost forever.

When Pansy had been milked to the last drops she was taken back to the paddock; the milk was poured into large white bowls in the spotlessly clean dairly and Ronnie and Elfrida went into the barn to look at the pigs.

The twenty small pigs had grown enormously; which was very satisfactory, of course, but sad to say they were not nearly as attractive as they had been when they were young and frisky and playful, so Ronnie and Elfrida moved on to the third pen which housed a large pink sow.

Ronnie had heard all about her and was aware that half of her belonged to Chowne and half to Elfrida Jane.

She was lying on a bed of straw, but when she realised that she had admiring visitors she rose in a dignified manner and came to speak to them.

"I always give her a bun," said Elfrida, producing one from her pocket. "She loves buns . . . it's a funny taste isn't it?"

"What's her name?" asked Ronie.

"She has got a proper name, but it's very long so Chowne calls her Pinkie. She's sweet, isn't she, Ronnie? I can't help feeling that it must be dull for her to be all by herself, but she's going to have lots of piglets . . . that will be fun for her."

"Oh, Elfrida Jane!" exclaimed Ronnie. "I do love you so frightfully!"

She looked at him in surprise.

"Oh, you needn't say anything," continued Ronnie in a low breathless voice. "I know it's hopeless . . . I've known it was hopeless from the very beginning and now there's another fellow, so it's more hopeless than ever. . . but it just came over me all of a sudden and I couldn't keep it in any longer. I love you so frightfully much——"

"But, Ronnie——"

"Didn't you know? Oh goodness, I'm just being silly! Of course you didn't know what I was feeling—how could you? Elfrida Jane! darling Elfrida Jane! I've been wanting to say it for ages, but I knew it was hopeless—and there aren't any words—and I thought I could go on like this, being your friend and chatting and having jokes and doing things for you—but I can't any longer. I can't, really, because I can't bear to be with you for a few days and then go away. I'll have to go away and never come back, because I can't bear it any more."

"But, Ronnie, I couldn't bear it."

"What do you mean?"

"I couldn't bear it if you went away and never came back."

"But—but I've told you I can't go on like this, and Mrs. Chowne said . . ." began Ronnie in bewilderment.

"Emma Chowne is very romantic."

"Romantic?"

"Very romantic," said Elfrida, nodding. "Lucius brought me roses and that was quite enough for Emma. Roses and romance go together, don't they?"

"She said you liked him! I thought——"

"I do like him; he's a dear. The Babbingtons have been awfully kind to me. I like Charlie Cobley, too—very much indeed—but I don't intend to marry him."

"Does that mean——"

"Yes, of course it does," she said, turning and putting her hands on his shoulders and smiling at him.

"I can't believe it!" he cried joyously and seized her in his arms.

When she was able to speak she said, "Oh, Ronnie, darling!"

He kissed her again.

After some time they sat down together on a sack of meal.

"When did you begin to love me?" asked Ronnie.

It was the age-old question of lovers . . . but Elfrida could not answer it.

"Well, never mind," said Ronnie. "You love me now, that's all that matters."

"Yes, that's all that matters."

"You looked so surprised when I said I loved you."

"I was a little surprised," admitted Elfrida. "We were talking about Pinkie's piglets, weren't we? I knew you loved me, Ronnie, but I didn't expect you to say it just then."

"You knew? When did you know?"

"That afternoon on the beach. I knew by the way you looked at me; I was 'certain sure' when you said I couldn't have done anything else except dash into the sea and try to save Patrick."

"You couldn't have done anything else!"

"Of course I couldn't! But you were the only person who seemed to realise that I couldn't have stood on the beach and watched him drowning."

"I loved you the very first moment I saw you in Uncle Bob's office," said Ronnie seriously.

"Not really?"

"Yes, really and truly. We sat by the fire together and I told you about Mountain Cross. I remember just how you looked. You looked a little frightened and I wanted to take you in my arms and comfort you and take care of you forever and ever."

"Oh, Ronnie!"

"Coming down in the car I loved you more every minute . . . but I thought it was quite, quite hopeless. I made up my mind that I should have to get over it, somehow or other. You were friendly and kind, but you were—you were sort of untouchable. It was like seeing a girl through a plate-glass window."

Elfrida thought about this; it was because her thoughts had been full of Glen—yes, that was the reason—but she did not say so. She said, "I didn't know. I thought we were just good friends until that day on the beach. When I was 'certain sure' you loved me, I told you about Glen because I wanted to give you a chance of changing your mind about me."

"Changing my mind?"

"Backing out before it was too late. You might have been put off when you realised I was a silly donkey."

"You weren't a silly donkey! Lots of girls——"

"Yes, I was. But I've learnt my lesson; nothing like that will ever happen again." She sighed blissfully and leant her head against Ronnie's shoulder; it was a nice solid shoulder clad in Harris tweed.

"I shall take good care that it doesn't," declared Ronnie, tightening his arm around her waist.

They were silent for a little while. It was very quiet in the barn; the only sound was the rhythmic snoring of Pinkie.

"Oh, darling," said Ronnie at last. "It's wonderful that you love me, but . . . but what are we going to do? There's Uncle Bob, you see. He has been so good to me and now I'm just beginning to get the hang of things and be useful to him."

"He said you had become good value."

"Yes," said Ronnie with a big sigh.

"It means we shall have to live in London."

"You wouldn't like that, would you?"

"Well, I *do* love Mountain Cross," admitted Elfrida. "But there's nothing else for it; we want to be together, don't we?"

"Darling, of course! It will be absolute bliss . . . but supposing you were unhappy in London? You hated it, didn't you?"

"Yes, but that was because I was so lonely. I was dreadfully lonely after Mother died."

"You won't be lonely any more."

"No, never any more," she agreed. "Let's make plans, Ronnie. We shall have to find a little house."

"Not at Uxbridge," said Ronnie hastily. "Too many people live there: Mother and Uncle Bob and Mr. Riggs and a whole flock of partners and relations. We want to be on our own."

"Yes, we want to be on our own . . . except for Patrick. I told you I'd got Patrick 'for keeps,' didn't I? He has been given to me to take care of."

"I know. I shall help you to take care of him."

"Good," said Elfrida happily. "I just wanted to be sure."

"What about Mountain Cross?" asked Ronnie. "You can't sell it, of course. We can come here for holidays. Could Chowne run the place?"

"Not by himself," replied Elfrida. "We must get a man to help him, but I don't suppose that will be difficult. You said there would be quite a lot of money when the album was sold."

"Oh, goodness!" exclaimed Ronnie in dismay. "I'd forgotten! I can't marry you! I shouldn't have asked you!"

"Ronnie, what do you mean?"

"Uncle Bob will be furious with me."

"Why should he be furious? We've agreed that we're going to live in London, so you can go on working in the office just the same. It will make no difference to——"

"It isn't that."

"What is it, then?"

"I've got no money," groaned Ronnie.

"You said the album was valuable."

"But it's yours," said Ronnie, getting up and standing and looking at her. "The album is yours, so the money will be yours. I've got no money except what I earn."

"Money, money, money," said Elfrida impatiently. "I thought you loved me."

"I do, terribly much, but——"

"There aren't any 'buts.' "

"There are lots of 'buts.' A man shouldn't ask a girl to marry him until he is making enough money to support her."

"That's a silly idea!"

"It isn't a silly idea; it's what Uncle Bob will say."

"Oh, Ronnie, we're quarrelling!"

"No, darling. I'm only trying to make you understand. It isn't what I think that matters; it's what Uncle Bob will think."

"It's our lives that matter."

"Listen, darling Elfrida Jane!" exclaimed Ronnie in desperation. "I shall have to do what Uncle Bob wants me to do. I can't possibly go against him, or do anything that he doesn't approve of, because he has been so frightfully decent to me. You see that, don't you?"

"Yes, I see that," she agreed, nodding thoughtfully. "Yes, you'll have to consult him . . . but are you sure he won't approve of your being married?"

"Yes," replied Ronnie, miserably. "He'll say I shouldn't have asked you to marry me until I was making enough money to support a wife; he'll say I shouldn't think of marriage until I've made my way in the firm."

"But you can't be certain what he'll say until you've asked him."

"I know his views about young men getting married."

"You'll have to tell him about us."

"Yes, of course . . . but I know what he'll say."

"Why not ring him up tonight?"

Ronnie looked doubtful. "I think it would be better not to ring him up. He doesn't like telephone conversations . . . and it would be difficult to explain."

"Yes, you could explain it all much better if you saw him."

"I'll go tomorrow."

"Tomorrow? Oh, Ronnie, need you? I hoped you would be able to stay two days at least! Why must you——"

"I can't bear the suspense," declared Ronnie. "I must get it settled as soon as possible. It's no good, of course; I know what he'll say . . . and Mother will back him up."

For the first time Elfrida was really alarmed. She knew Mr. Sandford (he was a dear and she could not believe he would "be silly about it"), but Mrs. Leighton was an unknown quantity. Ronnie had mentioned her several times in the course of conversation so Elfrida was aware that she liked going to parties . . . and liked Ronnie to go with her. She liked travelling abroad . . . if Ronnie went with her. She liked Ronnie to take her for a spin in the Wisp on a Sunday afternoon. Obviously Mrs. Leighton would not like a daughter-in-law.

"I suppose your mother won't want you to—to marry me?" asked Elfrida in a doubtful voice.

"I'm afraid she won't be too keen on it," admitted Ronnie. He added hastily, "She hasn't seen you, of course. When she sees you, she'll realise that you're a million times more lovely and sweet and beautiful than Anthea."

"Who is Anthea?"

"Oh, she's just a girl, that's all."

"What sort of girl?"

"Mother likes her," said Ronnie uncomfortably.

"Your mother wants you to marry her, I suppose?"

"Well, you see she's a Wilkins. It sounds silly, but it's one of the things in the firm. I mean people whose fathers or uncles are in the firm sometimes marry each other."

"Do you like her?"

"Oh, I've known Anthea all my life! We used to play together when we were kids."

"You had better marry Anthea Wilkins," said Elfrida. "Your mother will be pleased; 'Uncle Bob' will be pleased; everyone in the marvellous firm will be pleased."

For a moment Ronnie looked at Elfrida Jane in dismay . . . then he burst out laughing, swept her into his arms and kissed her. She did not resist.

It was quite a long time before they came to their senses.

Elfrida recovered first. "Goodness, look at the time!" she exclaimed. "We haven't fed the pigs or filled their water-troughs—and I shall have to cook our supper unless Emma has come back—and Patrick hasn't had any tea; he'll be wondering where we've gone! Oh, poor Patrick, how awful of me to forget!"

They fed and watered the pigs and hurried home.

37

When Ronnie and Elfrida got back to Mountain Cross, it was nearly seven o'clock. They were worried and flustered—they had run most of the way—but fortunately all was well. Emma Chowne had returned from Cherleigh and was trotting round the kitchen preparing the evening meal and Patrick was laying the table in the dining-room.

"Well, of course I came back," said Emma, as she opened the door of the oven and put in a large pie covered with puff pastry. "And it was just as well I *did* come back, Miss Elfrida. That poor child hasn't had any tea; he was sitting in the parlour reading his books as good as gold. Wherever have you been?"

"We were feeding the pigs."

"You look as if you'd been running races! Your face is flushed and your hair is all in a mess."

"How was the parent?" asked Elfrida, changing the subject.

"It's difficult to tell. He's such a worry; sometimes he makes a fuss about nothing and sometimes he makes no fuss about a lot. When he had pneumonia and was really ill, he was like a lamb . . . so you never know where you are. I told Ernie he'd better stay the night, just in case. He'll be back in the morning."

"Mr. Leighton wants to see him."

Emma nodded, "About that book, I suppose?"

"Yes, do you know about it?" asked Elfrida in surprise.

"Ernie told me about it this afternoon. He couldn't tell me before because he'd promised Mr. Ware. Oh, goodness!" cried Emma, throwing back her head and emitting a loud hoot of laughter. "Oh goodness, what a joke! There we were, hunting everywhere for that book! I'll never forget Mr. Whitgreave—he was hunting in your bedroom when I went up, but I chased him out of there in double-quick time! He was crazy to find that book, Miss Elfrida."

"I know he was."

"You remember I told you he'd upset Ernie when he came to the back-door before lunch? Well, he tried to give Ernie five pounds to find the book and send it to him unbeknownst to you. If Ernie could have talked, it wouldn't have been so bad—he could have told Mr. Whitgreave what he thought of him—but all he could do was slam the back-door in Mr. Whitgreave's face! Of course I didn't know at the time. I didn't know about any of it."

"None of us knew."

"None of us except Ernie. Oh dear!" exclaimed Emma with another hoot. "Oh dear, when I think of me hunting for that book it nearly kills me! I hunted everywhere I could think of for days and days. I even took up the floorboards in Mr. Ware's bedroom . . . but all I got for my trouble was the skeleton of a mouse, and Ernie brought the ladder and we took every single book out of the book-case in the library and dusted them and put them back! Ernie, as solemn as a judge, helping me to look for it . . . and never saying a word! Oh dear, it's the best joke I ever heard in all my born days! He had it wrapped up in an old torn pyjama jacket and hidden under the jumbo-cover. It was there all the time!" Emma pointed to the row of dish-covers on the top shelf of the dresser and subsided into a chair, gasping and hooting and holding her sides in a positively alarming manner.

"It was there all the time?" echoed Elfrida incredulously.

Emma nodded. She was incapable of speech.

"How amazing!" exclaimed Elfrida, beginning to laugh.

It really was absolutely amazing, not only because the house had been turned upside-down in Emma's search, (and 'the Red Book' had been within a few yards of her head as she trotted about the kitchen), but also because Emma considered the whole affair to be a good joke. Many a woman would have been annoyed to discover that her husband had deceived her . . . but Emma was never annoyed with her beloved Ernie.

Presently the hoots and gasps subsided and Emma recovered; her recovery was hastened by a glass of water which Elfrida fetched for her from the pantry.

"Well, there now," said Emma at last, wiping her eyes with the corner of her apron. "I haven't laughed so much for years. Ernie's clever, isn't he? That reminds me Ernie wrote a letter to Mr. Leighton before we went to Cherleigh—it's a beautiful letter. Ernie wrote it all down because he can't talk properly and he wanted to explain what he'd done . . . and anyhow we might have been delayed at Cherleigh if the parent had been on his last legs, like he said. It's there, on the chimney-piece, Miss Elfrida, behind Henry James's photo. You'd better give it to Mr. Leighton.

"Now I must get on with the supper," added Emma, rising from the chair and beginning to bustle about. "I'm all behind, like a cow's tail."

Realising that she had been given her *congé*, Elfrida took the letter and went away.

She found Ronnie and Patrick in the parlour. Ronnie was reading Mr. Jeremy Fisher and Patrick was curled up beside him on the sofa, listening with all his ears. (It was ever so much nicer to be read to than to have the bother of reading to yourself . . . and Mr. Leighton made Mr. Jeremy Fisher talk in a hoarse, croaky voice which was excruciatingly funny!)

"Hullo, Elfrida Jane!" said Ronnie. "Is supper nearly ready? Patrick and I are hungry; we didn't have any tea."

"It won't be ready for about twenty minutes; Emma is all behind like a cow's tail," explained Elfrida, beginning to laugh again.

Ronnie nodded. "We heard strange noises coming from the kitchen. I thought it was a motor-horn, but Patrick said it was Mrs. Chowne laughing. What was the joke?"

"This beautiful letter will tell you all about it," replied Elfrida, giving it to him.

The letter was addressed to "Mr. Laten," clearly written in a round, schoolboy hand.

Ronnie raised his eyebrows and opened it.

Mountain Cross

Mr. Laten
Dear Sir,

We have to go to Cherleigh to see the parent so I am writing to tell you about the book of stamps. Mr. Ware give it me before he died all tied up and sealed with his seal and he said I was to keep it secret and safe till the new owner of Mountain Cross was settled in for 3 months and then send it to Mr. Sandford by a sure hand. Well she is settled so I did. When Mr. Ware give it me, I put it under the jumbo-cover on the top shelf of the dresser because its the only place in the house Emma dossent clean. I clean them myself once a fortnight because I like them nice and shiney.

Yours faithfully,
Ernest Chowne

Ronnie smiled when he had read the letter; he handed it to Elfrida without comment.

"Is this what you want?" she asked.

"It's perfect," declared Ronnie, chuckling. "Couldn't be better! You see this makes it absolutely safe. I must ring up the senior partner and tell him about it; he'll be tickled to death! What is the jumbo cover, when it's at home?"

"You've seen the row of silver-plated dish-covers on the top shelf of the dresser, haven't you? The jumbo cover is the biggest one, of course. It's big enough to be used for a baron of beef—I thought of that the first time I saw it—so it would fit quite comfortably over 'the Red Book.' Emma told me herself that she wasn't allowed to lay a finger on the covers, so it was a perfectly safe hiding place."

"That was clever!" exclaimed Ronnie. "You wouldn't think Ernie was clever."

"You would if you knew him better. I used to think he was stupid, but I soon found out my mistake." Elfrida added, "Don't forget Grandfather wanted him to be 'suitably rewarded.' "

"He deserves a substantial reward," said Ronnie very thoughtfully indeed.

38

Ronnie decided to leave Mountain Cross at half-past-six next morning; he had said it was too early to have breakfast before starting, so Elfrida came down at six o'clock and made coffee and they had it together in the kitchen.

They talked about their plans last night, but the conversation had gone round and round and had led to no satisfactory conclusion. This morning they began to talk about Mountain Cross; Elfrida explained that the only way to run the place as a paying concern was to buy back some of the fields and grow crops; to buy more breeding sows—like Pinkie—and a couple of pedigree boars. The barns would have to be altered and the farm would have to be modernised and run on a large scale to make it worth while.

Ronnie was surprised and impressed by her plans; it was obvious that Elfrida Jane knew what she was talking about.

"It's Chowne, really," she explained. "He was with Sir Henry Champion at one time and looked after a big herd of pigs. Chowne has taught me a lot . . . but it's all in the air, isn't it? There may not be enough money to carry out the plans, or we may be going to be married and live in London."

"I hope so," said Ronnie with a sigh. "I shall do my best to persuade him . . . but I know what he'll say."

They were back where they had started. It was useless to talk about the future, but they could talk of nothing else.

When they had finished their coffee Elfrida went out with Ronnie to see him off. Dawn was breaking, the sun had appeared above the eastern horizon veiled in the early morning mist. It looked like an orange and there was an orange-coloured path across the sea. A gentle breeze wafted the smell of seaweed up the cliff and stirred the leaves of the trees.

"How fresh and lovely it is!" said Ronnie. "How I wish I could stay here and never go back to London and that stuffy old office."

"How I wish you could!" said Elfrida with a sigh.

This was the third time she had said goodbye to Ronnie . . . and it was different. There was no pretence of cheerfulness; they clung to each other and kissed with a sort of desperation.

"Oh, Ronnie, when shall I see you again!" she cried.

"Tomorrow," said Ronnie firmly.

"Tomorrow?"

"Yes, I'll come back tomorrow. I'll come and tell you what he has decided. I'll come . . . even if it's just to say goodbye."

"We can wait," she said. "We can wait for a year . . . or even two years. I can't be worse than that."

"No, it can't be worse than two years (at least I don't think so), but two years is an awfully long time to wait."

"I'll see you tomorrow, Ronnie."

"Yes, but don't expect me until late. He usually plays golf at the week-ends. If I can't get hold of him tonight, I shall have to watch my chance to have a private talk with him tomorrow. It all depends on what he's doing; it's no good rushing him because I want to get him in the right mood. Au revoir, Elfrida Jane."

"Au revoir, Ronnie."

She waved until he had turned the corner and then went back into the house. She had not told him to be careful and not to drive fast. He would drive too fast whether she told him or not.

The day stretched before Elfrida like a desert; she wandered into the kitchen to wash up the coffee cups and found that already they had been washed up and put away. Emma was on her knees scrubbing the floor and humming cheerfully.

"You're early!" exclaimed Elfrida.

"I like getting up early on a nice bright morning. The work gets done much quicker if it's done early."

"Why does it?" asked Elfrida.

"Why?" repeated Emma, sitting back on her heels and looking up in bewilderment. "Well, I don't know why, exactly . . . but it does."

"Has Chowne come back?"

"Not yet, Miss Elfrida. He said he would phone from the call-box about nine o'clock."

"You weren't frightened of being alone in the flat?"

"Frightened? I've been alone here dozens of times. Did you think I was the sort of person to be frightened?" asked Emma with scorn.

"No, I didn't."

"Well, why did you ask?"

"Oh, I just wanted to make sure." She smiled and added, "I'll go and milk Pansy and feed the pigs. Patrick can have his breakfast in the kitchen."

"Yes, him and me will have it together. He's good company is Pat. By the way, Miss Elfrida, there's more about that film in this week's paper. Would you like to see it . . . or not?"

Elfrida hesitated. She did not want to see it, but perhaps it would be just as well to know what Glen was doing.

"I'll get it," said Emma, rising from her knees and producing it from beneath her ironing blanket in the dresser-drawer. "I just got it last night, so I hid it until I had time to look at it properly. I didn't want Pat to see it if there was something awful in it about his father. There's a picture of him riding a camel. I hope it bites him," she added revengefully.

The paper was spread on the kitchen table and they looked at it together; there were several pictures of Glen: Glen Siddons riding a camel; Glen Siddons having breakfast at a small table beneath a coloured umbrella, Glen Siddons dressed as a

Bedouin Sheik. In the middle of the page there was a very large picture of Glen Siddons arm-in-arm with Clarissa Downes; they were wearing charming smiles . . . but little else. The caption read:

"Glen and Clarissa Off for a Swim."

"Look at that!" exclaimed Emma, pointing at it with her stubby forefinger. "I thought he said he couldn't swim!"

Elfrida did not reply. It did not seem to matter whether or not he could swim. In fact nothing about Glen mattered any more . . . except that he was thousands of miles away from Mountain Cross.

It was a good thing to have something definite to do. Elfrida walked up to the farm; she milked Pansy, fed the pigs and filled their water-troughs; then she sat down on a sack of meal and thought of all that had happened to her.

She had come a long way . . . and she had changed. Yes, she was quite a different sort of person from the girl who had gone in fear and trembling to see Mr. Robert Sandford. All the wonderful things that had happened to her had begun on that fine March afternoon.

Miss Martineau did it, thought Elfrida. I never would have gone to see Mr. Sandford if it hadn't been for her . . . and it was she who showed me how silly I was about Glen and told me to "get over it" and come to Mountain Cross. What a lot I owe her! thought Elfrida. I can never repay her, of course, but now that I'm going to have some money, I could ask her to come here for a holiday and pay her expenses. I wonder if she would be bored in this quiet place . . . but I could have her for a week or ten days and give her a proper rest. I must think about that.

Then Elfrida thought of her arrival at Mountain Cross with Ronnie and of all she had seen and done. She thought of "the ladies' breeze," which had wakened the land and made it as beautiful as a dream of Paradise. She thought of her wanderings in the flowery lanes and sun-bathing on the beach and swimming in the cool clear waters of the bay. She thought of the dear old house . . . the knowledge that it was her very own possession was one of the things which had changed her and given her confidence in herself. She was no longer a waif, living from hand to mouth amidst other people's belongings; she was a woman with a home of her own.

Then Glen had come. Elfrida did not want to think of Glen (and of the horrible things that had happened when he was here) and she need not think of him. All the foolishness was over and done with.

No, she would not think of him, nor would she nurse a grudge against him for the way he had behaved. He had taught her a valuable lesson . . . and he had given her Patrick.

Elfrida smiled at the thought of Patrick; he was such a dear little boy and he had become part of her life. She knew his secret now; it was such a big secret that he had not been able to conceal it any longer, besides he wanted Miss Ware's advice . . . so he had taken her up to the wood and dug up the acorn.

"It's my present to the wood," he had said, holding it out for her to look at.

"What a lovely present!" Elfrida exclaimed. "It's a much better present than roots and bulbs because it will grow into a big tree and the birds can make nests in its branches."

"Yes, but why hasn't it begun?" asked Patrick, turning it over and over in his small brown hands.

"Trees take a long, long time to grow and they like to be left in peace. Let's plant it carefully," suggested Elfrida. "Let's leave it quietly in its little bed until next spring; then we'll come up here together and perhaps we'll find a tiny green shoot."

"We'll come on the twelfth of April," said Patrick nodding. "That's my birthday and I'll be nine."

This had happened yesterday morning before Ronnie had arrived . . . but Time had got jumbled up again and it seemed much longer ago. Elfrida thought of Patrick's acorn and wondered where she and Patrick would be next April . . . perhaps in London!

Ronnie would be getting near London now; she wondered where he was at this moment. She wondered when he would be able to have his talk with Mr. Sandford and what Mr. Sandford would say.

Elfrida was less worried than Ronnie about the future; she was less impatient. If necessary, she could wait two years for Ronnie . . . and meantime she could get on with her plans for the farm and make Mountain Cross self-supporting as her grandfather had desired. Two years was a long time, but Ronnie was worth waiting for . . . she could see him sometimes and they could write to each other.

Ronnie had told her that he had loved her "from the first moment"; he had asked, "When did you begin to love me?" but she had not been able to tell him. Even now, looking back and thinking about it seriously, she could not tell the precise moment when her feeling of friendship for Ronnie had changed to love . . . but it had not really "changed," thought Elfrida. Her feeling of friendship had grown and deepened and ripened. That was what had happened. It had not taken long—just a few days—but they had been days of close companionship and Ronnie was so crystal-clear that she knew him as well as if they had been friends for years. He was "real"; he was absolutely honest and natural and he had a boyish awkwardness that appealed to her heart . . . Elfrida was sick and tired of airs and graces!

She remembered how he had hastened towards her across the beach and flung himself down on the rug at her side with his arms and legs in a careless and somewhat inelegant attitude. He had not been thinking of his arms and legs; he had been thinking of Elfrida Jane and how "splendid" she looked! Then she had told him about the accident and, later, about her infatuation for Glen and in each case he had shown the right reaction. He was good and kind and dependable; he was understanding and considerate; he was full of fun. She had watched him with

Patrick and had seen him gain the boy's trust and affection without the slightest effort, but simply by being himself.

All this time Elfrida had known that Ronnie loved her and gradually she had realised that he had become very dear to her heart and she could not be happy without him. She wanted to be with him, caring for him and being cared for, all her life.

39

The day seemed very long to Elfrida—she had been up and about before six o'clock—so she went to bed early. It was a warm night, not a breath of air was stirring, and presently there was a growl of thunder in the distance. Elfrida could not sleep . . . she began to feel less hopeful about the future. She had made up her mind that if necessary she could wait two years for Ronnie, but now she began to wonder whether Ronnie would wait two years. He had said two years was an awfully long time to wait . . . and there was that Anthea girl, thought Elfrida as she turned over and over restlessly. The Anthea girl was a Wilkins, and lived at Uxbridge, so Ronnie would see her nearly every day; Ronnie's mother liked her and wanted Ronnie to marry her . . . the "whole flock of partners and relations" who lived at Uxbridge wanted Ronnie to marry her.

"Don't be a fool," said Elfrida to herself, as she sat up and shook her pillow and turned it over with the cool side uppermost. "Ronnie loves you dearly; you know that, don't you? Why can't you be sensible and go to sleep?"

The thunder, which had been rolling in the distance like Drake's drum, came nearer and nearer. Suddenly the room was illuminated by a blinding flash of lightning, followed almost immediately by an ear-splitting crash of thunder; the clouds opened and the rain came pouring down, hissing and splashing on the roof, gurgling in the gutters.

Elfrida got up, shut the west window and lay down again. She felt better, now that the rain had come, and presently went to sleep . . . but the Anthea girl haunted her dreams in a very uncomfortable manner.

In spite of her bad night Elfrida got up early and went to church. It was a lovely sunshiny morning and everything was fresh and sweet after the heavy rain. In the cottage-gardens the roses were in their second bloom scenting the air with fragrance. The world was so beautiful that Elfrida's spirits rose and her "night thoughts" seemed foolish.

As she walked along, she remembered the Sunday morning when she and Mr. Sandford had gone to church together. They had talked about Ronnie. Mr. Sandford had said that Ronnie was "a good boy" and had added that he could not be fonder of Ronnie if he were his own son . . . so he would listen sympathetically when Ronnie spoke to him and give his consent to the marriage. Elfrida felt sure of this . . . or almost sure.

The little church was dim and shadowy after the brightness of the outside world and the congregation was small. Elfrida prayed for Ronnie; that he might have a long, happy, useful life and that she might share it. Her heart went soaring up beyond the dark oaken beams into the bright blue summer sky.

Judith Doubleday was in church this morning, so Elfrida walked home as far as the post office with her. She was a pretty young woman with quiet eyes and a gentle manner—not in the least like either of her parents. Elfrida had seen her before quite often, but had never spoken to her alone, so it was rather pleasant to have this quiet chat.

They talked about the roses.

"The second bloom is early this year," said Judith. "It's lovely, isn't it, Miss Ware? I do love roses."

"So do I," replied Elfrida. "I want to get the rose-garden at Mountain Cross tidied up and put in order."

"I hope you like living here," said Judith anxiously. "We were afraid you might find it dull after London. Dad is so happy about the pigs; he's always wanted to keep pigs, but Mr. Ware wouldn't let him. It's made such a difference to Dad having pigs to look after . . . and when Dad is happy, Mum is happy too."

Elfrida saw the point of this little speech, but it was difficult to know how to answer; her plans were so chaotic . . . but Judith was looking at her and waiting, so after a slight hesitation she said, "I love Mountain Cross."

"That's good," said Judith. "I was just wondering, you see. I was going to ask if you'd let Mum bring Pat to tea with us this afternoon. It would be nice for Henry James."

"It would be nice for Patrick," said Elfrida, smiling at her. "Thank you very much, Mrs. Doubleday; I'm sure he would enjoy it."

"They'll be going to the Children's Service, so they can come in afterwards," said Judith, nodding.

They said goodbye at the post office and Elfrida walked on by herself; she was pleased to think that Patrick was going to the Doubledays. In some ways he was too old for his age, but that was the fault of his upbringing. He had never had the life of a normal child.

When Emma heard of the invitation, she was delighted and agreed that it would be "nice" for the boys to make friends. She would take Pat to the Children's Service and they would go to tea at the post office—it was an admirable arrangement. Patrick was not so pleased; he was shy of strangers and was perfectly happy at home. In spite of Emma's assurances that he would enjoy the Children's Service; there would be chocolate cake for tea and a clockwork railway to play with, he went off with her somewhat reluctantly.

Elfrida could not help smiling as she watched the two figures trotting down the avenue. They made a funny pair.

Yesterday had seemed a long day, but today seemed even longer. Elfrida had slept badly; she had gone to church early and had spent the morning on the beach with Patrick. The house was quiet, now that Emma and Patrick had gone, so she decided to take a book and sit in the parlour and read.

It certainly was the sensible thing to do, but unfortunately she was too restless to settle down quietly. She read several pages of the book and discovered that she had not taken in a word. She discovered that she was thinking of Ronnie and wondering when he would come. It was hopeless trying to read, so she put down the book and decided to do some weeding. Weeding was a peaceful occupation. . . and useful too. There were plenty of weeds in Mountain Cross garden.

She saw Chowne, who was in charge of the house this afternoon, and told him she would not come in for tea; then she put on her gardening apron and sallied forth.

Elfrida weeded a whole row of late peas very carefully by hand. Then she started on a row of runner beans. She tried not to think; she had thought and thought about the future, sometimes hopefully and sometimes in black despair.

Ronnie had said he would come today, even if it were just to say goodbye . . . but she could not bear to say goodbye to Ronnie! No, she could not bear it! She sat back on her heels and looked round the garden; it had become familiar and dear to her, but without Ronnie it would be a desert. It can't be worse than two years, she thought. I could bear to wait two years . . . if Ronnie could bear it . . .

She seized the little fork and continued her task. She decided not to think about Ronnie; she would think of Emma and Patrick. They would be having tea now, sitting round the table at the Doubledays and eating chocolate cake. She hoped Patrick was not feeling shy; it was horrid to feel shy; it made you dull and stupid—she knew that by bitter experience.

When would Ronnie come? But it was silly to keep on thinking about it and expecting him. He had said he would be late, so it was no good expecting him to arrive until after supper; perhaps not until nine or ten o'clock!

Elfrida had just made up her mind, quite firmly, that she would not *begin* to expect Ronnie until nine o'clock when the green door burst open and here he was!

He ran down the path and took her in his arms. "It's all right!" he cried joyously. "It's all right, darling!"

"Ronnie, do you mean . . ."

"Yes. He's pleased!"

"Pleased?" she asked incredulously.

"Yes. Oh, goodness, I'm so happy! I'm so frightfully happy that I feel as if I'm going to burst!"

"You told him . . ."

"I told him everything. At first he was surprised, because Mother had been prattling to him about Anthea, but when I explained that Anthea was Mother's idea—not mine at all—and that I had fallen in love with you, head over heels, the very first moment I saw you, he understood at once . . . so it was easy to go on and tell him everything."

"He didn't mind?"

"Not a bit. He understood, you see. When I told him how marvellous you were, how sweet and dear and beautiful, he nodded and said you were very like your mother."

"What has that got to do with it?"

"Everything," declared Ronnie.

"I don't understand."

"No, of course you don't understand, darling. I'm so crazy with happiness that I'm telling it all back to front. Let's sit down and I'll try to be sensible."

They sat down together on the seat by the lily pool and Ronnie put his arm round her waist.

"That's better," he said. "I've got you safe now. All the way down in the car I kept on thinking that something awful might have happened to you."

"What could have happened to me here?"

"You might have been drowned or the house might have gone on fire or you might have been run over by a car on the way to church or you might have——"

"Ronnie, do be sensible!"

"Yes, I must be sensible," he agreed. "I'll begin at the beginning. I told you Uncle Bob was fond of you, didn't I? I told you when we were coming down here together in the Jag—but you didn't believe me. Well, I was right; that's the beginning of everything. He loves you because you're like your mother.

"Long ago he was in love with Marjory Ware. He had known her when she was a child—he often came to Mountain Cross—and he had watched her grow up into a lovely young girl. He knew Marjory was fond of him, but she was so young, barely eighteen, that instead of telling her that he loved her dearly and wanted to marry her, he decided to speak to her parents."

"People did that in the old days, didn't they?"

"Yes, it was the right thing to do and he knew that the Wares liked him—they were always pleased to see him whenever he could come—so he thought they would be sympathetic and kind."

"But they weren't?" asked Elfrida.

"Anything but! They were astonished and dismayed; they said Marjory was just a child; they wanted her to go about and meet people and see the world before there was any talk of her being engaged. They pointed out that he had only just become a junior partner in the firm and ought to be sticking to his work instead of thinking of marriage. Finally Mr. Ware asked what his income was and whether he thought it sufficient to support a girl like Marjory who had lived in comfort all her life."

"Goodness, how awful for him!" exclaimed Elfrida.

"Yes, awful," agreed Ronnie. "He tried to explain that he hadn't expected their consent to an engagement. He had just wanted them to know that he loved Marjory; he thought the honest thing to do was to tell them. He said he was willing to wait until she was older; he would wait as long as they liked before saying a word to Marjory. They wouldn't listen. They said he had no right to think of marriage until he had settled down and was making a good income."

"Just what you thought he would say to you!"

"Yes. I'm pretty certain that's the reason he didn't say it to me."

"I see," said Elfrida thoughtfully. "Did Mr. Sandford tell you all that? It sounds——"

"No, he didn't," replied Ronnie. "He told me some of it, but afterwards I had a chat with Aunt Millie and she filled in the gaps. She told me that when Uncle Bob came back from Mountain Cross, after his interview with the Wares, he was terribly upset and miserable. All the more so because the Wares had told him that he wasn't to see Marjory or correspond with her for at least a year. After that they would "reconsider the matter." Uncle Bob was obliged to accept their ruling—there was nothing else to do—so he went back to London and threw himself into his work. His father was the senior partner at the time and gave him plenty of interesting work to keep him busy.

"Uncle Bob waited for a year," continued Ronnie. "He had worked hard and won the respect of the partners in the firm and he was making a better income, so his father (who had been very sympathetic) advised him to write to Mr. Ware and remind him of his promise, but by that time Frederick Thistlewood had appeared on the scene . . . and you know what happened."

"Oh dear, how dreadful!" said Elfrida sadly.

"Aunt Millie was rather bitter about it. She said Marjory was very fond of Uncle Bob and if they had been allowed to go on being friends and seeing each other it would have come all right . . . Marjory would have grown to love him. But the Wares interfered and sent him away. Aunt Millie said the Wares wanted 'a good match' for their daughter; they thought Bob Sandford 'not good enough.' They were sorry afterwards, when it was too late, because, in their opinion, he would have been better than Frederick Thistlewood."

"He would have been much better."

Ronnie was surprised. He had been careful to say 'in their opinion' because, after all, the man was Elfrida Jane's father.

"Well, go on, Ronnie," said Elfrida, after a short silence. "You haven't told me what Mr. Sandford said about us."

"I know," said Ronnie remorsefully. "I've put it all back to front. What he said about us came at the beginning of our interview. I told him that I didn't want to leave him in the lurch when I was beginning to be useful; I told him we were willing to wait for a year before getting married . . . but he interrupted and said, 'No, no, Ronnie! That won't do. If you're in love with

Elfrida, and she's willing to marry you, there must be no waiting.' "

"Because of what happened to Marjory?"

"Yes. He didn't actually say so, but that was the reason, of course. Then I repeated that I didn't want to leave him in the lurch—because of all his kindness to me—and he glared at me as he always does when I mention his generosity. However I took no notice and went on to say that you had suggested we should get a house in London so that I could continue working in the office just the same. I told him that we would like to keep Mountain Cross and come here for holidays. Chowne could run the place with a man to help him.

"He nodded and said that was a good idea. He wouldn't like Mountain Cross to be sold because, if possible, he was anxious to carry out Mr. Ware's 'last wish.' He asked if I thought it practicable to make the place 'self-supporting,' as Mr. Ware had suggested. I told him yes, if we could buy back some of the fields and make it into a large pig-farm. I told him all your plans; I could see he was impressed.

"Then I repeated for the third time that nothing would induce me to leave him in the lurch—and you felt the same about it. He thought for a bit and I remained silent. At last he said it was true that I was useful to him and, if you were agreeable, he would like us to get a flat in London so that I could stay on in the firm for six months or so until he could find and train someone to take my place."

"Ronnie!" exclaimed Elfrida. "Do you mean that after six months in London we can come home to Mountain Cross?"

"It may take longer than six months."

"That doesn't matter! Even if it took a year it wouldn't matter!"

"No, it wouldn't matter because we'd be together . . . and we could look forward to coming home to Mountain Cross."

They were silent for a little while.

"I want to tell you everything," said Ronnie at last. "All the time we were talking I was expecting him to say something . . . but he didn't, so I said it."

"What do you mean?" asked Elfrida in bewilderment.

"I said you were going to be very well off and I hadn't a penny."

"Oh, I see! I suppose he told you it didn't matter."

"No, he just smiled and said if I felt uncomfortable about it I could work like two men on the pig farm . . . and so I shall," declared Ronnie. "It's the kind of work I like: looking after animals and growing things and grubbing about in the good clean earth. I told him that. He said he had always known I wanted to be a farmer, but it had seemed an impossible ambition so he had put it out of his mind . . . but here was my chance and he was very glad indeed that I was going to have the life I had always wanted."

"How unselfish he is!" exclaimed Elfrida.

"Yes," agreed Ronnie. "He said I was doing well in the office—I was pleased about that—but he knew it was more because I was conscientious than because I was really interested in the work."

"What did you say?"

"I said I enjoyed working for him . . . and it's true," declared Ronnie earnestly. "I enjoy working for him because I'm fond of him. So then he smiled and said that I ought to be interested in the work for its own sake."

"But you aren't?" suggested Elfrida.

"No . . . and I wasn't going to tell him a lie. I just repeated that I enjoyed working for him. He said, 'I know that, Ronnie. You're a good boy!' "

"He'll miss you terribly!"

"I'm afraid he'll miss me a bit," admitted Ronnie. "You see I know his ways. I know what he likes and (even more important) I know what he doesn't like; but it won't be so bad if we can find a good man to take my place. We shall have to stay in London until I'm sure we've got the right sort of chap . . . and then I shall have to get him into Uncle Bob's ways. It may take some time."

"You'll have to stay until you're quite sure it's going to be all right."

"Yes. You don't mind, do you?"

"Of course I don't mind! It's wonderful, Ronnie! It's better than we dared to hope for . . . better than our wildest dreams! How good and kind he is! I wish I could thank him."

"You can."

"Oh, I know! Of course I shall thank him, but I mean I want to thank him now—this minute."

"You can thank him now—this minute," declared Ronnie, laughing happily. "He's here."

"Here?"

"Yes, sitting in the parlour. He came down with me in the Jag. If he hadn't been with me, I'd have pushed along and been with you a great deal sooner. He was determined to come with me; he said he wanted to see you."

"If he's here——" she began, trying to rise.

"He's all right," said Ronnie, tightening his arm round her waist and kissing her ear. "I left him talking to Chowne. He told me to go and find you and not to hurry. He's all right—he knows everything—and he's pleased."

"Your mother won't be pleased."

"She'll love you when she gets to know you, darling. Anyhow, we needn't worry. Uncle Bob can manage Mother; he can twist her round his little finger; she always does what he says. We needn't——"

"We must go to him," interrupted Elfrida; she unclasped the arm round her waist, not without difficulty, and rose.

"He said not to hurry," murmured Ronnie.

Elfrida took no notice but walked up the path to the house . . . so Ronnie ran after her and took her hand and they went on together.

"You needn't worry, Elfrida Jane," said Ronnie. "He's happy about it—really happy. He talked a lot coming down in the car and he said this had taken away some of the sadness of the past. He felt it was a good ending to an unhappy story. He talked about our wedding; he wants it to be soon. He said Mother would want the wedding to be in London, but he hoped we would decide to be married here, at Mountain Cross."

"Oh yes!" exclaimed Elfrida. " We must be married here in the little church . . . but not too soon."

"Why not?"

"Because . . . well, because I've got to get used to the idea of being married."

"How long will it take you to get used to the idea?" asked Ronnie anxiously.

Elfrida did not know how long it would take. She promised to think about it. "What else did he say, coming down in the car?" she asked.

"He said he hoped we'd ask him to stay with us sometimes."

"As often as he likes!" exclaimed Elfrida.

"Yes. As often as he likes," agreed Ronnie.

They found him sitting in the parlour, reading *The Sunday Times*, and Elfrida was glad to see that Chowne had produced refreshments for him.

He rose when they came in and held out his hand to Elfrida, but she put her arms round his neck.

"Thank you . . . thank you . . . thank you!" she said. "It's all your doing, dear Uncle Bob." Then she kissed him very gently and hid her face against his shoulder.

"Why all these thank yous?" he asked in a gruff voice.

"For giving me Ronnie," said Elfrida.